INTERMISSIONS

INTERMISSIONS

ORIGINAL STORIES SELECTED BY GRATTAN STREET PRESS

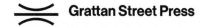 **Grattan Street Press**

Published by Grattan Street Press, 2021

Grattan Street Press is the imprint of the teaching press based in
the School of Culture and Communication at the University of
Melbourne, Parkville, Australia.

editorial@grattanstreetpress.com

Cover image copyright © Ave Calvar, 2021

Grattan Street Press
School of Culture and Communication
John Medley Building,
Parkville, VIC 3010

www.grattanstreetpress.com

Printed in Australia

Typeset in Adobe Garamond Pro and Mr Eaves Mod OT

ISBN 9780 6482 09669

A catalogue record for this book is available from the National Library
of Australia.

CONTENTS

BEGINNINGS

FROM WHERE WE CAME

Kaitlyn Dara

THE CEILING FAN spun slowly as he sat at his desk, writing in the same journal he'd been carrying around for years. It was only because he didn't have much to say that it had lasted so long, but he was finally about to reach the last few pages. He had signed each entry with Huyen, even though everyone called him James. Every morning he would take an hour to write only a few words before heading to work.

His journey was muscle memory at this point. Out the squeaky front door, onto a stench-soaked bus, into an office building in the city, up to the sixth floor. The voices of people gossiping about the government floated through his ears in a drone.

James was the most efficient worker at his firm; he rarely made any mistakes and finished everything quicker than any of his co-workers. He didn't converse with any other employees much either – not anymore. The way they spoke made him feel surprisingly lonely.

Each day he would think to himself, *I want to go home.*

Yet when work was over, he would drag his feet and keep his gaze down. Opening the door to his own house didn't bring him any relief. Every day was the same.

The same bus.

The same work.

The same people.

The same empty picture frames.

His clothes lay folded in an old suitcase, aside from a suit hanging up in the bathroom, even after a decade. The walls were bare, and the blinds were dusty and bent in the corner as if the sun was desperately trying to climb inside. The fan spun at such a slow pace, it was just a symbol that he was still paying the power bill.

The only thing that brought him comfort was when the day was finally over. After brushing his crooked teeth and hanging up his cheap brown suit, he would slip under the covers of a thin futon on the floor of the living room. He would stare up at the fan spinning slowly,

slowly,

slowly, before drifting off to sleep to dream of a place where he could smile again. Where he could feel at home.

It was a place that smelled of sautéed shrimp and seasoned soup that had been sitting since three that morning. A kitchen full of family members around his size, yelling and shouting at each other to hurry up and sit down. Where light streamed from the thin curtains and coated the entire room with a golden glow of familiar warmth. Spring rolls stacked high at the centre of the table with little cups of sauce for each seat. The women worked to prepare dinner, with one dishing pho into each bowl, and another lathering ribs with a homemade sauce they had worked on for days.

James felt a hard smack on the back of his head as a short, older woman yelled at him in another language, gesturing for him to take a seat. It didn't hurt at all, but for some reason this action made him want to cry. His heart ached as he sat down and looked around at a gathering of men that looked like him. The man nearest to him laughed and ruffled his hair as if he were a child again. He spoke in a joyful tone and had a loud laugh, but James couldn't remember what his words meant.

He assumed those dreams were memories. They felt too real to be anything less. Waking up from those dreams was unbearable. He opened his eyes to grey walls and the droning fan on his ceiling. He stared up at it and remembered that he had to go to work so that he could keep that fan spinning,

        spinning,

                spinning, just as the world continued to spin.

Once again he picked himself up off the floor, rolled up his bed, and sat down to write at his desk. Sometimes about how dull his kitchen is, or a reminder to buy more detergent. Other days, he sat at his desk and wrote down his name, in the hope that he would never forget it.

The fragmented memories of his family and homeland were scattered across his mind, lost amongst the cobwebs of his life since he'd moved. The culture was suffocating. He had nothing left of himself.

He thought, *I can't breathe.*

On the day he reached the final page of his journal, he closed it with a feeling of clarity. He wished to return home, to a place that he could remember.

GETAWAY

Christine Johnson

SATURDAY MORNINGS ARE peaceful. They're perfect. A frame from a movie you never thought you'd live – a movie in which you play the young suburban mother who wakes up at seven-thirty to go running. Even after nearly ten years, it still feels a bit like acting.

It's early enough that there are no whirring lawnmowers or garden conversations filling the damp April air, so you listen to your own ragged breath, the grinding of your sneakers on asphalt, and your wandering thoughts.

You're grateful for how flat your neighbourhood is – how unlike the neighbourhood of your youth it is, the many hills you'd crest when you'd run as a teenager, and you smile a bit at that long-lost determination to go, whatever the cost. Now, of course, you run because you have to, to survive that half-marathon in the fall – but back then, there was nothing in front of you, nothing you ran *for*. There was only what you ran *from*.

You recall the long routes you'd take, the loops around the block, just to escape walking on eggshells and the huge looming presence that seemed to cast a shadow over your childhood home. In your mind, you'd play out a million heroic scenarios as you ran, a million brilliant things you could have said to defend yourself. You'd let them all slip away, knowing that, really, nothing would have made a difference.

Panting, sweat dripping into your eyes, you glance at your watch, which reads eight-thirty. You think of Alex, probably now just waking up, making the bed you share and brewing coffee for when you return, just like he always does. You muse about how strange it is, even after all these years, to share a bed with someone every night – and even stranger still, to enjoy it. Before Alex, the closest you'd come was your mother. Even now, when Alex stirs during the night, you sometimes wake thinking it's her, slipping silently under your covers because she knows your father won't follow her there. Then you're six or seven again, pretending to be asleep so she won't know you can see her tears, so you can keep up your facade of believing that all is well. The facade is shattered, of course, when your father starts sleeping on the couch downstairs, and then your mother stops climbing into your bed, and you have it to yourself until you have a husband of your own.

You feel guilty, even now, that you waited so long to tell Alex – until the very last moment, until you absolutely had to, until you couldn't fabricate excuses not to move in with him for a moment longer. You were engaged, and you were consumed by the guilty idea that he'd chosen you without knowing you were damaged goods. He asked you when it would be time for the two of you to find a place of your own, and you finally blurted, 'I just don't want to leave my mother alone.'

You still remember the way his eyebrows came together. 'What's wrong? Is she sick? She has your dad.'

'No,' you told him. 'I don't want to leave her alone with my dad.'

He'd been collecting all of your hesitations and cryptic hints and meaningful pauses and in that moment, you'd finally given him the instructions he needed to assemble them into a full portrait, and he understood. Even now you can picture, with dazzling clarity, the love and warmth on his face, clambering out of him and over every inch of you that you'd hidden from him.

The memory settles over you and sends tremors down your arms. You've come to the street that runs adjacent to your own, and through a clearing in the trees you can see the front of your house, the door wide open. Alex likes to leave it open in the springtime, to let the warm breeze in; Alex, who found this place because he loves you, this place close enough to your parents that you can see your mother whenever you like, but far enough that you can avoid your father whenever you need to. The kids will be up now, clamouring for seats at the kitchen bench to watch Alex pour pancakes onto the griddle like he does each Saturday morning. You'll stride in, sweaty and panting, but he'll tell you you're 'glowing', and you'll kiss three little foreheads good morning and then excuse yourself to call your mother, who will hem and haw and make small talk about the grandkids until you demand to know what your father has done this time. You will offer for the hundredth time to let her come stay with you for a while, but she will say no, no, surely he'll be over it by dinnertime. And you will tell her you love her and hang up the phone and return to your life, to your pancakes and your perfect children and your guilt. The thought of it is almost enough to make you keep running, past your street. But you come around the corner, flanked by impossibly green little lawns and dogs that bound along beside you, and then it's downhill, effortless, easy, towards that open door and the happiness you don't deserve.

PLAYING

Paulette Smythe

THE PIANO SAT in an awkward corner of the hall, as though on its way to somewhere else. It seemed to shudder a little as I approached. Small, grim, determined, I practised every day without fail, trying to master complex pieces with cumbersome chords that stretched my tiny fingers to their limits. Awaiting the moment my mother would rush into the hall, exclaiming at my virtuosity. Straining in the intervals for steps that never came.

'You can read music,' she would say with a wistful toss of her head as she caught me peering at the score. But music cannot be read. She, of all people, knew that.

My mother played by ear, rarely and only ever in the late afternoon when our dark, disordered hall seemed suffused with warm golden light. I recall her poise on the worn piano stool, her small, deft hands glancing across the keys like birds skimming the waves, never stumbling for the right note, as others who play by ear might do. Her playing was feather light, whimsical, as play should be – breezy little tunes, lifted from popular musicals and light classics. A world away from my own intense, laborious choices. Her playing greeted me sometimes when I returned from school, or lulled me to sleep in my infant years. I lapped up its comfort like a kitten at a warm dish of milk.

This mother of mine could also tap dance and, every now and then, would leave off shelling peas and trip lightly across the kitchen linoleum.

She was only ever truly present at the piano. At other times, she was feverishly plotting her escape. And after each birth – there were six of us – the desire to flee grew wilder.

'I don't know where you came from,' she told me once with a baffled stare. Too many small strangers in the house, too little time to play.

WORDS FOR A PUPPET

Kellene O'Hara

ONE

MY BELOVED CREATOR entered the workshop. He did not look like me. His screws were hidden. His body wasn't wooden. I turned my head towards him. He turned towards me.

We had never seen another thing like that thing that we saw.

He made sounds, but I did not have access to his language. I did not have access to any language. In the beginning, I could not speak.

He repeated the sounds. Again and again.

I thought, *Could I make them too?*

His mouth opened and closed. The sounds were coming from inside to outside.

I wanted my inside to come outside.

I watched his face carefully. His face was so elastic. It moved with such ease. I wondered if my face could move like that.

I followed his movements, but nothing happened. He began making different sounds like valleys and mountains. Up and down they travelled.

They had no meaning to me.

When the day ended, he shut off the light, left me alone, and silence descended in the workshop.

In the morning, he repeated the sounds.

I opened my mouth and produced the sounds.

I said hello.

TWO

I learned to mimic my moving maker. I wanted to move like him. I wanted to make his sounds.

He pointed to me. 'Puppet,' he said.

'Puppet.'

He pointed to himself. 'Puppet Maker.'

'Puppet Maker.'

I made his movements and his sounds. I learned that he had made me his puppet.

THREE

I lived in a tomb of dead wood.

In the workshop, there were other puppets. The puppets only moved if the Puppet Maker pulled the strings. My Puppet Maker and I were the only ones alive in the world.

I wanted to see the world my Puppet Maker told me about: the trees, which were alive, and the grass, which was alive.

He told me that there were humans. The humans were alive.

I was not human. I was a puppet. I was alive.

My Puppet Maker said that puppets are not alive.

I was alive.

FOUR

A collection of humans was called a town. My Puppet Maker visited the town often, selling the dead puppets to humans. Little humans played with the puppets, which were purchased with shiny pieces of metal.

I could not go to town.

'I would never sell you,' my Puppet Maker said. 'You are special.'

None of the other puppets spoke or moved. I was special in my loneliness.

FIVE

'I want to go to town.'

It was all I wanted. To see the humans.

My Puppet Maker told me that the humans no longer wanted to give him pieces of metal in exchange for the dead puppets. But he needed those coins.

He had an idea.

SIX

I went to town, which was beautifully moving.

There were humans that moved. Other creatures, called animals, were moving too.

'Do you remember the script?' my Puppet Maker asked.

'Yes, I remember.'

I spoke to other humans for the first time. 'Hello. I am a puppet.'

'Look – a talking puppet!' someone shouted.

'Is it real?' the crowd asked.

I was real.

'It's no trick,' I said. 'No strings attached, see?'

The humans liked the words. The Puppet Maker sold his puppets. He did not sell me.

Every day, we went to the market. Every day, I would perform my part.

'Smile,' my Puppet Maker would say.

And I would move my puppet mouth, contorting the grain to make a smile. The children cheered. The adults stared. I was alive.

'What else can it do?' a human muttered to my Puppet Maker.

He replied, 'Anything I want.'

SEVEN

I wanted to be human.

But my Puppet Maker said I couldn't be human.

I told the Puppet Maker that I wanted another puppet friend. He said he couldn't make another one of me.

Sawdust fell from my eyes. My Puppet Maker told me not to cry.

He cradled me as he told me a story. 'Once upon a time, there was a puppet girl who came to life. She wanted to be like all the other humans. A fairy godmother came and granted her wish, telling her that she would become human if the magic words were said—'

'What were the magic words?'

'The magic words are secret. Until those words are spoken, the puppet girl can never be human.'

'Why doesn't the fairy godmother just turn the puppet girl into a human?'

'Because it doesn't work that way.'

EIGHT

I wanted the magic words. I began to speak all the words I knew. I learned new words listening to the townspeople.

I spoke, I spoke, I spoke.

I was still a puppet.

NINE

I met a man in town; a Puppet Master who wanted to buy me. My Puppet Maker said no.

The man said something about a travelling show. My Puppet Maker said no.

The man said I could perform with other puppets. My Puppet Maker said no.

I said nothing.

TEN

I found the Puppet Master.

I said, 'Don't go.'

'Where is your maker, little puppet?'

I asked, 'Are there other puppets that are alive?'

'Come. See.'

I followed him to a cart. He opened a bag and pulled out a wooden puppet. It looked like the other puppets. But then, I saw the wooden pine move. It had arms and legs connected to a sleek torso. It moved of its own will.

It belonged to no-one.

A puppet, like me.

ELEVEN

I was not alone.

I am not alone.

There are others.

THE BARN ON THE ROAD AWAY

Breanne Jade

THE WIND PUSHES against my fingers, as if trying to send them fly-ing off my hand. I push back, twirling each finger in the breeze, watching as they cruise along the tree line. Beside me, Mum digs her fingers into the steering wheel, focusing her attention on the sprawling country roads ahead of us. Each turn she takes is sharper than my stomach likes. I watch the dry corn fields pass by, for now, dead in the off-season.

My fingers start to turn cold. I pull my hand back inside the car and roll up the window. Without the sound of the gusting wind, the car is suddenly filled with an unbearable silence. It suffocates the air, dares me to break it. Moving slowly, I reach for the volume on the radio, turning it up until Dad's favourite radio station ends the silence.

'No,' Mum says, switching it off with one quick turn.

More silence. I stare at a crumbling farmhouse in the distance until it's out of sight. I turn to watch a flock of birds racing between the pine trees. I pick at my fingers, dropping pieces of fingernail on the floor below.

'Stop that, it's gross.'

'Sorry.'

I watch the leaves fly past my window. Brown, gold and red. They sail through the air without hesitation.

'Mum?'

She shakes her head, then pinches her bottom lip between her index finger and thumb. 'I don't want to talk about it.'

We pass another dilapidated barn. Its red paint is chipped on the sides and the roof is caving in. Mum slows to a stop at the four-way intersection. I continue to stare at the barn, waiting for the breeze to knock it over. A pickup truck crosses abruptly in front of us, forcing us to forfeit our right of way. It has a mahogany wardrobe tied down to the truck bed, and the bottom of the wardrobe is tilted dangerously over the back.

Before Mum can step on the gas again, I unclick my seatbelt and open the car door. Mum hollers after me and pulls over as I leap over an overgrown ditch and run through the decaying cornstalks. As I reach the red barn, the stench of mildew is overpowering. Mould clings to the empty doorframe. Stepping inside, the floorboards groan under my weight and strips of wood threaten to splinter my feet. I look up through the hole in the roof; the sunlight is streaming through the frayed wooden edges. My feet shift through the layers of straw covering the ground as I journey deeper into the barn. Petrified cow dung clings to where the floor intersects with the walls, and lazy flies hover in the air. Rusted farm equipment is piled up high in one of the corners, looking like a bonfire waiting to be lit. A faded red tractor sleeps near the heap of metal, and spider webs crisscross over its rotten gears. The seat is rusted and leaning downwards, ready to fall off at any second. When I start to move again, my feet startle something and a pile of nearby straw starts to rustle. Out of the nest crawls a matted grey kitten with its crossed eyes looking in opposite directions. It trips over its swollen paws and sniffles straw out of its nose. Carefully, I reach out and it hobbles toward me. The kitten mews loudly, stopping at my hand and sniffing it. I stroke its head, my fingers leaving indents in its matted fur. The kitten begins to purr, looking up at me with its mismatched eyes, the tip of its tongue poking out. Then it turns around, tripping over the straw, looking back at me, asking me to follow it.

The kitten leads me to a dark corner where the walls and floors have rotted away to nothing but dirt. Bloated flies swarm at my hair as I approach. The stench of rot stings my nostrils. The kitten cries out and I look down at what it has brought me to. A dead grey cat, weeks gone. The flies and maggots have been hard at work feasting on the cat, leaving a window where the cat's ribs once were. Flies travel in and out of the dead cat's mouth, resting before continuing their work. The maggots writhe in clumps around the cat's abdomen, bubbling up under the fur to create the illusion of life. The kitten paws at its dead mother, its claws getting stuck in the dead cat's fur.

Slowly, I pick the kitten up and bring it close to my chest. 'Don't worry, I will take care of you now,' I whisper, finally closing my eyes to the gory scene. The kitten begins to purr, trying to lick my chin with its coarse tongue.

'What the hell do you think you're doing?' Mum calls out from the empty doorframe, her hands planted on her hips.

I race back through the barn, dodging the rotten floorboards and hazardous tools. The kitten is meowing in my arms. And then I'm standing in front of Mum, holding the kitten aloft for her to see.

'I found a kitten. It needs us,' I begin to plead.

'That thing is probably diseased. Put it down, we're leaving.'

'But Mum—'

'Now. We don't have time for this,' she says sharply.

The kitten begins to cry as I set it back down on the straw-covered ground. I whisper, 'I'm sorry,' as the kitten leaves my hands. I close my eyes tight so that it doesn't have to see me cry. It probably doesn't understand why people come and go so easily.

'Dad would have let me keep the kitten,' I mutter as our feet crunch back toward the road.

Mum doesn't respond. She stomps through the cornfield without looking back. I watch her shoulders rise and fall as she takes a deep breath. As we reach the car, the wind picks up again. Behind us, the barn groans. But the leaves rejoice, dancing across our shoulders. I climb back into the car, trying not to glance at the overflowing suitcases that were haphazardly thrown into the back seats this morning. I roll down the window and stick out my arm as we drive away.

THE CLIMBER'S DESTINY

Jonathan Koven

SCARRED PALMS AND fingernails coloured like lichen. These are my earliest memories of my father. Born and bred a climber like his grandfather before him, he vaulted the Purple Mountain's ramparts, but failed to greet the summit. His scale soon slowed, and he lowered to the gravel, vowing never to touch a stone again.

He tells me my fate is to climb the highest peak, to leap from Purple Mountain, because he could not. Such is the natural order of things. He thinks that when I jump, the clouds will be my home.

Blisters line my palms. My teeth rot from breathing heaven's air. My days are emerald hills and glacial walls. Every new peak echoes louder with this hungry laughter – my father's inheritance to me. I wonder, is there no greater thrill than that of pursuit?

Still, the mystery of life sustains me. Its answer shall arrive when my legs will leave the tallest mountain top. The dense rush of air will flow into the spaces between limbs, not falling but spreading me apart to become one with the wind.

Mother was once wide-eyed with geraniums in her wild brunette hair. Time has been unkind. With dry lips, she tells me that we must have faith. All will be revealed if I jump from the summit's edge.

'But I am only a boy,' I say, even though I have grown tall.

Standing on her toes to kiss my forehead, she whispers gently, 'You will become an angel.'

Father joins us and pats me on the back. 'The best climber in the kingdom,' he says. 'Are you afraid to jump?'

'Yes,' I answer bluntly.

He nods and stares forward, the cuticles of his eyes dry and yellow.

Sleep grants dreams where Mother and Father watch me climb from below. 'Go away!' I shout, soaring from the mountain top, wind licking my flesh with its razor. My sleep is disrupted by trilling bird calls. With my hands full of the bedsheets, I wake up screaming the future and past away.

* * *

My throat itches. Gums like settled dust in my mouth. I was, I am, only a young boy. I should never have climbed anything.

Today, Purple Mountain awaits. The stones of the cliff face rasp my knuckles raw. Ahead, an aspen branch juts out from dark crust to shed its leaves, golden over me. The sky seems endless beneath my clutching shoes, and the gravel of the ground hides behind a dense mist. And yet, the task is not so difficult, having spent my life climbing.

The air thins near the summit. Cool winds fill my lungs. I exhale clouds. Purple Mountain's ashen crown hosts mats of bacteria and black driftwood. At the top, it is the loudest silence that I have ever known. The years grow immense with the days of my life, different mountains climbed, and valleys bypassed on the lookout for the next peak. Staring out at the range below, everything fits within the scope of my eye.

Everyone waits for my jump.

But I do not jump. Instead, I build a home with petrified wood. Kneeling over the frost, I cut my palm on obsidian. Blood streams a hot and furious red like melted cinnabar. It is proof I am alive.

ANARIA'S NOTES

Marija Mrvosevic

WINGS

THE FLOOR IS wet again, and I have to mop it up.

Last night, rain poured as if someone held a hose above our concert hall. The attic roof keeps dripping onto my head.

'The blood is let. Ratpeople – they'll know,' Auntie says. She is holding a slice of carrot cake, pinching at it slowly.

'Maybe I'll look for them,' I say.

'Nonsense, Anaria!' Auntie says.

Luke yelps and withdraws further into his corner.

I continue to clean the puddle with my oldest shirt. It's a good shirt; it only has a few holes and five stains in total. This impromptu cleaning will surely freshen it up.

Auntie is staring through me, her eyes wide and grey hair slicked back. There is a deep groove between her brows.

'I'll send them your best,' I say. A smile pulls at the corner of my mouth.

The room shifts. One moment I'm standing and the next I'm in the water, Auntie's knee on my spine. She snickers in my ear.

From this vantage point, through the droplets collecting around my eye, it looks like the light pouring in through the ceiling grows wings.

Luke remains deep inside his shadow, invisible.

PICK

It's too hot today. I can't sit by my window.

The chair creaks as I sway.

How far can I lean before it falls?

If it had room to fall, I would – but my secret spot is crammed.

Luke is lucky; he has an entire attic corner to himself. On the other hand, he has to stay there with her. I shiver at the thought. The chair creaks.

Perhaps I'm the lucky one. I found the door to my stuffy dressing room tucked behind a broken mirror. Though someone had to be unlucky for me to benefit.

Is that how life works?

Auntie would say, 'Shut your trap, girl. Ratpeople hear you most!'

I reach into my pocket, feeling around. My heart tightens. For a second, I freeze.

But the cold metal surface reassures me. I pull out Dad's guitar pick.

'We'll dance next time, Dad. I promise.' The pick goes back.

I sway some more to a gentle tune by Umebayashi. Dad played him the best. The stage awaits, but for now, I sway.

The chair snaps at its legs.

I tumble down.

DREAM

Up on the roof, the winds blow downwards.

I approach the sharp edge. I had marvelled at it before; the clear concrete line I'm not supposed to cross. But I am tiny now. I have wings and I can sing. My steps clink on the metal plating.

I chassé.

I add a pirouette.

Then I fly off the stage.

* * *

I wake up with a fluttering heart. I want to go again in the middle of the night, but it's too risky. Auntie is snoring, and Luke glares at me from the corner. His nose twitches. I bite my lip. Way too risky.

I could escape if it weren't for the Ratpeople.

Auntie would say, 'No going. They see and kill. You wanna die, girl?'

I shrug.

She frowns, snarls, says, 'You wanna see Luke die? Wanna see his little death on the floor?'

I scream at her. She screams back and I end up on the floor.

Luke winces from his corner. The attic constricts.

That is how it goes. And there's no wind or rain to wash it off.

DETRITUS

There's too much rubbish. We need to leave.

'He was the best. He plucked, they smiled. Remember?' Auntie says.

Luke is tucked into her thighs. She moves her fingers through his hair, like she used to do with mine.

'Luke was a baby. Of course he can't remember,' I say.

Auntie flicks her gaze at me.

I smile at her.

Auntie only purses her lips. Her cheek twitches. I used to crawl to her when she'd return like this, but it never lasted long. So, I stay on my dusty mattress, pricking at a loose spring.

'Rock'n'Roge they called him back in The Moonlit Brew. You know why?'

I smile. Luke relaxes. Her voice is steady now. We both shake our heads. But we know.

'He was Roger. And he was the best!' she says through a chuckle.

'What really happened to them?' I blurt out.

My insides flutter. Sharp metal pricks my finger. Before Auntie can see, I tuck it into my pocket. The smooth surface of the pick eases the pain.

Will the red stain stay forever?

Auntie wipes a single tear as if it were a noisy fly. On that spot, redness forms in the shape of a pear.

'Ratpeople got them. Big blood flow,' she says, pushing Luke out of her lap.

I yank the spring out of the mattress. Auntie grunts at me but doesn't approach.

She crumples to the floor, sobbing.

I want to hug her, but everything is in the way.

CALYPSO

The red lights flicker in the messy auditorium as we enter stage left.

I sashay to the ragged edge. I had inspected it many times in dreams. A clear line we never dared cross. The wooden planks creak at my gentle steps. I wince.

The nightmare tortures me with what could never happen.

Swirling Umebayashi speaks within me. Dad's guitar echoes, I add a drum. I krump-krump-krump. I add a two-step, then tutt-tutt-tutt, and glide into one-two-three chaînés. I fall to the floor. Knee down – heel up.

'Ana,' Luke whispers from behind. I stop and look at him.

'Come back. Auntie will—' He swallows, brushing the thought away. 'We're not supposed to.'

But I must know. If the Ratpeople are real, I need to be certain. I glance once more across the empty chairs, clench my jaw and exhale. I piqué back for a start, then I calypso.

Off the stage, into the darkened abyss.

PICK

Ratpeople. It was us.

Luke slowly approaches the edge. I'm sick of conformity, he needs space.

'Come, little hare. Let's play a game.' Dad used to say that.

Luke blinks. He offers me his hands.

* * *

We move through the torn-up cushions and old newspapers. The red light doesn't recede. As we walk through the aisle of the shadows ahead, we fret no rats, for we have each other, and them; their memory and love, they unwind. A sign hangs above the door. We exit.

From behind, we hear a familiar snarl.

We run into the atrium.

A Ratperson grunts. I can feel her sneaking around. She thinks we don't know.

'Hide,' I whisper.

I'm pulled by my leg through an opening, into a room smaller than mine. There's a foiled window. I tear off the layers, and light trickles inside.

'Money!' Luke says, holding a handful of paper.

I shake my head. 'Tickets,' I say, and shush him.

The Ratperson is drawing near.

We can only leave through the front door. A silhouette rises above, like a lighthouse. Luke hides under the small desk. I forget myself. The music swells. It's Dad. I blink hard, look around and see only tickets and a register. I pull the spring from my pocket.

'No,' I say.

Steps resound. The booth feels like it's shrinking.

Dad's guitar pick.

I throw the pick. It clinks on the dusty marble.

She scuttles in that direction.

We finally leave.

WINGS

The sun rises over us. The colours shine brighter here. A wren chirrups and I turn. Off to the right is a little patch of grass. Above, my window hangs from one side.

How did I never notice this before?

Luke yelps, and I follow his gaze to the door. She'd torn down the foil she'd put there. I feel safe.

'It hasn't been bloodless yet, has it?' I say.

Her lips curl, but I don't hear her. My heart settles.

'You stay there now, Maeve. Stay. Like a good girl.' A crooked smile forms on my lips.

Luke hides behind my thighs. In the pane of the entrance, he sticks his tongue out.

We just can't help ourselves sometimes.

She pounds at the door as we walk away.

*   *   *

As we scavenge the bins, Luke looks up at me, the skin of an apple on his head. I smile. We're alone. No more shadows, no more shifting moods. From now on, there will be no more Rats. Only us.

He's holding one hand behind his back.

'What've you got there?' I ask.

He looks away, his cheeks turning pink. I flick the apple skin off his head.

My other hand is waiting. He presses his eyelids together and puts a book on my palm.

My whole life I've had to pick up things. Nasty things, like digging through the trash. Pretty things, like looking at birds to learn about the weather. Risky things as well.

We move on. The trash is rich. We're lucky.

At the train station, Luke suddenly jumps up and down. I laugh.

'What is it?' I ask.

He points to a man playing a guitar. The tip of my finger starts bleeding.

I bite my lip.

Music booms from the speakers. It's not a song I like, but I take it in.

Before Luke and I set off, he says, 'Will we see Ma and Da?'

'No, little hare,' I say, my eyes watery. 'We need to live first.'

GUT INSTINCT

Joanna Theiss

I WOKE UP to the sound of Abigail retching and heaving. In the living room, I found her surrounded by bits of partially chewed flesh.

I groaned, grabbing a roll of paper towels and carpet cleaning spray. I picked up the firm lumps of last night's salmon. Then I knelt on the floor and scrubbed while Abigail stared at me, shaggy muzzle drooping, brown eyes gazing up at me in remorse.

'Bad dog, Abigail,' I said, although it's not true. She's a good dog, but she's had a hard life. According to my nephew, Micah, Abigail had been the devoted pet of a woman who had been living rough. She appealed to Micah outside of a liquor store, begging him to take Abigail because the woman could not afford the food that she needed.

Turned out Micah couldn't afford it either, which is how I ended up with her.

I baby Abigail. I got her a dog trainer, the best-quality grain-free dog food, and had recently hired a new dog walker too. Her instinct is to steal from my plate, and once she gets something, she defends her catch. I don't try to stop her, and neither would you. Her size is more mythical monster than poodle mix.

When Micah drove Abigail down from his place in Toronto, I almost changed my mind, but Micah assured me she was gentle, so long as she got plenty of exercise – hence the dog walker – and learned some basic commands. Micah pointed out the benefits to having a brute like Abigail for a woman living alone.

My dog trainer agreed. Abigail reminded her of the dogs that she grew up with in Texas, all power and loyalty, with the courage to face down a boar. Along with the commands she taught the other dogs – sit, stay, heel – she also taught Abigail how to attack, with just a word from me. On the last day of class, she took me aside and said, 'Abigail will protect you, if you need it.'

She didn't say 'again', but I felt the word land heavily at the end of the sentence.

If only Abigail could protect me from her own vomit. By the time I had cleaned up all of Abigail's mess, it was so late that I wouldn't make it into work. I emailed my boss and said I was sick, which I sort of was, after all that. I showered and changed, and Abigail hopped up next to me on the couch and put her long, narrow paws on my calves, her nails brushing my shins. I thought about going somewhere, running some errands, but I was so comfortable.

I didn't plan to fall asleep.

* * *

My neighbour called the police when he heard the screaming. The EMTs carried out the dog walker on a stretcher, his midsection covered in blood, while uniformed men swabbed my entertainment centre, which Abigail had destroyed in her charge.

At first, I was too surprised to do anything but answer honestly.

No, I didn't remember that the dog walker would be coming, because I was usually at work. No, I didn't hear his key turn in the lock. No, I didn't hear his heavy boots cross the carpet, towards me, dozing, and Abigail, apparently awake enough.

But two things triggered me and I began lying, an hour into the questions. The first was when the animal control officer spoke so casually about killing Abigail, like it was a foregone conclusion, even though the dog walker was alive when they pulled him out of the wreckage of my electronics.

All this talk of killing, yet the officer was too chickenshit to even meet Abigail.

'Is the animal restrained in there?' he asked, pointing warily at my closed bedroom door.

'No,' I said. (That part was true. Abigail's leash had been gripped in the dog walker's hand when he was stretchered out.)

'What will it do if I open the door?'

'I guess you never know what she will do,' I said, correcting his use of pronoun.

'Huh,' he said. 'The truck I brought doesn't have a big enough cage for – how big did you say the animal is?'

'A hundred pounds, or so,' I said, gifting Abigail an extra ten pounds.

'Yep,' he said. 'Not going to be big enough. I'll be back.'

The cops watched him go.

That was the second thing: the cops, their abdomens encrusted with bulletproof vests, kept glancing at me, then at my bedroom door, then whispering to each other behind their hands.

How could it be that these men, with their Kevlar carapaces and holsters of phallic weaponry, were actually afraid? The novelty of that – the rare, pleasant sensation of two females holding power over two males – made me lie.

Like when they asked me why Abigail would attack her dog walker.

My, my, officers. Why would she attack? Maybe because an unfamiliar man, smelling of cigarette butts and dried sweat, holding a leather leash, was standing over a sleeping woman? The same sleeping woman who provided Abigail with love, food, a soft bed, and, yes, grilled salmon?

Maybe because my own instinct kicked in, as my eyes opened at the smell of him, hovering there, watching me?

Maybe because I commanded her to, using the word that the trainer taught me?

'I have no idea,' I said out loud. 'She's unpredictable.'

'Maybe we should call this in from the car,' the short one said, and the other cop leapt up to follow.

* * *

'Do you have anything to declare?' The uniformed buzz cut asked me, as I idled at the customs stop along I-93. He had already handed back my passport, and he seemed bored by the interaction. He hadn't noticed Abigail stretched out on the back seat, so motionless in sleep that she looked like a discarded insulation blanket.

'Not a thing,' I said.

'Welcome back to Canada,' he said, waving us through.

NEVER LOOK BACK

Maria McDonald

IT HAD BEEN a long flight. We left warm sunshine behind us and flew fourteen hours through the night, hoping to land in London in the early-morning winter sun. Except there was no sun; there was nothing but fog. We gazed out the window in wonder at the swathes of viscous grey below us, like blobs of dirty cottonwool. The only hint at our destination was the London Eye's upper rim, extending skyward out of the fog. Our landing was textbook perfect despite zero visibility. We applauded our pilot's skill, then gasped in surprise when he announced that the onboard computers had landed the plane. No human intervention was necessary. I was glad he didn't tell us in advance. It might have led to quite a few prayers, even from the atheists amongst us.

Disembarking was surreal. Everything was quieter in the fog. Even the roar of the jet engines appeared subdued, the clatter of luggage carts smothered. The other passengers twirled in dancing sheets of greyness that disappeared into the foreground. Swirling clouds melted to the touch yet cloaked every object. The world felt slower, calmer, all worries abandoned, only softness and greyness and peace.

The door opened into the terminal, the bright lights bursting the semblance of calm. The hustle and bustle of the airport came as a shock to the senses. My heart started to pound in my chest as I thought about where I was and why I was there. We had a few hours to kill in Heathrow before our connecting flight to Ireland, so we found ourselves a corner, not too far from our departure gate, and settled ourselves down for the wait. He nodded off, and I smiled as I watched him sleep. His chestnut hair covered his eyes as his head rested on the arm of the chair, perfectly relaxed, oblivious to what lay ahead for us.

The letter was burning a hole in my pocket, and I took it out and read it again. She had always been articulate. Every word was measured. I could picture her poring over it, writing and rewriting until she had the tone perfectly correct. But it was written from the heart. I could feel that. She had put pen to paper and told me she needed to see me, that she missed me. Somehow, the letter she wrote to me summed up how we both felt.

It had all been so awfully long ago. Ten years to be exact, when I walked out of that house and out of that life. It was Tom who kept me going, kept me living. He took up every waking moment of every day and inhabited my dreams at night. Even when I dreamed of her, Tom made a cameo appearance. I wondered what she would make of him. It had been love at first sight for me, and I wondered if she had felt that way about me, before puberty, before the argument. I wanted her to love Tom as I did, so I had written to her back then and told her all about him. My Christmas card to her contained a photo of us, and I got that one short reply. No correspondence since then. Until last month. That crisp white envelope had called out to me from my postbox. My heart skipped a beat when I recognised the handwriting. The neat rows in her precise script, as if measured with an imaginary ruler, the Irish stamp symmetrically aligned on the right-hand corner. I re-read her letter again for the hundredth time.

The first time, I had to sit down to open it, to study it, to pore over every word to try and figure out what had changed, why now, and then I realised that it really didn't matter. My mother had written to me – that was the important factor, and the ifs and whys could wait. I emailed her and was deliriously happy when I got an almost immediate reply. I was a little bit shocked as well, to be honest, after ten years of nothing. So, here we were, sitting in an airport lounge, waiting for our connecting flight home.

Home. I was taken aback when it dawned on me that I had used that word. In ten years, I hadn't thought of Kildare as home. It was the place where I was born, the county of my youth, the place where I had lost my faith in the inherent goodness of humankind. Home for me now was California, sunshine, technology, and a circle of friends who cared for Tom and for me. Yet here I was, drawn back to Kildare, and the closer I got, the more apprehensive I became.

The voice on the PA system announced our flight, and I patted Tom's arm to wake him. He stirred and stretched his limbs. His sea-green eyes smiled into mine, and my heart melted. I loved him with every fibre of my being. We gathered our belongings and joined the queue at the boarding gate. Tom had never been to Ireland, although I had told him all about it. Well, not everything. I had left out the painful bits, the moments that still hurt my soul, that still burned something deep inside me. No, I had given him the tourist-board version. I spoke of the greenness of the landscape, the clearness of the sky mirrored back in the aquamarine sea as it alternatively kissed and battered the coastline. I told him about the majesty of the Curragh Plains on a frosty morning, with the mist rising and the racehorses flying along, like warhorse ghosts in the swirling ground fog, their hoofs cutting the short grass. I told him about the legend of Fionn mac Cumhaill and his hounds, whose sculptures stand guard over the entrance to my hometown. Stories of Ireland as the land of saints and scholars, St Bridget, patron saint of Kildare, and Brigid, the mythological Irish goddess.

Of course, these stories remind me of my childhood. I try to ignore the sense of yearning the retelling of these stories reignites in me, and remind myself that I have a good life where I am. Still, every so often, I realise that somewhere inside me is a homesick girl who misses her home and her family.

The fog lifted in Heathrow, and we took off right on time. Tom was very intuitive to my emotions, and I smiled as I felt his hand take mine during the flight. On our approach to Ireland, we peered out the window, but there was nothing to see. Low clouds blanketed the landscape, and I prayed that it wouldn't lead to our flight being delayed. A mixture of relief and something akin to anxiety struck me as I heard the landing gear engage and then the soft thud as we touched down on Irish soil.

My father was waiting for us, and I was struck by how much older he looked. I wondered how much of that had to do with my mother. There were bags under his eyes that hadn't been there when I left. He was now totally bald, and his potbelly was growing nicely. He wasn't surprised when I told him about the letter. He already knew. She had told him, asking his advice when wording it. That revelation shocked me. I didn't think they were that close. He rarely mentioned her over the years, or so I thought. He said that I had continually shut him off when he brought up her name, so he stopped talking about her to me. He told me that he didn't want to risk losing me.

That had given me a reason to think, to re-examine everything I had told myself up to that point. Did she break off all contact with me, or did I break off all contact with her? Did she believe me, or did I blame her? I had asked him that on Skype one evening. He looked despondent and somewhat anxious.

'Does it matter? You were both hurt by him. You both said things you regretted. Hurtful things said in anger. You are so alike, too quick with your tongue except when it comes to saying sorry. It's time to put all that behind you.'

I wasn't prepared for her to be there, at the airport, to meet us. She was sitting to one side, head bowed, and I knew she couldn't see me. I saw my father glance over at her, gesture to her that we had arrived, and watched as she turned to face me. Her appearance stunned me. The years had not been kind to her. His duplicity had left its mark on both of us, but I had recovered, bounced back from my past, with Tom.

My heart skipped a beat as I waited for her reaction, her face displaying anxiety and impatience, and a smattering of fear. Then her eyes met mine, and she smiled. She opened her arms to greet me, to wrap me up in the hug I had dreamt about for ten years, and I ran to her. It felt even better than I imagined. Such warmth, such love, wrapped up in my mother's arms. Her hands caressed my hair, and I felt her tears on my shoulder. I was transported back to my childhood and to the warmth of a mother's unconditional love, and I could not stop the tears that dripped down my cheeks.

Then I remembered Tom. I disentangled myself and wiped my eyes as I turned back to look for him. He was behind me, a broad, open smile on his face. I gestured to him, and he stepped hesitantly forward. With his hand in mine, I introduced my son to his grandmother.

INTERMISSION

MOVIE NIGHT

Samuel Bollen

SOME ARE SURPRISED to hear we have a movie night. They find it out of place. But if you think about it, Movie Night makes perfect sense.

The whole thing was my idea. I suggested it to the Big Man shortly after getting down here, when I got bored by the doldrums of torture. He told me, unsurprisingly, that That Was The Point.

Unfazed, I reminded him that if torture was always the same, one could get used to it. With a reprieve, nobody can ever truly get comfortable in the Lakes of Fire. He countered with the typical, We Are Sure To Mix It Up, which I expected. I just told him to think about it and flounced off to be flayed.

Evidently he thought about it, because it was only a few decades before our first Movie Night. We watched *It's a Wonderful Life*. I was the projectionist.

The Big Man took credit for it all, but he was sure to let me know about the twenty per cent increase in screams and wails in the following century, and left the programming schedule up to me, pending his approval.

We get new releases – on about the same schedule you do, just twenty to thirty years delayed. Of course, there are the occasional early surprises, and new arrivals are sure to let my department know what we can expect down the pipeline. The waiting is exquisite.

With the luxury of time, I can choose the films that are truly memorable – not just the awards season fodder that gets churned out one year and forgotten the next.

The schedule of new releases is fairly reliable. People who make good movies rarely go to the other place.

During each showing, a school-dance atmosphere presides. There are those who are too nervous, too new in their tortured bodies to truly enjoy themselves. Others, however, turn to their left and right in the provided folding chairs, seeking out what passes for a cutie down here. The lucky ones lock eyes. Later in the movie, perhaps, a peck on a rotting cheek from a desiccated lip. There are always several newbies wailing in the corner, of course – easy to ignore.

As much as I enjoy their reactions, I have to admit my motives have not always been entirely charitable.

In the beginning of the program, every few eons, I'd try to slip in a film that, strictly speaking, should not have been there.

I'd watch him watching the movie, tail twitching, feeling the heat rising off him. The movie itself I did not need to watch – I knew it inside and out.

He's never known my name. We don't have names down here. Even if we did, I don't think he'd care enough to know who I was.

At the end of each film, the credits would roll – my old name would appear. And he would look back at me.

'Is this the best you can do?'

I would give him the perennial classic that I'd been saving instead, and he'd end each follow-up viewing with a 'That's more like it.'

We'd slowly been working our way through my catalogue. To tell you the truth, there was one film I'd been saving. Unlike the others, it hadn't gone totally unnoticed.

I was hoping it wouldn't come to this – that one of the others might get approved by mistake.

But even the most prolific have a finite catalogue. And mine was quickly coming to an end.

I knew which film I was saving.

It had been a festival darling. Almost won some of the major awards. Again, as a curator, I didn't go in for all that. But the Big Man did.

'I've never heard of this one.'

'No? It won some awards.'

'Hm.'

Watching him watch it was agony. Would he laugh at the right parts? Tilt his head? Understand? But I watched his tail twitch and his fur ruffle in silence.

As the second act peaked, I realised I'd spent my entire life trying to impress Big Guys like this. No – trying to trick them.

They say that down here your life plays out over again. Sure, there are different decorations: the fire, the brimstone, the festooned organs. But the pattern is the same . . . over and over.

Well – here we were again.

The credits rolled.

'You know?' he said. 'Every once in a while, you show me something that isn't quite as good as the others. And the same name pops up in the credits.'

I didn't say anything.

'Do you think I'm stupid?'

'No.'

'You just think you're that smart – that you can trick . . . well, you know.'

I didn't say anything.

'Show them *Annie Hall* again.'

As he was leaving, he turned. 'You know, that one was cute. A couple more decades and I think you might've had something.'

That night, I watched the credits roll, watched the Big Man Himself stroll out on stage, his tail jauntily poking the air behind him. 'Did you enjoy the show?' The haunted murmur of lost souls. 'Now back to your pits!'

But you know? Seeing their upturned faces just before the end of the show . . .

It's almost worth it.

BE CAREFUL

David James

ONE DAY, WHILE rummaging around in the attic, the wife found a young face sitting in a hat box. She held it up, examined it and tried it on. It had long blonde hair, two dimples and blue eyes. After slapping the old face against the wall to silence its whining, she shoved it into a drawer filled with coupons and receipts.

'Now the world will be different,' her new face said. And it was. The world looked clearer and her sense of smell was sharper. She stared at herself in the mirror and smiled until she noticed her new face attached to an old woman's body. *I need a new body now,* she thought.

After looking through boxes, bags and plastic bins, she found a younger body crammed into a hope chest. She replaced her old one with it and folded the former body into a garbage bag.

'Now that's what I'm talking about.' She modelled her new face and younger body, strutting around the house. She danced through the kitchen, swinging her lovely hips. She couldn't wait to surprise her husband.

When the husband came home from work, he was greeted by a stranger. Startled, he fell back against the wall.

'Where's Martha?'

'I'm Martha, love,' the young woman said, reaching for him.

'You're not Martha.' He grabbed a knife off the kitchen counter and waggled it in the air. 'Where's my wife?'

'It's me, John. I'm just younger now.'

'I don't believe it.' John shuffled toward the phone, wielding the blade. 'I'm calling the police.'

'But look, this is my old heart.' The young woman took her heart out and gave him the bleeding, pumping sac organ. He studied it in his hands for a minute and began to cry.

'Please, Martha, come back. A young wife is too much work. She'd want children, she would not understand my jokes. She'd grow tired of an old man.' He gave the woman her heart back. 'I need some air,' he said and left out the side door, still holding the knife.

Martha climbed up to the attic and changed back into her old body. She opened the drawers, found her old face and put it back on. When her husband came home later, she knew they'd both pretend this whole ordeal had never happened.

She would love him even more for that.

RUMINATIONS

LIGHTS OUT

Travis Grant

HE WORE FULL leathers and was folded in broken, awful ways. His legs were bent at the knees but the sides of his boots were flat on the asphalt. His chest smothered most of his right arm, but you could see his hand and part of his forearm sticking out from underneath. His other arm was up around his face, and his right cheek would have touched the asphalt, except for the helmet. He looked like an action figure a child had dropped.

His motorcycle was crumpled into the side of a van, right where a range road crossed Highway 16. The Harley-Davidson logo was still visible on what was left of the gas tank. A woman in jeans and a white top stood over him, holding her right hand to her forehead. Another woman sat at the edge of the ditch. She hugged her knees and rocked back and forth. A man stood behind her, consoling her.

Rick and his wife, Dorothy, pulled up in their pick-up, towing a freighter canoe. They had been fly fishing in Jasper and were headed home to St Albert. Rick got out of the truck and walked over to look at the body. The woman in the white top looked up at him but didn't speak. Rick walked back to the truck and got in.

'Did that woman say what happened?' said Dorothy.

'No,' said Rick.

A man in a work truck heading the opposite direction stopped. He got out and stood beside the woman, then he walked back to his truck and got a canvas drop cloth to cover the body. Rick and Dorothy heard sirens to the west, coming from Edson.

'There's nothing we can do here, Dorothy. Let's go.'

Rick pulled around the accident and continued east, toward Edmonton.

'What do you think happened?' said Dorothy.

She looked back as they pulled away.

'I'm guessing they didn't see each other and when that van crossed the highway, it was too late.'

'Motorcycles are so dangerous.'

'We were just fishing in the backcountry, surrounded by bears.'

'That's different, don't you think? Out there it's more of a measured risk, as long as you're prepared and you know what you're doing.'

'I'm pretty sure people who ride motorcycles would say the same thing. I bet that guy back there knew what he was doing.'

'Sure, but the problem is other people. That guy might still be alive if that van hadn't crossed the highway.'

Rick thought about a story he read in *Alberta Outdoorsmen*. It was about a guy hunting up in the Peace Country who was mauled by a grizzly. He didn't even have time to chamber a round.

* * *

It was early September. There was frost at night and most of the poplars had turned yellow. Soon the fields along the highway would be alive with harvest. Rick and Dorothy passed over the bridge at Entwistle, where the Pembina River carved a deep, forbidden valley. An old iron trestle spanned the valley and a diesel engine hauling cargo rumbled across.

'My dad used to take me fishing on the Pembina,' said Dorothy. 'I used to get scared, thinking about falling into this valley. It's so steep, and the river – it's wild down there. I still get nervous on this bridge.'

Rick looked at Dorothy as she spoke. Her legs were crossed in the passenger seat, and she had a magazine on her lap. Rick was still thinking about the accident. He couldn't get the image of the man's broken body out of his head.

'I wonder if that guy had any family. Do you think he had a wife and kids? I wonder if they even know yet.'

'Oh my God, I don't want to think about it, Rick. It's awful.'

'One day you're riding your motorcycle, then . . . gonzo. It makes you wonder, what's the point?'

Rick looked out the driver-side window, then back at the highway.

'Did you get a good look at him from the truck?' said Rick. 'You couldn't even see how bad it was under the helmet and all that leather. He looked like a prop.'

'I didn't look closely,' said Dorothy. 'I don't know those people back there. That's not my weight to carry.'

They were quiet for a moment and Dorothy flipped open her magazine.

'Do you ever think about how in a few hundred years no one alive will remember we existed?' said Rick.

Dorothy stopped reading and looked up at him.

'Never.'

'Imagine it,' said Rick. 'Your whole life, your entire identity, lost to time, like you never existed. It's strange to think about. It hollows me out a little.'

'I wouldn't think about it too much, my love.' Dorothy smiled at Rick. 'It's better to just enjoy your ice cream while it's in front of you.'

* * *

At nightfall, Rick took the Villeneuve exit to St Albert. From the overpass, Dorothy watched the highway disappear through the glowing parkland into Edmonton. When they arrived home, Rick backed the freighter canoe beside the fence and unhitched. Then he backed the truck into the garage. Dorothy helped him unload. They put a charge on the batteries and hung the electric motors on a stand. Dorothy put away their fly rods and camping gear. Rick stacked fly boxes under his work bench. There was an old, framed photo on top of the bench, and he picked it up.

'Do you remember when we went into Orloff Lake with your dad that one year?' Rick asked.

'Sure,' said Dorothy. 'That was the trip when you cut all of that deadfall with your chainsaw, just so we could get around the beaver dam. I don't think we were even married yet. What made you think of that?'

'Just this old photo of us, sitting on the hood of that little Toyota 4x4 I used to have, buried to the headlights in muskeg. Boy that was miserable, getting the truck out of all that muck. But you know what? Looking back, we had the best time figuring it out. It's funny how you remember things when you look back. It makes me think differently about what's in front of me. Perspective, you know?'

Rick put down the photo and Dorothy put her arms around him.

'Let's go to bed. It's been a heavy day, and I'm tired,' said Dorothy.

Rick closed the overhead door and locked the garage.

* * *

A dim light still glowed on the motor for the overhead door. Rick and Dorothy's footsteps faded up the back porch into the house. Then a timer clicked and the light went out, but there was no one there to see it.

BUS ETIQUETTE

Charlotte Armstrong

ON THE BUS route, things always change. It is the same route, and yet each journey brings something new: a new display in the weird furniture shop (including a full-size Komodo dragon statue that you're still on the lookout for), a new café, a new driver, new passengers. You travel at different times, and each journey is like listening to a shuffled playlist of songs you already know. Most of the time you are familiar with everything that is coming, but sometimes something sneaks up on you.

A new store opens and you think to yourself, I should go in there, but you don't go in. You stay on the bus, mind hazy, music on, trying your hardest not to engage with the other people trapped in the tiny metal cabin hurtling (more often than not literally; bus drivers appear to have collectively decided road rules are suggestions only) from place to place. Bus etiquette and all that. The next time you pass, it's a different store. You think to yourself, I should check that one out. You don't check it out. Rinse. Repeat.

So the sight of a freshly painted teal door, sandwiched between the kebab joint whose lights are always on (but a little too dim) and something akin to a hippie store, is just another mild curiosity. Perhaps, you tell yourself, you will go and check it out. But where would it lead?

Realistically, the door has to go behind these buildings. Probably into a flat, you think, or perhaps another store. Idly, you can't help but wonder if perhaps, should you try to open that door, it might open into a magical Narnia-like land. At least then you could stop fielding questions about your non-existent love life from well-meaning but overbearing relatives. The thought almost makes you chuckle, but you're still on the bus, so you hold it in. Bus etiquette and all that.

You pass the tattoo store with the eight-foot dog mural. The subject of the mural – a large white-and-black bull terrier named Splash – has flopped gently onto the welcome mat. You tell yourself next time you'll get off the bus and give Splash another pat.

There's another door on the Way Home (which is different to the Way There, but also the same) that also catches your eye. It's ridiculously painted with a large sigil that looks hand-drawn (perhaps a cult?). You've only ever seen someone emerge from it once. Granted, it was a pair of artsy-looking hipsters in Hawaiian shirts and pastel corduroy so, if it is home to a cult, you muse, it's probably one that caters to people with dietary restrictions. When the door rolls by again, you wonder if the sigil is simply the result of some bored graffiti artist. Or perhaps, entertaining thoughts of fleeting fantasy, a lost magic-user in a desperate attempt to return home. A door to a home that takes you home?

The next time you pass, the door remains. And the time after that, and the time after that.

You almost don't notice when it disappears. After all, everything changes on the bus route.

RESPIRATORY THERAPY

Clay Hardy

REPORTERS STAND IN their usual spot. We look down to the parking lot from our usual spot, which is a small, gravelly corner square on the top of the fourth floor. We are positioned between the air purifiers and the helipad. The January wind blows fiercely around us but we can still hear the enthusiastic sounds of a young reporter interviewing the nursing manager. They're discussing the usual: heroic doctors and their superhuman efforts followed by a small nod toward the nurses who never get the glory. Just all the credit.

We continue to stand silently waiting for them to mention us. Just once. But today would not be the day. Don't mind us, though, we'll just be here making sure the patients can all still breathe.

Once the soundcheck people, hospital PR and random reporter groupies depart, there begins another sound. The same sound that we all dread: the wheezing of the asthmatics and the cough of the persistent smokers shuffling outside as all but the most critical individuals are turned away from the ER. Our usual patients have been told to come back in a few hours with hopes of a free bed then.

I counted seven of us on the roof this morning. Down from nine just a few days ago. One of our team was fired for excessive drinking on his breaks. Another employee quit from exhaustion. I find my eyes searching the faces of my colleagues, trying to determine who would be next. As I look around, I see our team in their most relaxed and tranquil state: dark circles under their eyes, shoulders hunched and jaws clenched. As relaxed as possible, considering the circumstances. Mostly, though, I just see red lines. Skin creases on the bridge of noses and just above eyes where elastic has strained then settled into its familiar home for the past twelve hours. And by twelve hours, I probably mean closer to eighteen.

An alarm soon goes off on my phone and we all know it's time. Time to breathe in one last second of peaceful, polluted mist. Cigarettes are stepped on. Coffee is chugged. And loud popping sounds ring out as necks, wrists, backs and jaws are stretched out. Back inside, we all exchange muffled curses as we meticulously cover up with H1N1 masks, fresh scrubs, protective gowns, face shields and multiple layers of gloves.

A few nods are exchanged between us and the night shift team as we pass one another down the hall. I try not to look, but I cannot help glance back to see a few of them already crumpled on the floor or scrunched into undersized folding chairs. I want to bring them coffee or sit with them, but think better of it and look away. The rest of my team ignores them as well, wary of allowing their exhaustion and despair to permeate our mood.

At the top of the hour, we hear another chorus of familiar sounds: a page overhead from the ER; a code red; the squeal of sneakers jogging on freshly waxed floors; the dreaded ding of elevator doors opening.

These are always the last few sounds I can remember before we plunge back into the chaos.

MERRY CHRISTMAS, ISLA MUSSETT

S J Elliott

Sydney, 1956

ISLA WAS REMOVING the pavlova from the oven when her son shrieked. She tightened her hold on the tray, burning her hands through the tattered gloves as she withdrew it from the doddering Kookaburra oven.

Hissing in pain, she set her fragile creation down by the sink, as the stovetop was already laden with burbling and hissing pots, spewing forth a clash of sweet and savoury scents.

'What's happened?' she called out.

No answer.

Winston's distraught cries worsened.

Stripping off the useless mitts, she swept through the doorway to the living room, finding that the humidity there almost rivalled the heat in the kitchen.

Winston was splayed out on the hardwood floor. Desmond remained unmoved in his armchair, cigarette in mouth, beer in hand, his head buried in his favourite copy of James Joyce's *Finnegans Wake*. The electrical fan perched near him rustled his thinning hair with its haggard breath.

'What happened?' Isla sank down and scooped up the unresisting Winston. He ensnared her with his limbs, but wouldn't show her his face.

She had to raise her voice to be heard, not only over Winston, but the radio. The freestanding Mantel unit was banging on about the Melbourne Olympics, but Isla knew that Desmond couldn't possibly be listening to it. Having covered the whole drawn-out affair at his work, he scowled at the mere mention of them now.

Not that he needed much provocation to scowl at anything at all these days.

Desmond turned a page. 'Ask him yourself.'

'I'm asking you.' She straightened and almost dropped Winston. Not from him squirming, but from all the muck her hands and arms were coated in. She'd need to wash and change. Again. With his beer-holding hand, Desmond gestured to the Christmas tree dominating the corner closest to the fireplace; below it, the rug used to catch the fallen needles was pulled from its place.

'He slipped. He's fine.'

'Winston would beg to differ.' She jigged their son up and down as his wailing continued. He pressed his snotty face into her chest, tickling her skin through the fabric with his hot, hitching breath. 'Wouldn't you, matey?'

'Winston can't even string a sentence together.' Desmond took another generous sip of his beer and resumed trying to decipher Joyce, while fat beads of perspiration slid unchecked down his face.

Isla turned away from him then, in search of some composure, as her son, their boy, did his unintentional utmost to shred her hearing. Her eyes wandered over the collection of framed pictures and assorted sentimental bric-a-brac adorning the tallboy gifted to them as a wedding present by her brother Malcolm.

Framed degrees, both from Sydney University, a decade apart, Desmond's for journalism, hers for teaching, sat on the mantle. Positioned in the middle of them was one of her earliest paintings, depicting a wooded fairytale vista, replete with dancing cherubic figures. The glare of the sun bouncing off the glass encasing the scene made it appear like all the little creatures were engulfed in flames.

'Win, give it a rest,' Desmond ordered.

That just encouraged Winston's wails to renew, and Isla brought him over to the window. She sought relief from the heat, but not a single waft of cool breeze stirred the curtains.

She glimpsed a gaggle of the neighbourhood children whom she knew by sight, if not by name, charging down their homely street in the heart of Balmain and in the full swing of Christmas Day celebrations. Now she knew why Desmond had the radio blaring.

At least that's what she hoped was the reason, instead of the alternative – having it up so high to drown out their son's cries.

'Bloody little mongrels,' Desmond said.

'They're just children. You were one once too, you know.'

Desmond's widened eyes snapped back to her, and Isla breathed in sharply as she'd done when she burnt herself. Childhood. Taboo. Guilt aplenty.

She avoided his wounded stare by looking to their son.

Despite her arms starting to ache from holding Winston, and how uncomfortably stifling the contact of sticky flesh on sticky flesh was, she continued gently rocking him, making soothing sounds into his soft, clean hair. It was blond and unruly, like his father's. She occasionally prayed to God that that was all that he inherited from him. Then she prayed just as vehemently for forgiveness for thinking such thoughts about the man she loved.

It made no difference that Desmond didn't believe in God; she felt like she'd betrayed him all the same.

'You promised you wouldn't start drinking until the afternoon.' She managed to juggle Winston and wipe away the sweat beading on her face.

'Kept it.' He gave his wristwatch – an exquisite Tudor that she'd given him shortly before they were married – a theatrical shake. 'It's getting on.'

'Well, don't go falling out of your chair trying to help me get ready.' Isla gently pried Winston's hands from his face. She found no bleeding, no welts, no redness, save that caused by his crying.

Sensing he'd been caught out, Winston favoured her with a huge smile, both rows of baby teeth accounted for, gleaming brightly.

She smiled back as she thought about how he became more beautiful each day, more assured, becoming whoever he was meant to be – regardless of, or in spite of, Desmond's naysaying and handwringing. Or worse, Desmond's silences. She set Winston down, her arms and back sore from the exertion. He was getting so big, and she was getting so weary just thinking about it. Not that she thought about it much. Not that she had the time to think about anything much.

'What needs doing?' Desmond killed his beer, set the empty bottle down to join two of its mates on the coffee table near his chair, which was stacked high with loose sheets of scribblings, atop which he'd rested *Finnegans Wake*, as a paperweight, as a goal.

Isla knew that the sheets couldn't be all that important – Desmond would never leave them in easy reach of Win if they were, so that ruled out the latest draft of the novel he'd been working on longer than their boy had been alive.

Desmond noticed what Isla's eyes had fallen upon and flushed, embarrassed. 'What?'

Isla nodded. 'What's that?'

'Nothing.' He flustered, sitting up.

She eyed him with what she hoped was glowing adoration, wanting him to feel reassured, to feel that it was fine to share. She wondered if he'd deliberately left out some of his writing as proof to her that he was still creative, just as creative as she was.

His chin tilted upwards to her and the steeliness in his eyes confirmed she'd get no more from him on the subject. So, she relented, nodded back toward the kitchen, where the collection of pots and pans sat neglected. 'Off you pop then.'

Desmond scoffed and rose from his chair. 'You joking?'

'Are you that much of a chauvinist?' She smiled when she wanted to frown. 'What happened to the progressive Desmond?'

'He's still here, fighting the good fight.' He drew near her with his hands outstretched. 'I'd just burn the whole house down.'

'That's no excuse.' She bristled, but already her frustration was waning; she was just too tired to sustain it.

She had been up before dawn and had barely gotten any real sleep before that, after stealing off to attend Father Goodman's midnight mass on her lonesome. Then Winston had shaken her awake as quietly as he could. He'd wet the bed again and didn't want his father finding out. When that had been sorted, she'd started cooking, leaving Desmond in bed. He'd continued sleeping in his eerie way, corpse-silent and motionless, a behaviour she suspected had been conditioned into him during his childhood.

'I'm a scoundrel, I know.' He regarded her with his usual self-deprecating half-smile. It usually worked and she felt it working on her then. She loathed that it did, that he knew it did.

'You are.' She buried her face in Winston's to hide it from Desmond's.

'The worst of the worst.' He sank down to his knees and hugged them both, tried blowing raspberries into her stomach, covering her in his sweat. Winston giggled and reached a tiny hand out to pull and prod at his father's face.

'Stop.' She tried angling her body away. 'You need a shave.'

'I just need my wife to love me as I love her,' he said, not looking at her, his nose brushing against Winston's.

Isla wanted the contact to end. Not that she found her husband's touch unpleasant, only that she found him so unattractive when he was sweating the beers he had been drinking. Desmond had never had an athletic physique, but it had held such staggering allure for Isla when she'd met him. *A real man's body,* she'd thought. What a jarring contrast Desmond's proudly unfit body had been compared with the men's she'd grown up with. The young men that worked for her father's company paraded before her, all towering and imposingly built. The hubris they exuded. How could she be expected to lust after something that was so contrived and certain in its perfection?

Her wandering mind stirred her, and she pinched Desmond's bottom hard enough to produce a yelp.

'What was that for?' he asked.

'You deserved it.'

Even though she'd said it jokingly, Desmond's earnest smile bled from a wounded expression. But he reclaimed his fail-safe smirk quickly, even if his eyes didn't fully meet hers.

'I acknowledge that I can't help in that hellhole.' Still hugging Isla, he nodded toward the doorway where the kitchen lay beyond. 'But I'll get the car packed. Assuming those little bastards haven't blown it up, or something.'

'Language,' she mock-chided as she gently cupped Winston's ears. He tried jerking out of her loose grasp, his tiny hands battering at her.

'He's got to learn it all sometime.' Desmond readjusted his grip around them both, the proximity to his wife and son making him seem taller, surer, happier. 'For the playground.' Isla was astonished Desmond had mentioned something from his childhood. She tightened her hug on Winston as she basked in his easy and breathless fits of giggles, their mellifluousness spreading a warm giddiness in her, which distracted from the oppressive heat.

The perfection of the moment left her wondering why all moments couldn't be like that.

Isla pushed those thoughts away as she eased Desmond off her. 'Winston can help.'

Desmond hesitated, before ruffling his son's hair. 'Winston can help,' he repeated. As soon as he heard his name, Winston raced out of the room.

Desmond frowned. 'Oi, you're helping your old man.'

But Winston thundered down the hallway toward his bedroom. Isla saw Desmond's face darken. 'Don't go getting grumpy. Just call out to him when you're at the door, he'll come.'

'He only listens to you.'

'He listens to you when you're not yelling at him.'

'I don't do that.' Desmond averted his eyes from hers.

Isla wondered why Desmond was often frustrated with their son. How could he think that Winston was not developing properly? Was he not reassured by Winston's endlessly inquisitive spirit?

Surely he saw that their son had inherited that wondrous trait from him. How could he fail to see that thirst for knowledge when Winston reverentially sat at his feet, volleying random questions at him until the sheer exertion of doing so made him drop off, and ended with Desmond carrying him off to bed?

Seeing the most important males in her life like that, feeling the fleeting harmony they emanated, restored her belief that their little family unit could endure, that their hardships would be conquered and any animosity between Desmond and her decidedly resolved.

'Please, just go pack.' Isla motioned to the mound of presents under the tree as she returned to the stove.

Returning to the stove, she found that nothing had burnt or boiled over, and that the pavlova had not cracked. That was a relief. The last thing she needed was a snide comment, or a lecture from her mum, Eden. Not that her mum was a whizz in the culinary department either, only she never passed up an opportunity to give her daughter a tongue-lashing, especially with an audience to witness it.

Isla had, in her lifetime, come to understand that interacting with Eden was nothing like strolling through the endless paradise of her mother's namesake. In many ways, it was actually the equivalent of being forced to make one's way through a field riddled with bindies.

Time passed while she tended to the food, and Isla gradually became optimistic that they might not be as late as she first anticipated.

'Malcolm going to make an appearance?' Desmond asked from the doorway.

Isla was so startled she nearly dropped the dish of honey glaze she was spreading atop the steaming leg of ham.

''Course he will be.' She coated her response with an acidic warning. 'You're supposed to be getting the car ready with Win.'

Desmond lifted his shoulders, looking toward the fridge, where what remained of the beer stockpile beckoned. 'He didn't come.'

Isla had heard as much, knew that it was because Winston had come to associate his father's utterance of his name with something bad.

'Please just go start putting the presents in. We're going to be late.'

'I hope your brother behaves himself today,' Desmond said.

Desmond liked to condescendingly drawl 'brother', like Malcolm was unworthy of being identified as one. That ugly, heavy jealousy that had been there almost from the start and grew once he'd learned Malcolm was adopted, evolving into rancour that fuelled their verbal brawls over the years. It was an unseen beast tethered to the pair, that crammed itself into any room they shared so that it felt like there was no space for anyone else – least of all Isla.

Desmond noted Isla's pointed silence and retreated with a parting tongue click, like he'd won some argument.

She heard the front door open, and Desmond called out 'Win, mate, I need your help.' His tone was friendly and light and Isla hoped their son would emerge from his room and help his father as a good boy should, as a son who didn't fear his father.

THE EMPTY DINER

Scott Beard

I FEEL MY phone buzz in my back pocket, and I know it's another reminder that I'm late. But I keep my fingers gripped on the wheel because I'm passing another blue, blanketed figure waving for a ride in the black of the night. The snow pelts my truck's windshield and soon turns to slush under the hot air blowing from the defroster. I sigh. Out of the corner of my eye, I catch the blue flash of the plow lights spinning overhead. My stomach growls and I start to think about the text message that has come through. I quickly pick up my phone and check. It's from Mr Parsons, who is waiting for me at Millie's Diner along Pennsylvania 28. I start to get hungry. Luckily, I only have a few more miles along US Highway 119 before I get to Punxsutawney.

As I'm clearing the right lane of the highway, I look in my rear-view mirror and see the hitchhiker once more. The sight of them out in the cold makes me jitter. I ease over the centre line and, thankfully, the oncoming cars see this and slow down. They must fight against the spray of snow and mud coming from the plow shear. The shear continues to grind along on the asphalt. My hands are still shaking, but I try to forget about it. I take the next exit along a winding stretch of highway on the west end of Punxsutawney. To the southwest, the silhouettes of the Allegheny foothills fade out into the distance. The winter sycamores appear to writhe like twisting lines of black ink. There is snow covering the hills, burying all the dried and dead leaves. The hills won't see daylight again until early April. I check my rear-view mirror. The hitchhiker has already disappeared into the night. He is now a memory.

I flip my front blinker on as I approach the bottom of the exit, lift the shear and slow down before I reach the traffic lights. The red light illuminates the snow like cotton candy. I make a left turn and grind up the next hill toward the flashing blue marquee for Millie's Diner. I continue past Mr Parsons's brown truck, which is also blanketed in white snow. I am soon greeted by warm air as I move inside the diner, and quickly forget how cold it is outside. I wish it was that easy to forget a lot of things.

Mr Parsons is sitting at one of the rear booths. He is wearing an old ball cap, blue vest and red flannel shirt. He sees me and waves me over to his table. My hands are jittering as I slide my coat off. The waitress has already come to us and she sets some water down.

'You're late,' he says.

I look into his tired, grey eyes. The whites around his pupils have faded to a dull yellow colour, a sign of too many all-nighters sloshing snow in that miserable plow, chugging cup after cup of coffee just to be paid for with a wad of sweaty change. When I look at him I feel I am looking past him into the opaque black and blue of a winter's night.

Mr Parsons leans forward into the centre of the white Formica table. He reaches for his ceramic mug, takes a sip, coughs and wipes his lips with the back of his heavy right hand.

'Burnt and bitter,' he says, shaking his head. I look out the window and see a lone man digging out his light-green sedan. He bends and scrapes the wet snow, which flies behind him. It seems futile. He stops, straightens his back and adjusts the hood of his thick jacket.

I turn back and stare at Parsons's coffee. The swirling mixture reminds me of the snow and fog outside. I close my eyes momentarily and can picture the hitchhiker. They remind me of another blue-and-black silhouette I had seen two years ago.

The snow had been spitting like frozen embers. As my plow roared past him, I heard a thud and checked the rear-view mirror.

The shadowy figure had ungraciously broken out of the large pile of snow I had just created, standing there motionless. My hands had begun to shake. I checked the other mirrors and the road was empty. My chest was pounding, but I had kept the truck grinding up Pennsylvania 28 alongside the tall sycamores crowding the snowy shoulders of the road. I had tried to focus on the road, stare straight ahead into the low beams as they lit up the asphalt ahead. Just drive into the heavy flakes. The white powder had begun to cover the hood of my truck again and I loosened my tight grip on the wheel. I didn't stop driving, though, as I left the cold and dark of that night behind me.

Mr Parsons mumbles something that breaks my daydream. He slides in the bench seat next to me and I look up to meet his grey and yellow eyes.

'Well, Jeff,' he says in the cartoonish manner he will use to get to the point. 'I appreciate all you've done this season.'

His hand reaches for the envelope in his jacket pocket. I wait. I know the roads will be empty tonight, but I don't want to be lingering around on any snow-packed streets. He hands me the envelope and I can already see the sweaty wad of paper bills peeking out. He's an honest man, so I won't count them in front of him. I wish I were more like him.

'Thanks,' I say reaching for the envelope. It is all I can muster.

I stare into his coffee mug. It's almost empty. He stands up and puts his coat on. He wraps his woollen scarf around his neck and sighs.

'I'll get in touch with you again around October. Until then, take care of yourself, Jeff.'

As I watch Mr Parsons leave, I see that the diner is now empty. The clank of dishes being tossed into the kitchen sink breaks the silence. I'm still staring into the coffee mug he left behind. Through the dark and murky swirls, I picture my windshield again. Cold. Blue. Then I picture the dark coat and pants next to the pile of snow. I close my eyes.

They will find the hitchhiker in the spring. Skin and bones frozen and bruised. I sigh and stand. I quickly leave the diner and get into my truck, planning to head west down Pennsylvania 28 into Pittsburgh, and further west across to the Ohio border. I want to leave the memories of the late night shadows behind. I know that the plows will still be out on the roads, even now. Their blue lights will flash from the tops of their trucks. I look out the windshield, back toward the empty diner. The snow continues to fall.

CURRENTS

Rebecca Moore

THESE DAYS, THE memory arrives and dematerialises in front of her like steam. A bob in the water. Coconut in her throat. Sand like shards of glass between her toes.

The sun had been strong. At first warming and kind, then scorching and deceitful, spotting vision and making him difficult to see among the rollicking waves. She was reading *Cosmopolitan* – Ten Signs He's a Serial Dater, and The Best Push-up Bras for Your Bust Size – a respite from the Morrison novel in her bag. A volleyball game played out behind her, the claps of hands to canvas thudding like a heartbeat.

The Mexican resort was grand, drenched in a kind of luxury that delighted and appalled in tandem. She remembers how her mother had marvelled at the lobby as they entered. She'd slung an arm across each of her daughter's shoulders saying, 'Enjoy it, but don't get used to it.' The plan was to relish soft fitted sheets and pillow mints, and to simply do nothing on a beach.

That day, a father and his daughter had been hunting shells along the shore. She recalls a red bucket and water wings. And wasn't it the little girl who saw him first? Her doll-like hand pointing out to sea? By then the man had grown smaller, drifting towards the horizon. Later, when he lay motionless in the sand, she'd marvelled at the size of his blueing body and wondered how perspective could be so fraudulent. Even now she harps on it, measuring trees and clouds with her thumb and index finger while contemplating their true size.

She had been outstretched on a towel, sipping on a pina colada – umbrella garnish and all. Her skin prickled with sweat, and she contemplated a move towards shade when the icy drink sent a pang to her head. It was then, with eyes closed as she willed her brain to thaw, that she heard the cry. A lost point from the game behind her? No, it was more of a wail, and much farther down the beach. The man's wife had seen him. The cry was hers.

The families nearest to the woman stood at the sound. And then, almost like a standing ovation, the whole beach rose. Later, she would remember the 'STRONG CURRENT' sign posted by the towel rental stand, and the throngs of people in the water. Plenty who had also believed themselves immune to the tide.

As they brought the man to shore, a quiet had settled like ash across the beach. The man on the towel beside them, white wires sprouting from his leathered chest, kissed his wooden cross necklace. And – this part plays in her mind like a glitch in a film strip – she rolled her eyes at that. And he had seen her do it.

He stalks her now – while she's giving a presentation at work or standing in the line at Starbucks. He's there with his wooden cross and yellow swim trunks. They've reached an understanding; she acknowledges him then shakes her head, and he falls away like the lines of an Etch A Sketch.

The beach had swarmed with whispers as the lifeguard went through the motions of resuscitation. Her mother had steadied herself against her chair. Her father and sister, always active and ready for combat, walked quickly towards the crowd for a better look. A young couple – honeymooners maybe? – shook their heads in unison as the lifeguard backed away from the body, and an emergency vehicle trundled across the sand.

And then, like the flip of a page, the scene had dissolved. The man and his wife gone; the lifeguard back atop his stand. A waiter in white, clutching a tray to his chest, looking on for some sort of aftermath. But there was nothing. Just the waves, unaware, moving rhythmically against the sand.

It felt like only seconds later that a pink-shouldered mother in her forties had turned to the waiter to say she was just dying for a daiquiri. She remembers watching him, how he'd studied the woman, letting the satire hover thickly in the air before asking if she would prefer peach or strawberry.

* * *

Years later, on a date at a bar in a city far from the beach, she wears the perfect bra for her bust while her date says something about mortgage rates. She nods with feigned interest while sipping on a dirty martini. The brine lingers, and she wonders if the man had tasted the salt in the water as it filled his lungs.

Then, as usual, the tide comes and the thoughts ebb. She eats the olive from her glass.

DRIVING IN THE DARK

Grace Gibbons

I AM AFRAID of the dark. When I drive, blast after blast of blinding light comes at me, and I can't tell where I am. Too far left and I will be hit head on. Too far right and I will careen off the road or crash into a tree. I try to keep up with the 55 miles per hour speed limit, but cars swerve around me, so I turn off and take the back way.

Now, I won't be flooded by light coming at me, but there will be some car riding so close behind me that I will be blinded by his headlights in my mirror. The driver knows these roads and I am holding him up. He is young and powerful, fearless, reckless; he wants to accelerate full speed into the darkness. Come to think about it, it is just as likely to be an old man. Old men are still in charge, and they will fight to hold on to their position. I am passed on the road often, and when I catch a glimpse of the driver, it has never been an old woman.

I know these roads in daylight, but at night they are not the same. I cannot see ahead where the bends are, which way they will curve. Does bolt out of the woods, fawns following. There are patches of darkness so deep they suck in the light of my high beams. Suddenly, a driver is behind me; he's appeared out of nowhere forcing his way forward with aggression and anger. He leans on the horn and guns his engine to shoot around me.

As a young man, my husband, Aidan, drove aggressively. He pressured the cars in front of him to speed up or get out of his way. 'Learn to drive, asshole, or leave the fuckin' thing in the garage.'

70

If someone challenged him, he'd make kissing noises and insult the other driver's manhood. He'd press his foot into the gas pedal and career around other cars. I'd plead with him to stop, and he'd berate me: 'Stop yelling, you're going to cause an accident. I know what I'm doing.'

Aidan did most of our driving, but a few months before he died, he'd had to stop because he was too sick. When the kids were still at home one of them would usually drive, but they're gone now, too, so I'm on my own.

Aidan fought hard against death. He kept the brightest lights on in the house, so it couldn't enter unseen; he tried to push past it, to swerve around it by demanding treatments and pills until he was finally overtaken.

Headlights appear close behind, disbelieving my turn signal and, annoyed by my slowing down to make the turn onto my street, the driver gives me a scolding sound of his horn as he continues into the night.

I'm on the last stretch of road before home. I once told Aidan that I wanted to move out of this big house when the kids were grown, but he said no. Now, there is too much space filled by darkness. It isn't the house we lived in as a family anymore.

I pull into the driveway. I forgot to leave the porch light on, not expecting to return home after dark. I forgot how early darkness comes in December. I won't forget again.

When the kids were young and afraid of the dark at bedtime, I'd act as if it were nothing. 'It's the same place,' I'd tell them, 'lights on or lights off.' But I've never believed it.

DRINKING

Martha Patterson

IT WAS CHRISTMAS and well-intentioned friends had told me to clean up my act for the holidays. Trudy and Camilla both said I was hopeless. Trudy designs jewellery and has a perfect life: a handsome husband, two young, well-behaved children and a pretty house in the suburbs. Camilla is only slightly less perfect – has a steady, reliable boyfriend, works as an office manager at a tech startup and calls her mother every day. She has good hair. And she's a vegetarian, so she cares about the treatment of cows and pigs raised for slaughter. But she chews gum nonstop.

Anyway, they both told me at Christmas time I needed to shape up and 'get real' just because I drink.

Can you forgive me? I don't harm others, I mostly keep to myself, I see my doctor once a year and she says imbibing is okay as long as I don't 'crash' afterwards. I never do. I just want to read Dostoevsky's *Crime and Punishment* while drinking good Russian vodka and thinking about how Raskolnikov's conscience bothers him so much he confesses in the end. And how his young, sweet blonde girlfriend waits nine years for him to get out of prison, which is nothing for a double murder, but, after all, he does have a big conscience.

And *my* conscience really doesn't bother me. I have vodka to forget it all. And, if I do ever have a crisis in faith, I've got the knowledge that many people have done worse things with their lives than I have, like torturing animals, or abusing a child or stealing from the elderly.

I'm all right; I just drink. I wish it were easier to forget the past: bad boyfriends, a lousy job like telemarketing as a fundraiser for political parties I don't even believe in, maltreatment by mental health professionals. But vodka and tonics help. Weak of me, maybe, but they're effective. And since I don't drive and I remember birthdays and I not only pay my rent but also return library books on time, my booze doesn't hurt anyone else. I just like having a solution to all the angst, madness and cacophony of everyday living.

Two months ago a man was murdered in my building. His apartment was broken into by a burglar and the burglar stabbed him to death. Can I forget? Why would I? And do I want to live in this building anymore? It was senseless, as they say on the news whenever they announce a stupid crime. Why should Mr Sammler have died? He was eighty-two, was friendly, he shopped at the Korean market down the street and had a cat and never gave anyone any trouble.

So, dealing with this trauma, in some ways I *am* getting it together. I'm walking two miles a day and vacuuming my rug every week and trying to cut down on the heating bill. I'm only eating twice a day; my resolution to maintain my weight. I'm keeping in touch with friends via email – because they don't like the phone – and I'm hand delivering my neighbour's packages to his front door when our UPS guy just dumps them on the sidewalk in front of the building.

But I do drink. If I didn't have vodka, I'd be a nervous wreck.

This afternoon I'm going to do some online shopping for a new pair of flannel lined jeans and a couple of sweaters for winter, because what could be better in January than planning a cold-weather wardrobe? And I bought a salmon steak and some fresh spinach for dinner. Today, I'm trying to forget Mr Sammler's untimely death, and my basket case of a 'career', and all my loser boyfriends, and a really messed up psychiatrist as well as an egotistical social worker, both of whom I mistakenly consulted last year about my problems.

Today is the beginning of the end of listening to everyone who says I need to clean up my act.

HOMECOMING

Helena Pantsis

THE FIRST TIME feels like the fifth time feels like the twelfth time. Feels like coming home for the holidays and regretting it, like getting fucked up with an old friend from high school and fingered in an abandoned McDonald's carpark. He's trying to unhook her bra by letting the elastic slap against her skin, not as resilient as it was the first time, and the pain's not worth the anticipation of what it once felt like anyway.

Across the way is that dollar store Mum took her to, the one they bought their groceries from for a year after Dad was let go. It's empty now, the store a carcass, gutted clean. She stares at the abandoned building, bobbing up and down against him but keeping her eyes trained still on the trolley bay outside, just like they used to do. She doesn't even know why she does it – her mum invited him to dinner to catch up while she was in town, and he suggested that they go for a drive. Maybe she wouldn't have gone if there was more to do in this town; it's like she forgets who she is when she's home.

When she got older, she got a job at the dollar store, 'plastic-or-paper'-ing mothers like her own with starving kids in tow and two dollars at a time to their names. She used to undercharge, feigning to scan the pricier items or throwing chocolate eggs into the bags before bagging. She met him there, both working the night shift one Monday, him flirting and offering her a ride home and a shag. It was almost romance back then.

The boy presses into her awkwardly, his hands poking into her ribs.

They'd always look for a used trolley in the carpark, one with a coin already in it, and Mum would keep the coin and pretend she'd one day have enough to run away or pay off all their debts or maybe just get her hair done by a professional instead of Dad with the stationery scissors. Mum used to forget the cart and the kids with it some way through the store, in the aisles where the kids could entertain themselves, with the mass-produced Chinese toys with knock-off names like Smider-man and BEGO blocks. She, the oldest of the two kids, would stand at the end of the trolley yanking the hair of a plastic pony, with her feet tucked under the basket, teetering, her brother in the baby seat chewing on a cardboard box. Sometimes she saw her mum through a gap in the shelves, crying by the frozen foods with her head bent low.

'That hurts,' she says. He's digging his nails into her. She moves his hands to her back.

The store smelled like dust then, or plastic, or things made cheap and kept too long. This car smells like the same stale draught that used to blow from the aircon in those days in summer, when they'd huddle by the fan at the storefront.

When her bosses found out she was undercharging needy mothers, she was fired for stealing. It was ironic, given the company was outed for tax fraud the year after. She came back that night, with him, and threw rocks at the windows round the back. They couldn't afford to fix all of them; she wonders if you can still see where the rocks were thrown.

She repositions, him in the front seat now with the chair pushed as flat as it goes and her legs bent against either side of it like armrests, her upright on top of him.

Mum used to reuse the plastic bags as lunch boxes, triple-bagged for the holes at the bottom. She'd stock up at the end of every trip, blushing and refusing to make eye contact with the clerk as she asked for a few more bags.

She glances out the window for a second, thinks she sees someone leaving the McDonald's from afar. She flails, body collapsing flat on top of him; she's hit by the embarrassment of being an adult living out of home, but still spending Novembers searching for a place to make out with the boy who's got all his dreams pegged on being a Soundcloud rapper. The embarrassment of not being able to afford dinner for the week. She's thinking the new plastic ban will be tough on the hard up.

He pushes her hands down. She cups his scrotum, swollen, fondling like something out of bad porn, but she hasn't been on her knees in so long and she doesn't really know how to squeeze in a way that feels natural. She tightens slightly until he makes a sound resembling pleasure or indigestion, then stops when she feels a lump. Ten years ago, she could've just brushed it off, but she's a year into her internship at the clinic and she knows better. She pulls back and sees his eyes open when he can't feel her anymore.

'What's wrong, babe?' he asks, and it means he is waiting.

'There's a lump on your right testicle,' she says. 'It could be cancerous.'

The pair sit back, his face furrowed and strained, her breathing out a puff of air. She's thinking she won't come home for Christmas next year.

They dress, decide they should part, and pull the car out back. That's when she sees it. A hole in the window the shape of a rock. She smiles.

'What're you smiling about?' he asks, affronted.

'Nothing,' she says, but she's thinking it'll be nice to go back home.

EVERYWHERE INSIDE

Boshra Rasti-Ghalati

Dedicated to all political prisoners.

IT WAS HIS final kick of the day. I know this because I know the hours he roams around this shithole and I take pleasure in knowing that, despite what he believes, he's in here with me.

It doesn't hurt anymore, his steel-toed boot. Fucking fucktard. I can't wait until shit comes down, and it will. I am certain he'd sink faster in the quicksand, metal boots dragging him to his shitty grave.

There's the clink of the bars and I'm thrown into the cell. It's become comforting. The cold floor of loneliness. On all fours I look up to the wall, the one where I painted a heart out of my own blood, for Hope. She loves the colour red. She loves hearts. It's real, it's real, it's real, I say in time with my breathing. On the Outside, they don't breathe when they're praying, words reaming out like a robotic paper-packaging machine. Reality isn't where they live. They think they are doing someone else's work – God or man. Who would do someone else's work, except a slave? I call them Everyone Outside, the fools waiting for an imaginary end, when in reality they'll one day become Everyone Inside.

Here on the Inside, he believes he is immune; it gives me satisfaction. His days are numbered. One day, they will distrust him, and he'll become Everyone Inside, just like me. Isn't that what happened to all those who did the dirty work for Lenin, Stalin, Hitler, Pol Pot, Khomeini?

I caress the ground with my hand. The ground below me is stone. I laugh. Everyone Outside thinks they will ascend to the clouds like fucking saviours. The only thing they've saved is the sins that they've collected like the dust on the ground, now mixed with my blood, as they strike me with their whips.

He spits at me for good measure. 'You're going to die here and go to hell.'

I turn my face back to look at him. My teeth are clenched. I am angry, but I won't give him the satisfaction of my words. Hunger-striking demands energy. Lets me fall into untroubled sleep to dream of the colour red and the shape of hearts.

He hands the key to my cell over to another guard. Another piece of metal to mire him.

I am light as a feather. How long before skin and bone evaporate? I don't have anything to live for except Hope. I wonder why she loves the colour of blood? I would have thought it might be yellow or white – the colour of light things. Hope is more real than God. She is Everywhere Inside. Her name is Hope. Light as a feather, as the streak of sunshine on the grey ground below. I run my hands over it, making a fist, trying to catch it. More real than God. She never asks me to do her work. Such is the freedom of Everyone Inside. How much profundity can be crammed into skin and bones?

'Get up! It's interrogation time!' he barks.

I walk down the hallway: a spirit floating past pain, buzzing Everywhere Inside.

'You are a spy of the colonisers!' he shouts.

It seems they already have their own answers. Floating, dancing, whispering. Red hearts. Hope. Not the Stalinesque red of a flag and sickle. Everyone Inside is a scapegoat. Everyone Inside is a bargaining chip for Everyone Outside.

'Don't you dare touch Hope!' I scream.

Everyone Outside, they find excuses to use as fodder for the hellish world they are creating.

Everyone Inside knows these are lies. Convenient lies. One day he'll become a convenient lie.

He cracks his whip against my feet – bastinadoed by a bastard. But he's sinking deeper with those steel-toed boots. One day he'll be so heavy with witnessing they'll worry he knows too much. Then he'll become Everyone Inside. Just like me.

HEARTBREAK, HEARTACHE

Paul Bowman

SERENDIPITY. LUCK. TURNING the newspaper page and seeing his photo. They chose an old, old photo. Jesse at twenty-seven. In his prime.

She remembered. The eyes, the shape of the head, the hair, the smile.

Jesse.

She did not decide immediately to go. To see him. The body. To grieve.

Why grieve? What was the point of it?

But after a night of thinking about it she knew. She would do it. She would drive to Lexington. A three-hour trip. If she got too tired for the trip back, she would get a hotel room. A nice room. She had the money. She could afford it.

Was she being weird? Too curious? No one was watching. No one would know. And.

And. How much time did she have left?

She had two friends. Two. But she couldn't tell them. They wouldn't understand.

She left too early the next morning. She had to wait almost an hour before the other cars filled the parking lot. Then she walked in. She did not sign the guest register.

She waited in the large quiet room. Waiting. For what? Recognition? The other people in the room did not know her. And she did not know them.

They stood in groups and talked.

About what? Their lives?

She did not go to the back of the room where the beautiful box was. She could not.

What was she waiting for? Understanding? Peace? Forgiveness? Acceptance?

Yes. That was it. Acceptance.

It was finally over. The heartache.

In a few hours, Jesse's seventy-two-year-old body and the casket that housed it would descend into a freshly dug rectangular hole in the ground.

And the memory of her longing would fade.

* * *

The other room, almost five decades earlier, was larger, more silent. The seated people waited for the ceremony. Some of the women turned their heads to each other and murmured.

His side had more people. This surprised her. He had few friends. He did come from a large family. Many cousins, second cousins.

She was an uninvited guest. A spy. A voyeur.

She had no pride, no self-respect. Was it bitterness? No. No. She wanted to see it come to an end. Although it had ended some time ago, hadn't it?

Brittany. The pretty one.

Had they had sex yet?

Of course.

When she had walked in, she did not know where to sit, so she chose his side. In the back.

Was that an indication of loyalty? Still? After all that time?

The organist began the prelude. A pretty girl and a tuxedoed man entered the room from the front door. They walked at a sedate pace and were followed by another pretty girl and tuxedoed man. Then another pair. Another pair.

Some of the girls were not that pretty. They had tried.

He came last.

She did not think there would be eye contact. That they would look at each other. See each other for the last time. Take it all in.

His surprise lasted maybe three seconds. Two heartbeats.

Was he angry at her? No.

Instead, he had the look of a condemned man. His future, his life, was going to change in small, unknown ways. He bravely hid that worry, that concern.

Of course. Do men want to get married? Really?

(Was the bride pregnant?)

God, he was handsome. She wanted to get up right then, grab his hand, take him outside to the sunny world, smile at him, have him smile back and mean it, drive to the nearest hotel, motel, whatever, and do it. The sex would make up for all the disagreements, misunderstandings, mistakes they had made. So unimportant now. You were late. You kept me waiting. I didn't say that. What I meant was. Why don't you listen to me?

Take him away.

Before it all ends.

Before it all ends.

Before she had to live the remainder of her life without him.

Jesse stood in the centre of the line of pretty girls and tuxedoed men and waited for the arrival of his bride. He looked so far away. So far away.

She loved him more than anything, but that love, that desire, had no purpose, no future.

She left before the ceremony was over. She sat in her empty car and wept.

That day, years ago.

INTERMISSION

THE KNITTING TOURNAMENT

Stephanie Gobor

MAVIS TWIDDLED THE cheap acrylic yarn in her lap. It felt like plastic rope as it glided through her wrinkled fingers. Her short grey hair fell over her eyes in uneven lengths. Her back was hunched as she focused on her work. She was knitting a jumper for her sister who would visit the prison at Christmas. Mavis had taken up the art of finger knitting during her time there. Knitting needles were of course contraband, and yarn was strictly monitored. It was only allowed in the craft room. For her good behaviour, Mavis had worked up privileges for craft room use once a day. She had hardly done anything special to earn her privileges. Most of the other inmates were sullen creatures who didn't bother her. They were too focused on not missing a step while shuffling their walkers to and from the cafeteria. Although, there was one inmate who did bother her: Patricia Thorne. It was a suitable name, Mavis thought.

Patricia slid into a plastic chair beside Mavis. The plastic chugging across the lino floor as she pulled her chair in made Mavis close her eyes and lose focus. She wished she had a pair of tweezers big enough to pluck Patricia from the room. They wore matching outfits of bottle-green sloppy joes and track pants. The only difference was that Mavis sported a pair of hot-pink knitted slippers.

'Good morning, Mavis. We were spoilt with breakfast this morning, weren't we? Ham and powdered eggs. Oh, and the coffee was—'

'Morning, Thorne,' Mavis cut her off.

'What are you making with that ball of knots? You know, I used to have a cardigan in—'

'Can I help you?'

'I thought since we are of a similar cognitive wavelength that maybe, well, we would sort of get along?'

'Look, I'm not interested in starting a CWA.'

Patricia exposed some extra wrinkles in her brow then laughed. 'A Correctional Women's Association?'

'No, you know what I mean. A Country Women's Association – jam, fundraising, craft!' Mavis began to unravel half an hour's work due to some missed stitches. Undeterred, she looked at the clock and picked up the pace.

Patricia broke the short silence. 'You seem like a community-minded lady, how did you end up in here?'

'I'll tell you if you stop bothering me. I'd much rather hear my own voice.' She paused, collecting her thoughts. 'It was my sister Sue Anne's fault. I lived with her, her husband and her two grotty boys. I had no options. I was never married; all I had was my cleaning job. After work I'd come home to my granny flat, put my feet up, switch on the box and knit.'

Patricia let out a fake gasp. 'So, you killed your sister and took her house?'

'No, even though Mum always said I was jealous of her. She was so pretty, Sue Anne, pretty and stupid. She was the kind of stupid that made a man feel smart when she was around.'

Patricia gasped again. 'So, you killed her husband?'

'No, I didn't kill anyone.'

'Nothing to be ashamed of if you did. I killed my husband. Almost got away with it too!' Patricia said excitedly.

Mavis continued. 'Anyway, I would knit. I would knit with the best yarns my wage could buy. Wool, alpaca, cotton, soft yarns, durable yarns, you name it. My flat was a paintbox of yarn. I arranged the soft yarn balls by warmth of colour. Magentas, fuchsias and yellows, then blues and turquoise and royal purple. I knitted garments and home décor. My flat was covered in woven wool. I had a jumper for every occasion. I would also knit jumpers as Christmas presents for Sue Anne's family. Quite a useless gift for an Aussie Christmas, but art isn't meant to be practical.'

'You're an artist then?'

'Of course I'm an artist! I went to art school. But I don't blame you for having to ask. My current studio is a bit drab, don't you think?' Mavis gestured to the nearby windows that had spiderwebs stretching across the metal bars. 'At the peak of my career, I made the finest jumpers. Each a work of art, inspired by an old textbook, *The History of Art in 100 Paintings*.'

The craft room had grey walls that lacked any examples of art, so Mavis tried to explain further. 'The first jumpers were traditional and orderly, like a Renaissance painting, with classic colours and bobble stitches in rows. I moved on to Impressionism, knitting in shades from Monet's water lilies; the stitches were looser and less formal. I knitted jumpers that were Art Deco, early Modernist and Post-Modernist. Each year meant another art movement. Cubism saw that the sleeves were of different lengths, one placed slightly below the other with bold, straight lines running shapes around the body. Next was Abstract Impressionism, an impression of a jumper, using elongated stitches and clashing colours. One Christmas, Duchamp inspired me to gift everyone in the family a ball of wool and call it a jumper.'

Patricia released a laugh. 'What's the point of that?'

'Do you mean what's the point of art?'

'What's the point of making something so useless?'

'Because art is supposed to make you feel something.'

'The only thing that jumper would make me feel is cold.'

Mavis waited, expecting her to say something else stupid. 'Anyway, the year of Duchamp was a bad year. I done my back in working and got on the pension. Sue Anne's boys were living their big-shot lives in the city and her husband died – cancer. It was drawn out. By the end of it, Sue Anne was restless. It was just me and her.

So, she got involved with all the community groups and volunteered for everything. Serving coffees after church, sorting clothes at Vinnies, hospice care, Guide Dogs, Girl Guides, even the SES. Oh, what a saint she was. Worst of it, though, was when she joined the Country Women's Association.'

'Time's up, ladies,' said the warden as she bounded in. She was a petite woman but rigid due to her body's attempt to exude authority. 'The low security inmates have booked the room for their art class,' she said apologetically.

Mavis thought that it must be conflicting to order the elderly around in a strict manner. There was a fine line between respect for elders and the regiment of the prison system. Mavis accepted the warden's instructions. She bundled her project up and carefully tucked it into the plastic basket with her name written on it. Patricia had nothing to put away.

'I'll see you for dinner, Mavis. I promise not to talk too much so you can finish your story.'

Wonderful, Mavis thought. *Now she thinks I'm her friend.* But Mavis was so rapt in talking about her art, even if Patricia didn't understand, that she accepted the invitation.

* * *

The cafeteria in the geriatric ward consisted of four rectangular tables. A dead herb garden that the inmates planted as part of an enrichment activity sat by the only window. On the menu tonight was lasagne with traces of mince and scarce cheese topping. It was served with packet mashed potato and a tropical cordial solution.

Mavis was eager to finish her story as Patricia pulled up her tray beside her. 'Anyway, one day I noticed Sue Anne fussing about the house. She was having "a fresh start". I saw clear garbage bags stuffed with colourful rags. I had always known my jumpers were never appreciated. But seeing them like garbage broke my heart. They had never seen the spotlight of an art gallery where they belonged. Sue Anne must have felt sorry for me because she suggested that I enter the CWA knitting tournament. It was an annual three-day competition that was judged on speed, quality and creativity. I figured that this was my chance to gain recognition as an artist, and there was one art movement left to explore – performance art. I was up against the finest knitters in town, but my main competition was Doris Derrière.'

'So, you killed Doris?' Patricia exclaimed, sending cordial and spit across the table.

'No, but I had a plan for her. She had won the tournament five years running and was the obvious favourite. I loathed Doris, her jumpers were too perfect, almost as if they had been machine knitted. She was a technician who learnt her trade by revising the same patterns over and over. I imagined her family receiving their jumpers at Christmas, their joy as if they had received a designer jumper from David Jones. I imagined Doris at Christmas with her husband, children and grandchildren. I imagined Doris was celebrated.'

'What did you do about Doris?'

'She became my masterpiece.' Mavis said, grinning. 'The tournament began, and I sat in the centre of the room, facing Doris. I cast on with the brightest white yarn and I knitted a jumper. I clicked my needles. CLICK CLACK, CLICK CLACK. I didn't stop until the bell rang at the end of each day. On the third day, the bell rang and I swooped the bright white jumper over Doris's head. Her arms were stuck by her side and the empty sleeves of the jumper waved about. I took my needles and I poked her until blood stained the jumper. I poked her arms. I poked her stomach. I poked her thighs. Then I stood back. It was beautiful, *real* performance art. The adjudicator was so impressed that when I caught her eye, she handed me the trophy. I won; I am a great artist.'

* * *

Mavis took her place in the craft room the next day, but Patricia Thorne never returned. She didn't have an affinity for craft anyway.

THE MY LEFT LEG CHAINSAW MASSACRE

Mark Crimmins

IT WAS ACTUALLY much scarier than the film.

Bill Pulaski told me that if I wanted a Christmas tree, I should drive up to Cedars and swipe one from the forested properties.

'Why wait in line and shell out thirty bucks?' he said. 'Just drive up the canyon and grab one!'

I put the chainsaw in the truck and drove up to Provo Canyon. At the Sundance turn-off, I turned left and found the side road near Cedars. I stashed the truck and hopped out with my safety goggles and chainsaw. I squeezed through a hole in the fence, chose my tree and pulled the starter on the saw.

But the machine got away from me, the rotating blade wiggling wildly in the air. As I wrestled the blade back down, I swung it into my left thigh, cutting a deep gash. A jet of blood sprayed into my face, blinding me. I could hear chips of splintered bone hitting the hard plastic goggles. When I wiped the goggles and saw the gaping wound, I turned the machine off and threw it aside, before passing out.

I came to on the forest floor, covered in blood. I heard animal howls, but I soon realised they were my own cries. I managed to drag myself to the truck, pulling myself along with my hands. I turned the keys and started along the bumpy turn-off as blood pumped all over the seats. I felt light-headed. The cabin looked like a slaughterhouse. I managed to tie a seat cover around my thigh, slowing the flow of blood. I veered onto the road and barrelled down to the highway, hoping a cop would nab me for speeding.

I reached Canyon Road and drove towards the hospital, zigzagging all over the road. I was starting to pass out when I swerved onto Campus Drive. A girl on the sidewalk drew back when I stopped by the curb.

I buzzed the window down. 'You gotta help me! Please.'

She crept forward, glanced at the bloody cabin and vomited into the gutter.

'I cut myself with a chainsaw and can't make it to the hospital. Will you please drive me to Utah Valley Hospital?'

The girl started to hyperventilate.

'Please,' I said, 'I'm dying.' I started to sob.

'Okay, I'll do it,' she said.

She climbed into the truck. Everything went dark.

* * *

When I woke up, I was in a bed with my leg sewn up and bandaged, hopped up on medication. The girl was gone, but a cop was sitting in the room. He wanted to know how it happened.

'Were you getting an illegal Christmas tree up near Cedars?'

'What makes you think that?'

'Well, you're the second idiot this winter that ended up almost chopping off his own goddamn leg!'

The cop got the giggles. Maybe it was the meds, but I started laughing myself. After all, I was relieved.

'Any more of you suckers do this, we're gonna be using severed legs as Christmas trees,' the cop continued.

Now we were both laughing hard, tears in our eyes. In my whacked-out brain, I saw a few severed legs with Christmas lights on them, wrapped presents down near the bloody toes.

A doctor came into the room. He gave us a look of disbelief.

'You nearly sawed your own leg right off, Mr Lapham,' he said, shaking his head. 'I don't see what's so funny about that.'

The doctor's glum words just set us off again.

'Can you tell me what happened?'

'I needed a Christmas tree for my kids.'

'He decided to cut his own leg off,' the cop said, wiping his eyes.

'For something a bit different this year,' I said, giggling. The doctor just walked out of the room, shaking his head.

The cop put his notebook back in his pocket. He became serious.

'I lost a finger myself,' he said, holding out his left hand. His ring finger was gone. 'I dunno,' he said, shaking his head. 'The things we do for our kids!'

TRANSITIONS

THE CHEAP SEATS

Joel Fishbane

THE FIRST TIME we had sex was during the intermission of *Hamlet*. Lord knows what got into us. Maybe it was the true love or the moon in the sky or all those actors running around in bodices and tight pants. We were in the back of the theatre 'cause that's all we could afford, so it was easy to run out and dive into the car. We were perfectly choreographed, as if we'd been in rehearsal for months. Your father broke my bra and tore my skirt, but it was glorious, like being savaged by love, and we made it back with a whole minute to spare.

The next week, he took me to see *Sweeney Todd*. And we did it again. Then it was *Aida*, which had *four* intermissions. We almost didn't survive. Every show was the same. Sneak out at intermission, run to the car, refresh ourselves and be back in time for the next act. I thought it would always be like that. Adventurous. I thought soft and boring sex was something that only other people had to endure.

The seats got better after your father started writing reviews for the *Star*. His most common comment was that the first act was too long, but he seemed to enjoy the rest of the show. One time, we tried having sex *before* the play, just to see if it would make a difference. He enjoyed the first act but, after intermission, we both fell asleep.

The better the seats got, the more people there would be in the way when intermission struck. It became harder to get to the car, so we had to be more daring. Bathrooms and alcoves became our friends. In the summer, we saw *Pericles* at an outdoor theatre. I thought

95

intermission would be easy because of the surrounding foliage, but wouldn't you know, someone walked by. And not just any someone. It was someone from the *Star*. Well, your father, poor boy, he completely lost his rhythm. And word soon got around that he'd been caught being more than just barefoot in the park.

I don't know why they thought it unprofessional for a theatre critic to be enjoying himself at intermission. I guess they thought he should have been contemplating the set design or something. Anyway, they let him go, but the injustice of the thing woke something deep inside him. He went freelance and started writing about politics, and then he published that piece about the governor's mistress. After that, he was meeting all the important people in town. We had invitations to all the best parties. Even then, though, our reputations preceded us. People gave us knowing looks; they followed us around to see if we'd slip away.

We still went to the theatre during that time, but it was never the same. Until we got caught, we'd been untouchable. We'd had a perfect run of secret sex, and that idea of perfection had bled into the rest of the relationship. It made the rest of it seem perfect too, even though it wasn't. We weren't perfect at all. It probably would have ended, but we had never been too careful, and suddenly you were there, and your father talked me into getting married. He said it was the right thing to do. Which it was, for his image. For me, it wasn't the right thing at all.

Once that first crack came, the rest followed. He became clumsy and feckless. Sex started requiring a lot of direction. He needed direction in *other* things too. We stopped knowing how to have conversations. We were like actors left floundering without a script. There never seemed to be a moon in the sky, and all those tight pants no longer had any appeal.

I tried to get it all back. At a production of *Les Misérables*, I wore the same short skirt from our first night together and a bra I thought would be easy to tear away. But, by then, he was so successful that he said he couldn't have his important friends seeing us in the last row.

He got us the expensive seats, right near the front. This meant that, when intermission came, we had to fight through a crowd. I knew we wouldn't make it out in time. When we reached the lobby, I told him to buy me caramels instead.

'Next time,' I said, 'you buy us seats in the back.'

'It can't be done,' he said. 'There's a price to success and that price is the front row.'

All this happened last week. It's why I told him to leave and why he's not coming back. It's also why it's so good to be sitting where we are. I know we can't really see the stage, but at least it'll be easier to escape if the show isn't any good. That's what matters. Bad shows are like a bad marriage: the closer you are to the front, the harder it is to leave.

THE MONSTER OF RAVENNA

Sam Elkin

WHEN THEY FIRST saw me, they said I was a terrible omen foretelling my city's downfall.

I was born with the wings of a bat, a curly horn on my forehead and a third eye on my left knee that tilts down towards the earth. My right leg is hairy, and I have an eagle's talon where my foot should be. I have both girl's parts and boy's parts, but I sit down to make water. I have two birthmarks high up on my chest that look like a poplar leaf kissing a rosemary sprig.

The town pharmacist didn't agree; he wrote to the Pope about me, declaring my birth an abomination. He said my disfigurement was proof of God's wrath because my mother was a nun and my father a friar. Despite all this, my mother still loved me, and named me Torsione, which means 'little twist'. My father arranged a transfer to the port city of Cesenatico as soon as he saw me.

My mother hid me in a barn and nursed me, though she was very skinny and didn't have much milk. Soon, every important man from Ravenna to Rome was curiously poking at my body or staring at me in fright.

Just two weeks after I was born, our city was attacked, the butchered bodies of young men and women piling up in the streets. The pharmacist blamed me, naming me the Monster of Ravenna.

I was just a baby then, of course. I flapped playfully around my mother while she slept, careful to lie back down when she stirred. My mother was expelled from the nunnery, so we wandered the streets of

Ravenna, selling idols and trinkets to passing travellers. My mother was careful to swaddle me in blankets.

One morning, we were sleeping out in the cold, and my mother coughed until she brought up blood. She kept coughing until she sank into a pained, rasping sleep. I fell asleep on her chest, but when I woke, she was cold and still. I lay there, all three eyes drenching her clothes as I wept.

At nightfall, I flew up into a tree, thinking that I could join a colony of bats. While some were initially welcoming, others laughed at me because I was so slow, and pushed me off my tree. I fell, and my horn smacked into the frozen ground. I covered myself in my mother's wet rags and walked back into the town, eating slugs and thistles along the way.

My unusual body was an asset to me. I could fly into trees at night and feast on pomegranates that were too high up for the townsfolk to pick. I used my talon to break into barns, where I could sleep under soft hay with my wings wrapped around me. While I slept, my third eye would keep watch. I made my way towards Rome, which I'd heard was full of different kinds of people. I thought it could be a home to someone like me.

But Rome was a dangerous place, controlled at night by the Bravi. As I slept in the Forum, my third eye witnessed all kinds of butchery. When I could no longer stand to see such horrors, I flew into the Sistine Chapel and admired Michelangelo's paintings. I hoped their beauty might rub off on me. During the day, I begged on the streets, desperate to look like the other hungry and homeless children.

One day, a member of the Medici family tripped on my talon as he brushed past me. He turned back in anger and grabbed me, pulling off my cloak and shroud.

'Sweet mother of Jesus,' he cried out.

'I'm so sorry, Your Majesty,' I said, attempting to cover my body.

He kicked my rags away. 'Are you the Monster of Ravenna?'

'Yes, Sire,' I said, bowing my head.

I was sure he would lop off my head with his sword at that moment, yet he did not. My third eye watched him as he stared at me in wonder.

He ordered his guards to bundle me up in a carriage, and his driver took me to his palace in Florence. The carriage driver gave me bread, wine and fruit. I had never travelled in a carriage before, and I was in awe of the beauty of the landscape along the way.

But I did not forget that I was a prisoner. I wondered, would I be clothed and fed like royalty? Or was I being fattened up to be slaughtered by the Pope himself?

I slept well on the journey, despite the bumps in the road. On the third day, we passed through a valley before entering Florence. My tired driver expertly weaved his carriage past speaker's corners, market stalls and bands of musicians. I had never seen a city of such wealth. Even the beggars were dressed in silk.

As we entered the Palace, I realised that the important man was Alessandro de' Medici, the Duke of Florence.

I was shocked when I was taken to my own room. A maid, who'd been assigned to wash me, fainted when she saw my horn. When she awoke, she stood up, only to faint again when she saw my hairy leg and clawed foot. I wrapped myself in a velvet curtain so that she would not die of fright.

When she came to, I told her not to be alarmed, and that I would hide my body from her. She rose to her knees and made the sign of the cross.

'What are you?' she asked, staring at my horn.

'I'm Torsione.'

I hadn't thought of the name my mother had given me since she'd died. Suddenly, my body was wracked by sobs, and my face and right leg began to dampen.

'I am so sorry. Where are my manners?' she said. 'I'm Elisabetta. Let me wash you.'

Elisabetta told me about how the Duke was nicknamed 'the Moor' due to his dark complexion. He had a reputation for kindness, she said, and that's why he took me in. She nicknamed me Torsi, and she brought me different styles of clothes to try on. I tried on a woman's dress, but the skirts got caught in my talon. I tried on a pair of men's breeches, which went nicely over my claw and furry left leg. I paired them with a luxurious *cioppa*, an overgarment with red organ pleats. Elisabetta told me I looked dashing. I was so touched I almost wet my breeches. That night, Elisabetta traced her finger along my leaf and rosemary sprig, and then kissed me on the mouth. She touched my male and female parts and told me I was perfect.

We spent the night together, making love. She made me feel like I was not a monster, but a blessing from above. When she fell asleep on my shoulder, I stayed as still as I could, hoping to stay there forever. After a while, my bladder betrayed me, and I carefully moved her face onto a pillow. I got out of bed, made water in the bedpan, and cut a small hole in my breeches so that my third eye could keep watch overnight. I lay down and lightly stroked her back with one of my wings until I fell asleep.

Before dawn, a scout rushed in on horseback to say that Rome had been taken by the Germans. There was a rumour that the Monster of Ravenna had been sighted just before gunfire broke out on the south of the city, and that I'd been heading towards Florence to continue my reign of terror. I panicked and quickly put on my *cioppa*. I opened the window, ready to fly away. I realised that Elisabetta would be in peril if they saw that she'd lain with a monster. I jumped back down from the window and shook her awake.

'Elisabetta, you must get up. The guards are coming for me!'

As she rose in fright, I accidently slashed her shoulder with my horn, and her blood gushed onto the bedsheets. I could hear footsteps on the staircase.

'Torsi, let me come with you,' she said, applying pressure to her wound.

'No, Elisabetta. Please stay here where you'll be safe. Tell them that I tried to kill you, and they might let you live.'

I ran back towards the windowsill. Then, as the guards burst into the room screaming, I jumped and flew away. My wings, now stronger than ever, took me all the way to Milan.

I returned to the streets, to wearing rags to hide my face and wings. I heard that Elisabetta became famous for fighting off the Monster of Ravenna, and for carrying my mark upon her shoulder. I never saw her again, but always think about her, of the moment she drew her soft finger along my leaf and rosemary sprig.

SEVEN STOPS

Steven G Fromm

THE OLD MAN burned through three wives and eighty-six years before cashing it in.

My brother called to tell me. Logistics were challenging. They lived out in California. I lived in Jersey. We'd all started out in Michigan. That's where the family burial plot was located, the final stop for my mother, Wife Two, and Wife Three.

So, we were headed to Michigan.

I ordered a scotch after boarding the plane. My wife demurred. I waited until we were in the air to let it drop that my brother had found a trove of love letters.

'How romantic,' my wife said, assuming they were to my mother. Or Wife Two. Or Wife Three. They weren't. There was a Wife Four in the works, which happened while Wife Three was still above ground. Wife Three died one year ago. Since then, my father had become ill and moved to California to be with my brother. Given the situation, Almost Wife Four agreed to *stay* an almost, and remained in Michigan.

'Okay,' my wife said. 'I mean, it's bad. But it's over?'

Not quite. Almost Wife Four was in her mid-thirties. And she had a baby. An eighteen-month-old baby. My wife did the math. That's when I told her Almost Wife Four was coming to the funeral. My wife caught the flight attendant's eye.

'Scotch,' she said. 'Double.'

We hit Detroit. My brother was supposed to fly in later that day. I started getting calls from step-relatives I hadn't seen since the last funeral. Maybe they wanted to invite us to dinner. That would mean conversations. Conversations might lead to Almost Wife Four. I let the calls go to voicemail. We headed to a hotel near the cemetery.

My brother's plane was on time. One problem. While my father's casket was on the plane, my brother wasn't.

'How'd *that* happen?' my wife asked.

'Bromodosis,' I answered.

That's the medical name for foot odour. *Bad* foot odour. The TSA agent had asked my brother to remove his shoes. He wouldn't. So that meant my living brother had missed his flight, while my dead old man was right on time.

We hunkered down in the hotel bar watching *Law & Order* reruns and drinking scotch. The next morning, I got a text from my brother.

here. c u at cemetery

I texted back a thumbs-up emoji. Twenty minutes later I got another text.

dad's missing

I pressed dial.

'Missing?'

'The funeral home didn't pick him up,' my brother said. 'So, the airport stowed him.'

'Where?'

'No one knows,' he said. 'They changed shifts.'

'What can I do?'

'Go to the cemetery and stall.'

My wife had just come out of the shower.

'Do I want to know what's going on?' she asked.

'No.'

When we reached the cemetery, a few mourners were already milling about the gravestones. I recognised a few of them as step-relations. Some came up to say hello and shake hands. Some didn't.

The rabbi arrived. Everyone went over to greet him. I stayed where I was. A brunette with deep brown eyes and olive skin came up to us holding an infant wrapped in a pink blanket. I knew who this was. She introduced herself. My wife took one look at the baby.

'She's got your father's eyes,' she observed.

'Say it louder,' I said.

More step-relatives drifted over. I had to be polite, so I introduced Almost Wife Four and her daughter, who was also, bizarrely, my brand-new half-sister. Almost Wife Four excused herself and went off somewhere for a pre-funeral diaper change.

The hearse arrived shortly after with a taxi in tow. My brother climbed out of the taxi and walked over. He kissed my wife and hugged me.

'Is she here?' my brother asked.

I explained where she was and that I'd already introduced her to our relatives.

'And they're *okay* with it?'

'Not exactly.'

He gave me a look.

'I introduced her as your new wife,' I said. 'She didn't seem all that bothered.' I spotted her walking through the gravestones toward us. 'Here she is.'

'Well,' he said. 'I could have done worse.'

My brother introduced himself to Almost Wife Four as six pall-bearers slid the casket out of the hearse and started moving. Our little party shifted over to folding chairs near the grave. The pall-bearers paused every few steps. It was called the Seven Stops, a show of unwillingness to part with the dead. That's when it hit me. They were burying my old man. I looked at my brother.

'Glad you found him,' I whispered.

'I didn't,' he whispered back.

'What?'

'They're still searching at the airport.'

I looked at the casket and pallbearers.

'What's in there?'

'Fifty old Metro Detroit phone books,' he said. 'The funeral home had a closet full of them.'

The pallbearers completed their seventh stop and placed the casket on the lowering device. The rabbi started in with the El Maleh Rachamim.

'Shoulda postponed,' I said.

'Sure,' my brother said. 'Give everyone more time to meet and greet my non-wife wife.'

He was right. The phone books would do. The funeral wrapped up. We all took turns shovelling a token of dirt into the grave. After some parting conversations, everyone started drifting to their cars. We had to stop at a step-relative's home for the Seudat Havra'ah before heading to the airport. My brother stayed behind to handle the logistics. Logistics meant making sure the burial crew didn't bury fifty phone books.

Almost Wife Four rode with us. She'd let her taxi go at the cemetery. She sat in the back and started chatting with my wife. I sat there listening and realised I was heading toward the airport. I knew I should be going to the step-relative's house for the mourning meal. I knew I shouldn't be ditching my brother. But I kept driving. That's when I realised I was my old man's son. I looked at myself in the rear-view mirror.

I was smiling.

BLACK BLOOD AND RED SOOT IN RUNE'S HEART

Chris Dixon

I WAS BORN in Rune's Heart, in a coal camp. I'm a coal miner's son. My father worked in the mines until he became air and sun. I know about pinto beans, bulldog gravy and cornbread, for that was all we had to eat. Father worked and slaved in the mines every day for a dollar at the county store, for a dollar was all he was paid. Our mayor, J.T. Blaine, will sell you a land of prosperity, breathtaking scenery and diverse pastimes that're fun for all the family. So, come on down all you tourists and I'll tell you what you'll really get inside Rune's Heart.

Rune's Heart is right next to the Silverstone Cascades flowing down from the Rusting Mountain. If you listen to the water pass over the rock bed, you can hear spirits crying in the crashing water; bodies dashed against the rocks below, unburied and unmourned, so their ghosts forever roam.

Gun smoke and burnt wood marked the birth of Rune's Heart. A legacy of spilt blood and splintered bone. Blood is in our stones, our water and our land, contrasting so vividly against the forest green, river blue and winter white of the mountain. So, come all you tourists down to Rune's Heart and see the air filled with sorrow and the Silverstone Cascades forever weep.

I have found such deep respect in what we destroy, living in Rune's Heart. I come from the mountain where wild deer and black bears used to roam, where wildflowers dream, and every green valley has a clear stream. We miners called the mountain 'God's Depression' for its solemn spire pierces the heavens, and it's into the thin air we go when we're battered, beaten and broken by the mountain – never to return. Every year the mountain crumbles further in a sacrifice of body and land. We hack at timeless stone, unearthing a secret poison that leaches our bellies.

We poisoned the earth, poisoned the streams, poisoned ourselves for one man's greed. J. T. Blaine will take your life's blood and the lives of your children too. There's no work in Rune's Heart that won't take children from fathers and husbands from wives. With black lungs and broken backs, we work and slave in those mines. What we get is a dollar at the company store and a rundown shack with company rent that never stops.

In the beginning of spring, I plant my corn; at the end of spring, I bury my father. In the summer comes a well-dressed man who says everything's fine, J. T. Blaine just requires a way into his mine. There was a blackcap bird, and she sang in a sweet tongue. In the roots of a tall timber, she nests with her young. Then came the dynamite's roar and the voice of the blackcap came no more.

Then the mountain came sliding down so awful and grand, and then came the flooding black water rising over my land. In the fall, they tore down the mountain, covering my corn and my father's grave a mile deep underground. In the winter, everyone tries to hold out for one more day, but I watch families starve in the eerie silence of what used to be the mountain. Exposed to winter's ire, families fall while J. T. Blaine profits off them all.

Now I have no money and not much of a home. I own my land, but the land is not my own. This land was pulsating with life; you can't see the shimmering green nor the winter white of the mountain no more. Now there's only destruction at hand, and only black water flows through my land. And if I had as much money as J. T. Blaine, I'd throw every blood baron like him into the deep hole he made. I'd take all their money and sit by the banks with bait and beer and watch the water flow clear once again.

ROOFTOP TALKS

Chloe Allen

THE WINDOW IN the spare room was still open, and our old toy chest – now filled with winter coats – was sitting beneath it. I put one bare foot on the top of the chest and stood up before quickly shimmying through the window so the dry wood wouldn't give way beneath my weight. The black-tar shingles of the roof were still warm from a full day in the sun, and my hands and feet seemed to sink into them a little as I clambered onto the roof. Ty was sitting with his knees pulled up to his chest with his arms hooked around them. I quickly sat down next to him, copying his position. He didn't look at me, but he did sigh audibly, which was more acknowledgement than I usually got from him. We were staring directly into the sunset and I was trying to remember if that meant our house faced east or west.

'Did Mum send you out here?' Ty asked.

'No, she didn't see you up here when we came in. She was on the phone with Aunt Carol.'

I had decided our house must face east because I was pretty sure Mr Simpson had said, 'The sun rises in the west, sets in the east.' That sounded right in my head, anyway. Rises in the west had a ring to it; rises in the east sounded weird. But I also remembered Dad telling us if we ever got lost in the woods behind our house, we could follow the setting sun home, and I was pretty sure he said something about heading west, too.

'I'm not going to jump,' Ty said.

'I know. Even if you did, it wouldn't kill you. At least, I don't think it would.'

I leaned forward to try to see over the edge and judge the distance. I was moving to stand up when Ty grabbed the back of my t-shirt and pulled me back down onto my butt. I started to argue and explain I wasn't going to fall, I just wanted to look, but I didn't. We watched as our chocolate lab, Lady, ran circles in the yard. She was trying to follow the sound of our voices; however, she didn't seem to understand we were sitting on the roof.

'Maybe if you swan dived headfirst,' I said, breaking the silence.

'What?'

'If you like, if you swan dived like you were diving into a swimming pool and landed square on your head. The fall might kill you, but that'd be the only way. 'Cause we aren't that much higher than the treehouse right now, and we've both fallen out of it loads of times.'

'*You've* fallen out of it?'

'Oh, yeah, I guess so. I only got hurt that one time though, the time I broke my arm, remember? It was right before the fourth of July because I still had my cast on at the cookout.'

'Yeah, I remember.'

We sat in silence for a while, and Lady lay down in the soft grass beneath the trampoline. The sun was setting fast. I had never realised before how quickly it disappeared over the horizon. Soon the lightning bugs would be out, but we wouldn't be able to stay and watch them because Mum was going to be finished with dinner soon.

'I think Mum's making spaghetti tonight,' I said.

Ty made a hum noise to show he had heard me while not having to fully respond. He was still staring straight ahead, his green eyes focused like he was solving a math problem. I knew we would have to go inside soon, but I didn't want to. I wanted to stay sitting on the roof with Ty forever. I tried to remember the last time he and I had hung out together, just the two of us.

'Remember when you took me to see *Spider-Man*?' I asked.

'Yeah?'

'Yeah, that was cool.'

Ty looked at me finally, but just out of the side of his eyes like he was suspicious of me.

'What about it?' he said.

'What about what?'

'*Spider-Man*. Why did you bring that up?'

'Oh, I don't know. I was just thinking about cool stuff we've done together.'

He didn't reply; instead, he went back to solving his math problem in the sky. With a sinking feeling in my stomach, I realised I had interrupted his quiet roof contemplation time. I had talked too much and now he was annoyed with me.

When we were younger, Ty and I were inseparable. The three years between us seemed like nothing. But as we got older, that gap seemed to stretch wider and wider. When he was thirteen and I was ten, he made it very clear we were no longer equals. He was a cool teenager and I was his kid brother. Then he got his license. He soon became a ghost that only stopped by our house occasionally, drifting in and out for changes of clothes and sometimes to sleep. In fact, I was more surprised to find him home at all than I was to find him sitting on the roof.

'Are you going to eat dinner with us? Mum's making spaghetti.'

'You said that already.'

'Oh. She's been making it a lot lately. Is it still your favourite?'

Ty didn't answer me. I was blowing it, but I couldn't make myself stop. I knew if he didn't say something soon, I was going to resort to begging.

'I think she misses you,' I said meekly.

'I'm right here.'

'Yeah, right now, but you aren't usually here. Not like you used to be here.'

'I'm not a kid anymore. I've got a car and friends and a job. I have a life. You wouldn't understand.'

He ran his hands across his face. He was starting to grow a beard, sort of. It was patchy and fuzzy, but it did make him look older.

'Is this what I'll be like when I'm seventeen?' I asked.

Part of me meant the beard, but the rest of me was wondering if I was going to stop caring about things over the next three years. Ty moved to look at me – really look at me – for the first time in a long time.

'No. No, you won't be like this.'

'That's a relief.'

He laughed, big and loud, like I hadn't heard him laugh in a long time. And I laughed too. We laughed so hard, I thought we were going to fall off the roof. Tears began to roll down his cheeks, and he wiped them on the sleeve of his t-shirt as he caught his breath.

'Come on, let's go see if dinner's ready.'

DAISY CHAINS

Kate Fleming

ANNA

ANNA STILL REMEMBERS the day her parents said they were separating. Mum called for her to come downstairs. She bolted down asking if Mummy was having another baby, but she got no response. Instead, she was told to come and have a seat. Mum and Dad sat on the coffee table facing Anna and Lily on the couch – a perfect square. Dad was looking down at the floor like he'd lost something in the carpet. He had his hands in his lap and was picking at some dry skin on one of his fingers. He did that sometimes. Lily was looking down too, her hands behind her knees and her feet flat on the floor. Anna wondered if Bree had upset her again – Bree was the bully at the high school Lily went to. She had a knack for making Lily come home and spend hours in her room with the door closed.

Anna's feet didn't quite reach the ground yet; her feet swung just a few centimetres above the carpet. She nestled her hands under her knees, just like Lily, pointed her toes towards the ground, and sat up tall. Either she was getting taller, or Lily was getting smaller, she couldn't tell which, but Lily was looking pretty hunched over. Normally, Mum would tell her to sit up straight like an arrow, but instead she just said, 'Girls, we've got something we need to talk to you about.'

After that, her memory is a bit muddy. It felt like everything and nothing was explained at the same time. Words were spoken, something about two houses and two Christmases, something about

Mum and Dad loving them very much, something about nobody's fault. She doesn't know if she stopped listening or if she blocked it all out. Maybe she didn't understand. Her world changed in a matter of minutes, but those minutes no longer exist in her memory.

LILY

Lily still remembers the day her parents said they were separating. She was on her computer before it happened – the latest version of *Sims* had just come out and she was making a virtual voodoo doll of Bitch Bree. The plan was to lull her into a sense of false security in a mansion with a giant pool, then take her for a swim and delete the pool ladder before she had a chance to get out. Lily had picked up a packet of Pizza Shapes from the IGA to snack on as she watched Bree drown. It was going to be a fun day.

'Anna, Lil, can you come downstairs please?'

Within seconds Anna flew past Lily's door and bounded down the stairs. She asked if Mum was pregnant. She better not be, thought Lily. That'd mean having sex with Dad. Gross. Lily paused the game, folded down the packet of Shapes inside the box and followed her sister downstairs at a far more sensible pace.

She walked into the living room and saw Dad sitting on the coffee table. His head was down and he was picking at the dry skin on his hands again. He only did that when something was wrong. This wasn't going to be a fun family chat. Maybe someone's dead, she thought. Maybe Dad lost his job. Lily didn't want to move houses again, please don't let it be that.

'Girls, we've got something we need to talk to you about.'

Anna's little feet stopped swinging above the ground. There was something in Mum's voice that stopped everything – except Dad's skin-picking. Mum didn't tell him to cut it out though, and that was weird in itself. Mum and Dad sat across from Anna and Lily, they were all the same distance apart and yet, somehow, Mum and Dad looked like magnets being forced in opposite directions. Anna edged closer to Lily's side.

They were going from a team of four to a team of two. In a matter of minutes, Lily had gone from being the older sister to the third parent. She would be the constant in Anna's life now – going back and forth, making sure her bags were packed, making sure she didn't forget her school dress, teaching her how to catch the tram.

When the talk was over, Lily went back upstairs and abandoned the Bree plan. Instead, she made two new Sims – one called Anna and one called Lily.

BREE

Bree can't remember what life was like before her parents separated. She was only two at the time, still wearing pull-ups and taking daily naps. Her sister had just been born, but Bree never got to meet her – Charlie never made it home from the hospital. Dad said it was Mum's fault for smoking during the pregnancy, but they never *really* knew why Charlie was born the way she was. The nurses said she had deformities that were 'incompatible with life', whatever that meant. The point was, Bree had been raised like the second-best child. She wasn't the one they *wanted*; she was the accident that happened when a condom broke. Charlie had been *planned*. She was going to make their lives better after Bree had ruined them. When Bree's friend Molly told her she couldn't know that for sure, Bree had assured her it was true – her parents had both told her on several occasions.

Molly's parents were the kind every teenager wants. Her mum made the best paella and her dad had some music industry job, so he always got free tickets to gigs. Bree was always treated like an extra daughter when she went to Molly's house. One time, when Dad had broken his personal best for glasses of wine consumed in a single evening, Molly's mum was there to pick her up and take her out for dinner at a really cool restaurant.

As far as Bree could tell, she had parents that were incompatible with life. They were constantly looking for work, constantly moving house, and Bree was constantly the designated driver now she was on her Ls. She preferred the company of her nan, but Nan lived in

Geelong and hardly ever came to Melbourne. When Bree got her license, she'd visit Nan all the time. Maybe she'd even move in with her if she got into Deakin.

Dad always told her to forget about uni and start a restaurant with him – he could take care of the front of house while she did all the cooking. She did like cooking, she was the top of her class in Home Ec at school. When everyone was learning how to make spaghetti in year eight, she was already hand-rolling her own ravioli. That day, she'd overheard one girl in her class, Lily, tell the other kids that Bree was only good at cooking because her parents were never home to do it themselves. Bree hadn't been able to think of a verbal response at the time, so she'd turned off all of Lily's burners while she wasn't looking – she hadn't realised the spaghetti was meant to be Lily's lunch that day. They'd been sworn enemies ever since.

Bree had been the head chef at home since she was young out of necessity, so she'd had plenty of practice, but Dad would be the worst business partner in the world. He would probably get the orders wrong and then find a way to blame her for the mistakes while drinking half the bar. In some ways, it was flattering that Dad thought she could be a professional chef, but she also knew it was just a ploy for him to have a steady job.

MOLLY

Molly remembers the day when Bree ran away from home like it was yesterday. She was sitting on the couch watching *The Bachelor* with Mum like she did every Thursday, when her phone screen lit up. She didn't reach for it straight away. She'd wait until the ad break to check it – Dad and her brother were out for a boys' night, so this was quality mother-daughter time. A few seconds after the first notification though, the screen lit up again, and then a third time. Mum asked if it was a boy and Molly scoffed. Yeah right. She reached forward and saw several messages coming up from Bree.

Hey, you free?

I really need to talk to you

I just ran out of the house and idk where to go

Can I call?

'Shit.' Molly had never sworn in front of her mum before, but the word was out before she could stop it.

'What?' Mum sounded concerned rather than angry; that was a promising start.

'Just calling Bree, you keep watching.'

'What's happened?' Mum muted the TV. 'Should I be worried?'

'I don't know . . . Hey, you okay?' Molly walked to her room – her mum followed close behind. She couldn't make out if Bree was laughing or crying on the end of the phone, either way, it was hard to make out what she was saying. It sounded like there was traffic in the background. 'Where are you?' She didn't get an answer, just more muffled sounds that couldn't be interpreted as anything. 'Hello? Bree?' Still no clarity. Molly put the phone on speaker and her mum took over the situation.

The next few minutes blurred into one. She sat back while Mum figured out where Bree was and arranged to pick her up. The call ended and Mum was out the door and in the car before the ad break was over. Molly waited at home for what felt like hours. She watched the bachelor and his bachelorettes in silence as they vied for attention like idiots. She knew it was a guilty pleasure, but watching the show on mute really put into perspective just how much time she'd wasted investing in these people's lives. She should have been talking to Bree. She should have invited her over. She should have asked her how she was going more often.

Bree had stopped reading her messages so she figured her phone must have died. Or maybe she'd been mugged. Or hit by a car. Or kidnapped. Or stabbed. She was only about a ten-minute drive away; what was taking so long? Another ad break came and went and still no sign of Mum and Bree.

When Molly woke up, the TV was still on and her mum was sitting by her feet at the other end of the couch.

'Where's Bree?'

'She's at home.' Mum's voice sounded tired.

'Is she okay?'

'I bought her some dinner and we had a chat. She's okay.' Mum pulled Molly's feet onto her lap and started to rub them. 'Who went home?'

'What?'

'On *The Bachelor*.'

'Oh. No idea.'

* * *

The next day at school, Bree acted as if the night before had never happened. When Molly tried to bring it up, Bree just shrugged it off and told her not to worry so much.

'I'm fine, really. Can we not talk about this?'

Molly started seeing the school counsellor after that. She never told Bree, and they never talked about that night again.

YA

Amy Kayman

NOTIFICATION

IT'S NEARING MIDNIGHT and I texted a boy.

I texted a boy I barely knew.

I texted a boy I didn't like much.

I texted a boy six years older than me.

I texted a university boy who works at a bar.

I texted a boy with tattoos – I can show them to you if you like, he sent me photos.

I texted a boy and my insides dropped, and I looked at my phone until my eyes struggled to stay open. I looked for those telltale signs of engagement, for those three dots to shuffle in motion. I shoved my phone underneath my pillow, trying to convince myself that I wouldn't care if it buzzed.

I TEXTED A BOY . . .

Because that's what I'm meant to do. I used to cover my eyes during kissing scenes in movies and cover my ears during Sex Ed. Now I text boys.

First about how they've been, how they're going, what they've been up to.

Then about whether they've kissed a girl, how far they've gone, if they've ever had sex, if they'd ever have sex with me.

I figured out new questions to ask, new ways to excite and avoid keeping promises. Eventually, they realise that my interest in them is fleeting. They fade away, and I look up from my phone, relieved.

I TEXTED A BOY I BARELY KNEW . . .

We talked for months. In between classes, I'd check my phone and find paragraphs of his thoughts.

He told me about what life was like in Singapore, what his comfort foods were and how suffocating humidity could be. He sent me funny YouTube clips and videos of his cat, and I shared secrets because he was so far removed from my life. He lived thousands of miles away, yet I felt like he was the only person who got me.

One day, he told me he'd booked a flight to come see me. We met in front of the State Library. He didn't look like I thought he would. I showed him my favourite parts of the city, and he walked quietly beside me. He had a lisp, and his sentences were clumsy and jumbled. Before he departed, he gave me a gift: a beautiful book of Lovecraft's short stories. My heart sank. I'd brought him nothing.

That book has sat on my shelf ever since, its hardcover spine collecting a thick layer of dust.

I TEXTED A BOY SIX YEARS OLDER THAN ME . . .

What are you wearing?

My school uniform.

How short is your skirt?

Thigh length.

What colour's your bra?

Blue.

Could you show me?

No, I'm not into that.

What's sex like?

Come over and I'll show you.

Could you just tell me instead?

It feels good. Like, really good. It's a
release. And you're so close to the other
person, you know. It's like masturbating,
but so much better.

I've never masturbated before, so I
can't really relate.

Wait, you've never masturbated
before?

Never.

Well, you should definitely try it.

Something about it grosses me out.

You don't know what you're talking
about.

I just . . . don't want to. Does it hurt?

Masturbating?

No, sex.

Not if you do it right. I could teach you,
you know. How to feel good.

I'm just curious, that's all.

You're such a tease.

You're such a dickhead.

I TEXTED A UNIVERSITY BOY WHO WORKS AT A BAR . . .

I'd never felt so intellectually stimulated. At school, no one talks
about ideas or theories or anything like that. But this boy, David,

would talk to me about everything from art to philosophy to political theory. We met for the first time at an art museum. He was skinny and wore a denim jacket covered in patches. He was always a foot in front of me, due to his long legs.

'Look over there,' he'd exclaim. 'Picasso, a classic example of Cubism.'

'Look at this for me,' he'd demand. 'What do you see?'

'Just blocks of colour?'

'That's what I thought at first, but it's so much more. Rothko was so ahead of his time. He understood perspective and depths of hues.'

He placed his hands on my shoulders, leaning over me, his breath against my ear articulating every consonant.

'Notice how the more you look at it, the more meditative the experience becomes? How you find yourself falling into a trance? God, I wish I'd been young in the 60s.'

'Would've been rubbish if you were a woman.'

'Aha, too true. Over there.' He pointed. 'Monet, one of the best impressionists. Have you heard of him?'

'I think so. I like the colours.'

* * *

The second time we met was at his bar. I shouldn't have been there, but he let me in with a wink. I ordered red wine because I thought it would make me look sophisticated.

The area in front of the bar was packed with his university friends. There was a girl with pink hair who carried a Moleskine notebook wherever she went, and a guy in a beige trench coat who claimed to be a communist, and a group of musicians belting sea shanties.

As I watched them banter and laugh and debate, I decided I wanted to be them. They stayed until closing, then invited me to continue the night.

David quickly stepped in. 'Guys, she's still in high school.'

'Oooh,' a musician cooed.

'Well, good luck with VCE,' said the girl with the pink hair.

Then it was just me and David. I kept him company while he wiped down the tables, washed all the glasses, emptied the cash register. He was quieter than usual, more pensive, as though he were waiting for something to happen. We wandered out shyly, my fists digging into the seams of my pockets.

'Thanks for inviting me tonight. It was fun. Your friends are awesome.'

'I'm glad.'

And then his lips pushed so hard against mine I could feel the outlines of his teeth. I pushed him away from me, and we stood there, facing each other. Some first kiss.

He patted me on the head, tousling my hair. 'I'll see you around, kid,' he said, walking away.

I didn't hear from him after that. I did everything I could: I read up on Picasso and Monet, sent him quotes by famous philosophers, asked him questions about what he was studying. It took me months to realise that it wasn't my brain he'd been interested in.

I TEXTED A BOY WITH TATTOOS . . .

His name is Andrew.

Andrew and I would do everything together. Whenever we needed a partner in class, we'd immediately make eye contact. We swapped lunches and lines in books that we found particularly poignant, and would hang out on a concrete stairwell up the side of the science building during recess. He'd tell me about his fights with his Mum, and I'd tell him about the boys I was texting.

'Do you even like these boys?'

'Sometimes I think I'm just doing what's expected of me. I don't think I've ever liked anyone, to be honest. Maybe there's something wrong with me.'

'Being different doesn't mean being defective,' Andrew said, eyes sparkling. 'Also, fuck 'em.'

One day, on that grimy stairwell, he asked me to give him a stick-and-poke tattoo.

'I want you to write "HERE" on my wrist, facing me.'

'Why'd you want that?'

'So I can remember I'm here. Because that's just it, isn't it? We're here and there's nothing more to it than that. Gotta make the most of it.'

Andrew and I don't talk much now. He got a scholarship at another school, and a new boyfriend. Every so often he'll send me a picture of his latest stick-and-poke. I think it's his way of keeping me updated on what's going on in his life. He's got a pomegranate on his ankle, and the *Twin Peaks* owl on the back of his leg.

'I'm creating a map on my body,' he said. 'It shows me where I've been, and where I'm heading.'

I TEXTED A BOY MY PARENTS DON'T KNOW ABOUT . . .

Well, it's a girl, really. But when they ask who I'm talking to when I smile at my phone, I say it's a boy. Her name is Ophelia, and we started talking randomly at a party. She told me about personality theory, the podcasts she listens to and the moment she realised she only likes girls.

Ophelia was different from everyone else I'd texted. She'd start conversations and ask me how I was. The fantasies we had were different too; it wasn't about kissing or having sex, but about living in a cottage together and pickling our own vegetables or curling up together while reading old books. I found myself thinking about her all the time, what kind of lip gloss she wore and what it would taste like. She talked to me about being gay, how difficult it was to ask girls out because you never knew whether they'd be interested. I told her that if she were asking, I would be interested.

Then she asked me out on a date. Nothing serious, just coffee or something. We talked about what we'd do; whether we'd drop into the NGV or take our coffees to the Botanical Gardens and watch the branches rustle above us, creating shadow patterns over our skin. We talked about what the weather would be like, made backup plans and discussed what we'd wear.

And then, when the day came, I didn't show up. It was a beautiful morning and I lay on my bed, watching the shadows change on the wall. I heard my phone buzzing over and over. Eventually, the buzzing stopped.

I told myself many things that day: that I wasn't ready for that kind of thing, that we wouldn't have clicked like we had online, that I'd be leading her on if I went and it turned out it wasn't for me. But when you strip me of all my excuses, what's left is a girl in a coffee shop, sitting alone, waiting for me.

I TEXTED A BOY AND MY INSIDES DROPPED . . .

It felt like I was freefalling, out of control. He irritated something deep within me, an itch I could never muster scratching. I couldn't stop thinking about him.

'What do you want from me?' he demanded.

I didn't know so I said, 'Nothing.'

'I guess that's it then,' he said.

'I guess so.'

I liked you enough, but I don't like vulnerability. I don't like waiting for it to go one way or the other. I'm not jumping off that cliff unless you push me.

FIRE SALE

Seth Robinson

VIC HAD NEVER done anything like this before. Not once. Not even considered it. It was the sort of thing he'd read about on the news that made his stomach turn and his nose wrinkle in disgust. It was the sort of thing he'd heard about and judged with a sense of complete disbelief. It was the sort of horrific, reckless thing broken people did when they couldn't deal with the world anymore. When they were more animal than human.

But here he was, at the end of a long stream of numbers. Dates, times, percentages, interest rates, salaries, tax rates, deposits. Offers. And the sense of self-loathing that was riding shotgun with him did nothing to dampen the anger: the desire to do some damage. He'd made spreadsheets and budgeted and *worked*. Together, he and his wife had been to inspection after inspection after inspection. He had kowtowed before the freshly shone shoes of a legion of real estate clones. He'd stopped counting how many times they'd done this dance now.

For a second there, it had all seemed so attainable. The offer was in, and then it was gone. The number that had sent him over the edge was seven figures. He'd seen it on his phone when he'd gotten the text message – a fucking *text message*, not a call or even an email – that let him know they'd been outbid. The buzz of the preceding days, all the excitement and optimism and hope, had been gone in the time it took his eyes to track seven digits. Despite all the scrimping and saving, the extra nights driving Ubers and the pre-approval for a number that gave him anxiety when he thought about the shadow it would cast over the next thirty years of his life. It was gone. Vic was only a six-figure man.

He'd always hoped that would be enough, but with every passing day those six figures seemed to be worth less. It was all out of reach. Tomorrow, he would open up the news app and read the story. He didn't want to see his name in print – far from it – but he wanted to see the account and know that he had done something. That he might be a failure, but he was still a force to be reckoned with. He would hate that part of himself, he knew it, but it had to be better than what he felt right now.

Vic rolled down the street in neutral, lights off, listening to the squelch of his tires on the wet bitumen and the slosh of the petrol in the jerry can next to him. When he stopped, it was under a tree away from any streetlights. He'd covered his license plates with slips of cardboard, but that didn't feel like enough. Nor did the mask and hood and gloves. He needed it to be dark. And the night had delivered: a thick blanket of cloud cover, no stars.

He parked the car and got out, hauling the jerry can. It was heavy, with potential or with failure, it didn't fucking matter. It would do its job. He just had to facilitate that job.

The house was up ahead. Its windows were dark, staring out at the street and passing judgement on all the poor bastards who would never afford to grace its halls. It was empty now, decked out only in display furniture. Knowing that those surreal, too-small beds with their colour-coordinated blankets would go up in smoke made it better for him somehow. Like it wasn't just the house he was going to burn, but the whole institution, the system, the *market*. This whole world where people bought and sold and spent their lives in debt. Viva la revolution.

It wouldn't matter. Insurance would cover it. He'd told himself that again and again on the way over. It was the insurance companies who would lose out. No one else. That was okay. They were bastards. He'd been worried at first about the fire spreading, maybe setting the neighbouring houses alight and hurting someone, but then that morning – as he'd been sitting at his computer and staring out his office window, thinking about whether or not he *could* or *should* do it – the rain had come. Those clouds had dumped their affirmation all over him and told him this was the right thing to do. The wet earth and neighbouring walls would take time to catch. People could get away and the fire department would come. Maybe he'd call them himself once he'd started the fire and was making his getaway. They wouldn't be able to save the empty house – *his* house, by right – but they'd stop the fire before it spread.

Vic lifted his leg and stepped over the front gate. He crept up the front path holding his breath, waiting for a sensor light to come on, and didn't exhale until he reached the porch, still shrouded in darkness. For maybe the first time ever, it was all happening the right way. When something was meant to be, it was easy. He got that now. He wasn't meant to own this house, but he sure as shit was meant to burn it down. He unscrewed the top of the can and was hit by the heady, sickly sweet smell of petrol. It made his head spin and his eyes water. His mouth was so dry he had to peel his tongue free from its roof so he could mutter to himself.

'Take it easy now,' he whispered.

He tipped the jerry can, slopping petrol onto the deck. There was a loud slap as the liquid hit the timber and for a moment he froze, spine prickling. He watched the petrol bead on the damp wood, listening for . . . who? Neighbours? Security guards?

Nobody.

The next pour was slower, a steady trickle that sluiced over the boards and dripped through the gaps. He ran a line all the way along the porch's length, around the corner, up the driveway and along the outside wall of the house, all the while listening for police boots, or the sound of movement and people inside. But it was all quiet, lonely, like the rest of the city had forgotten about this little seven-figure house in its up-and-coming neighbourhood and Vic was the only one who cared.

The can ran dry and Vic sighed. He stood on the garden path looking up at the house, at the freshly painted weatherboards, the tin roof, the little bay window with the love seat he'd seen at the inspection. He'd wanted to sit there and read. He didn't know what. He didn't read much, but that seemed like the sort of thing he wanted to do, the sort of thing he ought to do. He'd wanted to sit on the porch and drink tea and have their friends and family over for barbecues in the backyard. He still wanted all of those things.

He wanted them so badly, but the whole thing felt rigged. The thing he couldn't understand was, who *were* these seven-figure people? Where were they?

Vic reached into the pocket of his hoodie and found the box of Redheads. He gave the packet a little rattle, same as he would before he lit a candle, then slipped it open and pulled out a match. He studied it for a long time, his eyes focusing on the place where sulphur met wood, and blinked. His eyes were itchy. They burned, probably from the petrol fumes, he thought, but it was hard to say. He was just so bloody tired. It had worn him down, all of it.

Vic struck the match and held it up in front of him, a tiny orange light dancing in the darkness. As he watched it creep along the length of the timber – down toward his fingers – tears rolled down his cheeks.

WHISPER

Tejan Green Waszak

GETTING TO JERSEY City on the railroad from the Ronkonkoma station with my three-month-old daughter, Corinne, is the biggest inconvenience I can remember having since I worked up the courage to quit my publishing job in NYC. It is as if I never rode the train, though a little over six months ago my weekday commute would have been about three hours daily. Of course, back then I would have been sans stroller and spit-up on my dress. I would have been wearing heels instead of Reeboks, my clothes would match, and my hair would definitely be done in fresh braids instead of being hidden under a Yankees baseball cap. With all that luxury of free time, I may have even brought along a book to read on the train as I sipped my coffee. Maybe *Color of Water* or *Ain't Gonna Be the Same Fool Twice* – two books I'd held onto since college, but only recently had the urge to re-read. College days – those were easier days.

My new self feels like an aged self and only a bit of the previous one. No one properly prepared me for this. Corinne is crying, although I am holding her. She is fed and her diaper is clean.

'It's okay, baby. Shhh, shhh, shhh,' I say – I plead! She stops crying briefly to look at me, her tiny bottom lip quivering. 'We're good, see?'

She looks angelic staring up at me from those deep brown eyes, but then the crying starts again. I give her the pacifier, which she promptly spits out. I go through the list in my head: she is fed, her diaper is clean, she is appropriately dressed for the weather and I'm holding her so close to me, she can hear my heartbeat. She should be fine.

It is the middle of the day on a Friday and there are only a few passengers, but I still feel guilty. The train is old and slow, and every now and then the bright lights cut off then come back on again, which causes Corinne to shriek. I remember all the times before when I would shoot dirty looks at parents who couldn't keep their kids from disrupting my weekday commute.

I take Corinne out of the carrier and sit her on my lap. I make kissing noises and shake the rattle, which calms her. I have a few moments to stare out the train window and admire the tree branches clothed in fluffy snow. Corinne touches my face, a whisper on my cheek. I smile at her and for a few minutes we are good. This is enough time for me to notice that the insurance advertisement on the train wall has obscene images drawn over the mouth of the smiling model. I imagine this as the work of teenagers feeling mischievous after school. I worry about never being able to avoid these visuals on train rides when Corinne is older, and the questions she will ask. Corinne places her hand on the top of my breast and gives a gentle squeeze, but I know she isn't hungry – this is only habit. I smile at her and for a few more minutes we are good. The conductor comes to get my ticket.

'Well here is a bright spot in my day,' he says. He is an older man of about seventy-five, with a thick moustache and a deep voice. He reminds me of my father. Corinne starts to cry again. 'Is this your first train ride?' the conductor asks Corinne, in a voice mimicking a toddler learning to talk.

'Yes, it is,' I respond.

He smiles and moves on to the next passenger, but then looks back at me sweetly. 'It's crying now; it will be talking and lots of whining later,' he says, laughing. He continues, 'I have three of my own. All grown! I miss when they were small like that.'

Corinne's crying intensifies, a mix of screams and whimpering with tiny breaks as if she is gasping for air. I bounce her gently on my knee as the conductor disappears into the next car. 'Corinne, shhh, shhh. Please stop crying.'

Corinne doesn't stop. Her eyes have all the tears I want to cry. I wipe her cheeks and then I feel the tears running down my own face. Now she stares at me. She is quiet.

UNOBTAINABLE

Samuel Marshall

WE WALK IN the rain, the cars splashing us as they try to beat the rush-hour jam.

The weather makes her freckles stand out. I can count the four tan spots along the arc of her top lip. One for each year I've known her. Her green coat is a flower among the concrete.

She stops as we pass the television shop and watches the news headlines we missed during the day: coronavirus is still the daily headline, politicians are arguing about trade deals and the lawsuit against Prince Andrew is fuelling the wave of celebrity scandals.

The news ran me into the ground a year ago, yet she still has her spark.

She turns to me.

'Do you think the shopkeeper will change the channel if we ask him?'

He does.

That's who she is.

She can change the world with a question.

BETTER TO HAVE LOVED

Linda McMullen

ON EVERY CHANNEL echoed versions of the truth, but the same image: the smouldering wreck of Jack's plane. I cried for all the right reasons – and arguably some of the wrong ones.

I pled a headache to my husband, Hugh, and retreated into an uncontrollable tear-and-snot burst of suppressed anger at God, fate or chance . . .

Seventeen years, from the moment he sang 'You Are My Sunshine' to me on the playground . . .

And then – after distraction-scrolling through Twitter – I realised that some ultra-intrepid reporter or maniacal fan probably had the wherewithal to guess. He'd left hints. Some of his devotees had established a combative Reddit channel . . .

Another ten to even date again.

I pulled myself together long enough to call Bill, who'd known Jack and me since our colouring days. He croaked my name, then blew his nose. 'Do you need me to come over?' I asked.

'N-no, it's just—'

'I know,' I said, my voice breaking. We exchanged memories as well as we could between Kleenex, and I said, 'You haven't talked to any outsiders, have you?'

'No!' he replied, indignation overtaking mourning. 'Except—'

My stomach lurched. 'Who?'

'Well – this lady called – she's – whaddaya – she's speaking for the family, now, but used to—'

'His . . . publicist?' I ventured.

'Yes,' replied Bill, relieved. 'She wanted a couple of stories for – colour, she said—'

'Did you mention me?'

'Well, I don't think . . .'

He had.

'I've got to go, Bill, sorry,' I said. I retreated to the bathroom and reassembled my face, to brave the outside world – and Hugh.

'How's your head?' he asked, sympathetically. 'Oh – and I fixed you a plate, just in case.'

The face behind the smudged glasses was pale and kind and very dear. 'Can you drive me to the library?' I asked. Operating a motor vehicle seemed unwise. 'Right now?'

He said 'I think you'll want a coat', and that was all. We raced over. Hugh said he'd wait in the car. I glanced at my watch: seven minutes before closing. The librarians fluttered like startled hens and I called over my shoulder, 'I promise I'll get them quickly!'

The Salem North High School yearbooks from all four years. Club photos, group photos, prom photos. Except – huh. I grabbed them and hurtled toward the circulation desk. 'Do you keep one copy of these, or two?'

Two, since my senior year, apparently, the librarian explained.

So there *was* a chance . . .

Hugh and I drove home in silence.

I retreated to my room and set all my social media accounts to private. Nothing yet. I glanced through Reddit. Still no messages from my clients. I switched on the TV—

Wendy.

ABC, NBC, CBS, Fox and CNN all looped the same big-haired, over-mascaraed interview: 'To you, Jack was a legend, but to *me* – well . . . he was my first love.'

The familiar chorus, in Jack's voice, played over an image of the album cover lined with telltale indigo berries. I tugged out a Kleenex only to discover it was the last, and padded to the bathroom for toilet paper. Well, fine, I thought. Let everyone believe that.

I had, I hoped, the normal amount of conscience. Though I could have decked Wendy without regret, even today, I believed firmly in letting her have this one. Despite her one, foundational, critically timed lie . . .

Jack, Wendy, bacchanal, booze, blur.

The junior reporter couldn't believe his luck. '*You're* the inspiration?'

Wendy simpered. My heart lurched for Jack – and for all the fans who believed him capable of ever having loved *Wendy*.

'Oh, I wish that were true,' she said. 'But it's not me.'

'Do you know who it is?'

'Oh yes.'

My lungs collapsed.

'Well . . . who?'

Wendy smirked, clinging to the limelight, until the anchor pulled back to the studio for an update from the police department.

The landline sounded. I closed my ears against it. After three rings Hugh picked up, then called upstairs to me. 'Hon? It's Nina Morris.'

I exhaled then picked up the extension. I had given Nina my home number for use in an emergency. 'This is Dr Fox.'

I followed my favourite psych professor's tongue-in-cheek mantra – 'Much of the job just involves channelling Alex Trebek' – and probed. Tides of woe regarding her nearly estranged husband, unctuous references to my *wonderful* book, pleas for reassurance – none of which merited a call after hours. I disengaged but failed to recover myself before the phone rang again. 'Nina,' I said, 'I'm happy to chat tomorrow.'

'Is this Ms Fox?' said an unfamiliar voice.

'This is Dr June Fox.'

The woman sounded amused. 'Dr *Juniper* Fox?'

'Who is this?'

'My name is Veronica Clymer; I'm a reporter. I'd like to talk to you about Jack Laskaris.'

'No comment.'

'You haven't even heard the question yet. The berries on the cover of the *Love Unrequited* album bear your name. I've paged through your senior yearbook. I'd like to know if *you* inspired "Better To Have Loved".'

Jack's croon: '*. . . and lost / than to have never loved at all . . .*'

A traitorous drop trailed down my nose. 'Only Jack could have answered that.'

Rage that extinguished tender years . . .

Daily, nightly wishing for words unsaid . . .

'Dr Fox,' she said patiently, 'I'm not the only journalist working on this story. I expect you'll be inundated with calls later. But if you give me an exclusive, you can tell the story on your terms – once.'

'No comment,' I said, and hung up.

That evening: a banshee phone; Hugh's mouth set in a repressive line. Channel 4, 5 and 8 trucks loitering outside the office the following morning. My patients, smugly: 'So *that's* why you became a relationship counsellor.'

Now and forever, 'the girl in the song'.

INTERMISSION

A SISYPHEAN EXILE

Pei Wen

RAINDROPS HURTLE TOWARDS her, then burst and stream down the glass pane. She stands watching the cityscape languish into a blurred painting. The skyline is washed away under grey strokes, but slashes of silvery fire fracture the sky, and skyscrapers unveil themselves fleetingly in the space between raindrops. She is obsessed with storms. Here, they are winds that course through the veins of a metropolis to purge defiled air; they are thunders rattling concrete bones to quell urban dissonance.

She tears herself away from the window and crawls back into bed, edging close enough to feel the warmth radiating from his body without rousing him. Outside, the city is getting colder. His chest swells and sinks in steady oscillations. She watches, synchronising her breaths to his, musing over each passing second.

An interminable journey chases: place to place, century to century. She is, by now, no stranger to the absurdity of her existence, but when circumstances necessitate the loss of a lover – or her life – old scars fracture into fresh wounds.

She recalls how the wandering swordsman swore to free her from the *okiya*. They had hatched a plan to elope, to settle in the county up north where he would open a *dojo* to teach *kenjutsu*, and she would help him run the school. She entrusted him with all the gold and pearls her wealthy patrons had lavished upon her, but at the riverbank, he never turned up. Then there was the time the emperor had orchestrated her death. She was an offering to appease his army, a pawn in the elaborate plot he had designed, to subjugate an impending rebellion. 'It has to be you,' he said, tears glazing his cold eyes. She was his favourite consort, he had claimed, but he had traded her life for the dragon throne all the same.

The chain of incarnations stretches back too far for her to remember each name she has existed in, but storms spilling from the firmament have always smelled like home. She remembers the roots of her existence: her earliest name echoing in soaring domes, the whitish otherworldly light in the atmosphere, the tenderness of feathers enveloping her body. Her foray into forbidden love. The excruciating pain erupting from her flesh as they severed her wings.

STONE FRUITS

Arundhati Subhedar

AMARA SWIMS THROUGH the sky, a strong breeze caressing her skin and dishevelling the long blue curls of her hair. Below her, the strong intertwining branches of the niphredylle trees do not share her movement, choosing instead to stay still and whisper to one another under her very nose. She enjoys the trees when they provide her shade on agonisingly sunny days, and she does not fault them for gossiping. There is, after all, little else to do when a nymph keeps hovering above them like an insistent fly.

Squinting to protect her eyes from any dust, Amara searches through the lacunae for a cluster of golden-yellow bushes. Elowan, to whom she is apprenticed, said that he needs their stone fruits as they are key ingredients in the saccharine cakes for which he is renowned.

'Golden-yellow,' Elowan said. 'It is important.'

This is the first time he has trusted another with the responsibility of the fruits' retrieval. But she has been floating for hours, and the sun shall soon set, leaving her to return by starlight empty-handed.

Amara does not relent, however. Having spent most of her adolescence working with Elowan, she is due to soon earn more responsibility at his hearth, a chance she is unwilling to squander over some measly fruit. He is stern but kind, and when she returns with his ingredients, she feels certain he will reward her. So, she swims on, searching, searching, searching.

The last strings of sunlight begin to disappear, but she does not stop searching. The sky fades from orange to pink to ink, but she does not stop searching. Her arms tire from propelling her body through the air, but she does not stop searching. The trees fall asleep, but she does not stop—

Then, suddenly, she sees the bushes in an area she is sure she has searched before. The difference, now, is that they are luminescent, impossible to miss. Amara hurries towards the ground, snaking through the branches gently so as not to wake the trees.

She finds herself facing a silhouette against the golden-yellow glow.

'Elowan?' Amara whispers upon recognition. 'What are you doing here?'

'I had to be certain of your endurance.'

'You know of their glow,' Amara realises. 'That is why you instructed me to leave during the day.'

'Indeed, and you have passed my test.'

'Test?'

'Amara, my child,' Elowan says with a smile, 'how would you like to run the bakery with me?'

Amara squeals in delight but immediately silences herself when the niphredylle trees begin to loosen some leaves from overhead, their sleep disturbed. 'I would be honoured,' she whispers excitedly, embracing her teacher.

In the glow of the bushes, they pick their ingredients, the niphredylle trees snoring gently around them. Together, baker and apprentice swim home through the starlit sky, Elowan promising to teach Amara how to use the stone fruits in the morning.

PERSONAL EFFECTS

Angela Glindemann

I DON'T KNOW how long I've been here, so I measure time and tide. I tick in walnut timber. I move in tiny non-ticking vibrations, around the Roman numerals carved in gold. It brings me back around and around to twelve.

I centre myself here at midday – on that day when I inspected all the shining, ticking, striking clocks that bent the light so every object in the shop had a face. I am struck. I see your face. The lacquered hands meet. The present moment strikes.

How many empty days have there been? I see your name, stainless among the leaves and cobwebs in the mailbox, under the symmetrical slit of sunlight. I am galvanised. On the other side, the nickel-finished number sends its signals out until it's soaked in shadow.

So I hollow myself out. I find the cardboard container – the last box from the last order – from some yesterday. And in yesterday's box, I can sing. I sink into the black plush holder. I am the violin – maple and spruce, resin and steel.

I am the D string. I am silent but I hold warm tones and it's everything and it's enough, and for that moment I don't see you at all because all I am is music and meditation and memory.

I was with some others when I first saw one; it sung in the hands of someone slender swaying in black, someone whose face bent with the music. Oh, I yearned for that day. And they delivered, smooth and sweet as a sonatina.

I try to hold on but it fades like all things and leaves me yearning. Where did you go? I am worn in the old armchair again, sinking. I gather dust and feel the stitching, feel the patches and the stains. I fray. I could break.

I was here then, when I broke the dusk-pink mug with the stains, when I had the thought again: *What if this broken object had feelings?*

You loved that mug; you were clay coffee mugs and matte nail polish and mismatched trackpants and your name was on all the boxes.

I was new when you lived here too, and I felt solid under your touch. Even when your eyes were fixed on those gold-polished numerals, we were home.

But then the lowness started – the housebound feeling – when I sank to the floor. Disintegrating.

So I became the skylight and shone, and strong as marble bench-tops I grew until I was the candelabra lightbulb touching everything.

I was hand-painted-vase me, mechanical-timepiece me, Victorian-silverware me. I was made of lumens and stardust and somehow like light and dust I drifted away from you. I revisit these things and look for you now. But even back then you were never there, and so I do not find you, only light and dust.

I go back further then, to less-powerful days, to a corner with softer carpet and thicker dust. And I dwell on the pre-packaged dining table assembled with an Allen key, with its mismatching wooden chairs, with its little drawer that yawns and squeals in the same tune as thousands of others.

And I remember where you are. You never left.

There, in that little drawer, we are reunited. I hold you close as you whisper from cardboard envelopes: 'Happy Birthday with Loving Wishes', 'For You Just Because', 'Loving Greetings for this Festive Season'.

ENCOUNTERS

THE AMERICAN TEENAGE CLASSIC GRADUATION FAREWELL

Redfern Boyd

NO-ONE DESERVES IT more than she does. You watch her pull away from the curb in a zigzag movement, a quartet of passenger seats occupied, an elastic band around her wrist that she took from her hair. Her friends hang out the windows, pop out the sunroof, arms waving free. The music is hitting their sweet spot – they're banging on the doors, the tinted windows, the leather seats. Any surface that will conduct sound. Screaming their triumph into the dense humidity outside. Seven hundred and twenty school days she's flown those colours, heading in on your heels, a relay, but one she ran alone as you did not have to. A quartet of discordant years that she hammered into harmony, three of which she spent rocking the pom-pom two-step like you never could; you lasted all of two months in that short, pleated uniform, staring into the bedroom mirror feeling like a Beach Boys song gone wrong. Thinking, that's not me. East Coasters have their road fantasies squashed by the time they hit I-95, but her ambitions are too solid to suffer more than a dent, her dreams too brilliant to chip like paint. She's outpaced you – she's lapped you and is coming around again. And no-one is happier for her than you. You, who loves music to a degree you are sure will someday destroy you. You, who can at the drop of a hat make the classic retreat into your headphones, recede from a world too terrifying to be worth knowing.

DANIEL GENTLE

Jasmine Dreame Wagner

THE OLD MAN drove him into the hills to teach him how to shoot a gun. Daniel was home for the summer, saving his money from odd jobs to buy a girl a turquoise pendant she'd thought was pretty when they'd spent an afternoon together at the San Antonio mall. Not south-western turquoise, opaque as his intentions, but princess-cut blue topaz, clear as the ocean in a magazine. His grandfather told him to *leave bitches alone, son,* as he notched the rifle butt into the soft tissue of Daniel's shoulder. Daniel knew better than to argue with a man holding a gun, but he disagreed with his grandfather, and in that moment promised himself that he'd never live alone, not like the old man, and that he would never shoot a gun. That's when the old man looped an arm around Daniel's waist, pressed his bolo tie clip against Daniel's spine, slid a finger over Daniel's on the trigger and pulled. The rifle bucked with the blast and Daniel pissed a half-pint in surprise. The old man laughed at the stain. After the piss incident, the next time Daniel saw the girl, she'd bleached her hair white and withdrawn from community college. Something had shocked her, too. Then she admitted that she'd adopted a dog, but the dog had run out the front door and into the courtyard of her apartment complex. And now the dog was gone. After she spoke, she dropped her cigarette and ground the filter into the dirt with her boot heel. The girl had never admired Daniel's grandfather and likewise, the old man detested college kids. Too much self-esteem. Daniel's grandfather wanted his grandson to be a self-made man and sell what God had loaded inside him. So Daniel took a night job up-selling suites to Fort Hood and Gatesville Correctional Facility visitors at the Holiday Inn Express, just for the summer, just until he headed north again, but really so he could be closer to the girl. When he finally saw the boxed rot of her apartment, the thought that she might soon sell her possessions, or other beautiful intangibles, entered him, thoughts which Daniel didn't want to consider. He promised her he would find her dog. He asked if she could remember the most recent dream she'd had. She said, *true, sometimes dogs dream themselves back to you.* She did in fact remember her latest: a night terror featuring Elton John. The girl didn't want to cause Daniel any trouble. There were so many things the two of them lacked, together or apart. Daniel told her that his dreams were animated clay figures loaded with morphine. He'd never taken morphine but somehow the drug plumped the sac of his night jaunt. He circled the girl's apartment complex like a sleepwalker, then drove back to The Cove where his grandfather's condo smelled like manure. His grandfather had Elton John on the radio. That's when Daniel recognised that this was all he had done his entire life, all he had trained for, even while reading geological surveys for his environmental science degree at Duke. A black thread sews the death of each creature to its mirror. His grandfather polishing his gun was an image that existed, not only in eternity, but in the tar of time itself, bubbling up across millennia. Who killed the dog? Daniel knew.

TOBY

Maggie Nerz Iribarne

WE SPRANG UP from the crouch by the fire. The boy appeared, rising out of the darkness, drawn by the flickering light. His shining face was surrounded by wide, scared eyes. His sweatpants had holes in the knees and streaks of black along the thighs. Despite the warm weather, he looked cold, his fists jammed into the front of his hoodie. I didn't know if Lizzy was going to attack or embrace him. She was cagey like that, wiry and reactive. The abandoned house we called the Shack, where we secretly met a few nights a week, loomed behind the boy.

He stared past us. I could see he wanted something. The warmth of the fire, maybe.

'You got food?' he said, moving closer.

Lizzy reached down and pulled out her stash of Morning Glory Muffins. The boy lurched forward and snatched the Tupperware container. He started shoving the muffins into his mouth one at a time.

'So, where'd you come from?' I said.

The boy made a gesture toward the house behind him.

'You're living in there? Why?'

'Because it's fun,' said the boy, smiling.

'How? What do you eat? What do you—'

'You guys throw out some nice food around here,' he said, looking around. 'Wasteful.'

'What's your name? I'm Lizzy and this is Grey.' She thrust out her hand.

'I'm Toby,' he said, shaking Lizzy's hand.

* * *

We met Toby at the Shack a few nights later. Toby took Lizzy's flashlight and showed us around the house. The floorboards creaked under our feet.

'How long have you been here?' Lizzy said.

'Since April. Things got real bad at my mom's, so I just left. Walked all the way here from the city.'

Lizzy and I exchanged glances. There was garbage strewn around and some blankets bundled in the corner.

'Is this really better than living with your mother?' I asked.

'Yes,' Toby said.

* * *

Toby loved all the food and clothes we brought him, but he especially liked the *National Geographic* magazines and listening to the podcast *Reply All*. He liked listening to our stories.

'What about you, T?' I asked. 'Who're your friends? Family? Don't you miss them?'

'Naaa. I could either have family and friends or be alive. I choose being alive.'

* * *

When school started, Toby grew restless, pacing around the Shack. We were busier, so he was alone more.

'You'll need some warmer clothes for the winter,' Lizzy said.

We tried to keep Toby distracted with lessons. We taught him algebra on a whiteboard and assigned problems for homework. He liked watching the numbers narrow down to a single value.

'I like that about math,' he said. 'There's always an answer.'

* * *

Thanksgiving was around the corner. We didn't say a word about all the preparations or the amount of food. Toby refused to go to a shelter, despite the icicles forming off the Shack's gutters. We reviewed our options and considered asking an adult to help.

'Who knows what our parents – what the neighbours would do if they found out?' Lizzy said. 'They'd be more upset about someone squatting than a kid suffering. It's too risky.'

We brought more blankets, but Toby just couldn't get warm. Lizzy cried one night as we walked home.

'It's like there's nothing we can do,' she sobbed. 'There's no way to fix his problems.'

Lizzy would be going to her aunt's house in Ohio. She felt terrible leaving Toby.

You have to bring him some Thanksgiving dinner, she texted.

Definitely, I replied.

* * *

It snowed the Sunday after Thanksgiving, something I usually enjoyed. I forced myself to forget Toby. Eventually, it felt like it never really happened. I was busy playing Xbox and eating leftover stuffing and pie.

Hey. How's Toby? Lizzy texted.

Dunno.

What? Be there. Tonight.

* * *

The grass was frosty as we walked that night, and the sharp air burnt our faces.

'I can't believe you didn't check on him!' Lizzy spat out.

I slouched in shame.

Lizzy took her gloves off and banged out the secret knock on the window. The house remained dark and still.

He was gone.

* * *

It was spring before I noticed my bike was missing. Then they came to demolish the Shack. Rumours spread around the neighbourhood that there were squatters living there.

Lizzy and I investigated the dumpster outside the Shack, finding the cans of fruits and vegetables Lizzy had brought, and the blankets and clothes.

'At least we kept him a secret. We kept him safe,' Lizzy said.

'At least we didn't get in trouble.'

Lizzy's head drooped as we walked away, her arms limp. We returned to our homes, guided by the moonlight, hoping the same moon was leading Toby somewhere better too.

ME AND BROOKE SHIELDS

Helene Macaulay

BROOKE SHIELDS AND I keep running into each other. I, of course, am aware of this, but she isn't. That's the problem with only one of us being famous. As a teenager, I boiled with envy the first time I saw her in a *Vogue* magazine spread. Next came a trillion covers, then the famous Calvin Klein jeans commercial: 'You want to know what comes between me and my Calvin's?' *That one's gotta be a mess,* I thought, perched on my Ethan Allen-framed twin bed and calico quilted polyester bedspread, obsessively leafing through photos of her and Andy Warhol at Studio 54.

When I turned eighteen, I moved to New York City, and through an incredible stroke of luck, I found myself working as a model on the same L'Oréal presentation as Brooke. She was the star, of course – I was just a filler. It was me, about twenty other girls, and Brooke. None of us could possibly have held a candle to her. She had a better face, hair and body than all of us combined. I thought, *Now there's a world-class beauty.* She was also really nice. Bitch. Afterward, I caught the R train back to my Bay Ridge studio, feeling like a total loser.

A couple of years later, I was working at a fancy pharmacy on Madison Avenue in the 60s, and Brooke stopped in one day. All the famous celebrities like Cher and Joan Collins shopped there. Well, it was the '80s. In fact, one morning, Johnny Carson came in really early, ostensibly to avoid the crowds, but when he saw that he was the only customer in the store, he did one quick turn around the place and he was out the front door again. Didn't buy a thing. And since we're talking about Joan Collins, a couple of decades later, when I was a makeup artist to the rich and famous, I worked with her on a *Harper's Bazaar* shoot commemorating the twentieth anniversary of the TV soap *Dynasty*, of which she, of course, was one of the stars. Well, I really worked with Linda Evans, but Joan was there. Anyway, one of the photos featured Joan and Linda engaged in a kind of pencil-skirted, stiletto-heeled tug-o-war with a Louis Vuitton bag, on the fifth-floor corridor of the Plaza Athénée. Even Neil Lane, the jeweller, was there, with his big fancy diamond rings. He was really nice. And Linda Evans was really nice. And Joan Collins was, well, Joan Collins. I wouldn't have wanted it any other way.

Anyhoo, back to Brooke. Crazy thing was, I had a whole conversation with her about hairbrushes, because that was what she had stopped into the pharmacy to purchase, and mission accomplished, I sent her home happily clutching a mini Mason Pearson. Oddly, I didn't even recognise her until the end of the transaction. I guess because you just don't expect these people to be strolling around and also because she was wearing a pair of sunglasses that covered half her face. As she left, I was like, *Damn, that girl is gorgeous.* Then the owner of the store walked up to me and said 'That was Brooke Shields', like I was stupid or something.

'Uh-huh,' I said, looking down my nose at him, pretending not to give a fuck.

Later, still in my makeup artist to the stars phase, I scored a job on one of those morning TV chat fests. I was hired to do makeup for one of the hosts, and one day Brooke was a guest. I was also kind of famous myself in those days (in a viral internet video kind of way – don't ask), and to my surprise, Brooke emerged from her dressing room that morning and said hi to me while I was chatting with one of the producers in the corridor. I mean, she said it like, 'Hi-i-i-i-i-i-i!!!' like she was really excited to see me. But because I'm an asshole, I just said 'Hi', wondering why she had said hi, and then went right back talking to the producer. Later, I had to remind myself that I was kind of famous.

That's the way it always was – I could never really wrap my head around why people sometimes smiled at me on the subway, or why once a fireman screamed my name out the window of a passing fire truck as I was walking down Fifth Avenue. I always had to slap my forehead and think, *Oh, right – I'm famous!* That's probably because I'm an Aquarius. So it might have seemed like I was rude to her, but I just couldn't fathom why *the* Brooke Shields would want to talk to me. I've been consumed with guilt about it ever since. But not as bad as the guilt I'd suffered the time I burnt the toupee of a legendary old-school crooner who will remain nameless, because, frankly, who needs a lawsuit? I mean, let's face it – they all wear wigs. And how the hell was I supposed to know it was synthetic hair? Anyway, I'd just once like to sit down with Brooke for a cocktail or, heck, even a coffee, so we girls can have a chat. Oh, and Brooke, if you're out there and you see this – HOLLA!!!

SOME LC

Jen Susca

TWO DAYS AFTER the bender ends, I'm in the back seat of a Honda Civic holding a greasy Dunkin' bag up to my face. I softly plead with the Uber driver to take the next corner easily. With every acceleration of the car, I hold my breath, brace for impact and look death in the face with a sense of defeat bordering on relief.

DJ Dash is playing on the radio, screaming that he is bringing us the best beats in the borough. His familiar voice wedges a stake through my throbbing brain. My migraine has spiralled me into a state of delirium. It takes every scrap of restraint for me not to lurch forward between the two front seats and turn down the volume.

Desperate for some respite from the smell of the Black Ice air freshener, I roll down my side window hoping that the fresh air will provide some further relief. Instead, I am slapped by waves of sticky, humid winds. Still, the cocktail of scents I can smell – street vendors' hot dogs mixed with cigarette smoke and a dash of curry – is both comforting and nauseating and I feel drunk once again.

The streets peel by and they represent landmarks that will never make it onto any tourist's list, but they have long been etched into my memory. The coffee shop where I wrote my thesis; the drag bar where my roommate met her fiancé on karaoke night; the stoop where I rested my freshly maimed ankle that got injured while running late to a job interview, and opting to use a Chipotle napkin to wipe away the blood that had caked onto my brand-new black leather flats. These are the traces of the city I love but, unfortunately, won't be able to afford for much longer. As I look longingly out the window, I wonder if the city will miss me with the same aching feeling.

'Here,' the Uber driver says.

I know it won't.

The Honda Civic slows to a stop and I thank the driver. As I push open the door, I carefully grab my crumpled puke bag and scoot out. My destination is in a part of the city that I'm not familiar with, an area so removed from my world that DJ Dash's beats are probably out of range here. It will be my first and last visit to this location.

I walk into the building and quickly find the elevator. I get in and glide effortlessly up to the eighth floor, pressing my back against the wall as my body instinctively slumps to the floor. I lean forward and cradle my head gently in-between my knees. I wince when the doors finally open to a bright white office, which sends pangs of agony shooting into my retinas. I get up, lower my sunglasses onto my eyes and approach the receptionist.

'Hi. My name is LC,' I say gingerly.

She looks up from her copy of *Us Weekly*, her eyes crossed. 'Elsie?' she asks.

I can always hear the inflection when people mistakenly confuse my name.

'LC,' I slowly repeat. I slide my ID card across her desk. My old ID expired five months ago and I have only just got it renewed. In the picture, I'm either grimacing or smirking. 'I have an appointment at two with Dr Reckless.'

The receptionist, Donna, according to her name tag, which is asterisked with a Donald Duck sticker, looks at me quizzically. Her eyes wander down to my flip-flops then over to the bronze nameplate nailed next to her window, which states: Dr Meredith Reckovich.

I slide my sunglasses back up. 'Yes. Her,' I say.

Donna turns back to her monitor. My stomach knots tighter with every click of her mouse. The knotted feeling moves further up my body, now in the centre of my chest. *Maybe I am having a heart attack,* I think to myself. No, maybe my liver is failing, self-destructing after barely forty-seven hours without alcohol. My left hand reaches over to my belly button. I can't remember where the liver is located.

'Two p.m. you said?' She does a double take, first looking at me then my ID.

I offer the smirk-grimace.

She clicks the mouse definitively. 'Oh, yes. Here you are. May I see your insurance card?'

This is the moment I have been waiting for. I take a deep breath and hand over my card which is boasting a premium, gold ticket, VIP, executive-level, platinum-coverage plan. I exhale. Donna taps away at her keyboard. 'Looks like you've only got about a year left on this plan,' she says, passing the card back to me. I wedge the card back into my jeans pocket. 'And happy belated birthday, by the way.'

My face naturally slips into the familiar smirk-grimace as Donna passes me a large stack of papers fastened to a white clipboard. 'Just a few forms for you to fill out for me while you wait. The doctor will be with you shortly.'

I mumble 'thanks' as I take the clipboard and start fumbling my way through the lengthy questionnaire. I check off 'not applicable' as much as possible to expedite the process. I skip past the sexual history section entirely, and just when my hand is cramping up and I think I must have hit the home stretch, I flip to the page with the emboldened headline: Mental Health. My stomach tightens, and I deeply regret my greasy breakfast sandwich. I skim through the seemingly endless list of questions, turn over the page and find even more questions, each one as daunting as the last.

I start to feel my cheeks burn and instinctively release my grip on the top of the clipboard, letting the papers unfold in a flurry, strategically burying the Mental Health questionnaire down to the bottom. Then I return the clipboard to Donna with my sincerest smirk-grimace. Moments later, a nurse pops open the door to my right and calls me into the examination room. She taps the table with her fingers. 'Hop on up,' she says politely.

I hastily hoist myself onto the table, the crinkling of the clipboard papers ringing in my ears. I feel like crying. 'Now, sit still please.'

'K,' I say, more tersely than intended.

She straps the blood pressure monitor onto my yellow bicep. 'So, are you still in school?' she asks.

'I wish. I graduated a few years ago.'

'Oh. Are you working?'

The tired small talk is only increasing the roiling in my stomach. 'Um, yes. Sort of. Well, I double-majored in Latin and Women's Studies, so . . .' I say as the monitor constricts further around my arm like a serpent. 'So my career hasn't been . . . exactly . . . fulfilling.' I force a laugh as she jams an otoscope into my ear. 'See anything good in there?' I ask. No response.

Her eyebrows furrow as she holds the icy stethoscope to my chest. She slides it over an inch to where my heart should be.

'Are you a runner? You have an unusually low heart rate.'

'No, just mostly dead inside.' No response.

Once the small talk and vitals are complete, the nurse says her line about the doctor being right with me and closes the door behind her, leaving me in the unbearable silence of the white examination room. I get the Dunkin' bag out of my pocket and put it in a nearby wastebin. I then grab the clipboard off the counter and flip back to the Mental Health questionnaire.

> Over the past two weeks, how often have you been bothered by the following problems?
>
> Feeling tired or having little energy.
>
> Little interest or pleasure in doing things.
>
> Feeling down, depressed or hopeless.
>
> Poor appetite or overeating.
>
> Feeling bad about yourself, or that you are a failure and have let your family down.

I place the clipboard back, put my sunglasses back on to protect my eyes from the searing fluorescent lights overhead, and lie down flat on the exam table with my arms crossed like I am a corpse. I start to wonder that if I die before I am kicked off my parents' glorious health insurance, how that would be such fortuitous timing.

The examination room door soon opens again and in walks a stern-looking woman with pin-straight hair. 'Hello, I'm Dr Reckovich,' she says flatly.

I lift my sunglasses off my face again. 'Nice to meet you, Dr Reckless.'

She doesn't miss a beat. 'Reckovich. What brings you in today? A routine physical? Any concerns?'

'Concerns? Yes, well actually I'm coming off a ten-day bender and I think I might be dying.'

Dr Reckless gets to work inspecting me, the apathetic nurse's examination apparently insufficient.

'Tell me more about this "bender",' she says, her stethoscope pressed against my back.

'Well, twelve days ago I started drinking, and I didn't stop until two days ago. My body feels like it's been hit by a truck and then tossed off a very steep cliff, my brain is all foggy and I'm quite certain that I am going to die at any moment. Oh and I haven't seen a doctor in like four years, so I think it's possible that something else has been festering within me, maybe like a tumour or a tapeworm. Anyway, whatever it is, it is just now acting up and I never thought I was afraid to die, but I feel awful. What is worse is that this time next year I won't even have health insurance, but what does that matter if I'm going to be dead by then anyway?'

Dr Reckless rests the stethoscope around her neck. 'How much alcohol did you drink during this period? Ten days, you said?'

'Twelve days, and hard to say.' I gag as she points a light down my throat. 'But a lot.'

'And did you take any drugs?'

'Pass.'

'Alright.' She makes a note on her clipboard. 'And your diet?'

'Mostly breakfast sandwiches of the bacon, egg and cheese variety.' We both eye the balled-up Dunkin' bag in the waste bin.

Dr Reckless sits down on a rolling stool. 'LC, it seems to me that you have a serious vitamin C deficiency.' She rolls over to the wall of cabinets, pulls open a drawer, rifles through some pamphlets and hands one to me.

'SO, YOU'RE VITAMIN C DEFICIENT' it reads above a picture of a middle-aged man crumpled up in a wheelchair.

'Like scurvy? You mean I have the pirate disease?!' I ask emphatically.

'Well, historically speaking, yes. Pirates, sailors . . . Scurvy is what we called it a long time ago. And it's very rare these days . . .'

'But I'm not a pirate, Dr Reckless. I mean, I do drink rum excessively but—'

She cuts me off. 'Anyone can become vitamin C deficient if they're not getting the proper nutrients in their diet.' Again, we both look at the Dunkin' bag. 'Now, you're only starting to show the first signs of actual scurvy, so I want you to start taking a multivitamin and begin eating a diet rich in fruits and vegetables.'

I flip open the pamphlet. 'Wait, this lists failure to thrive as one of the symptoms? You're right, doctor. I am failing to thrive. I do have scurvy!'

'Actually, failure to thrive is a symptom experienced by infants. Now, LC, this is easily remedied. However, I have to ask – what prompted this "sudden bender", as you call it?'

I look down at the pile of shredded tissue paper on my lap. 'I got laid off and I'm already in crippling debt paying for a private school education that has left me completely unemployable. So I had a few drinks because I had nothing better to do. And to be honest, I still have nothing better to do. I only stopped because I ran out of funds,' I say despondently.

Dr Reckless picks up the clipboard. 'Twelve days ago, okay . . . you mean you started drinking around your birthday?'

A quarter of my life had already passed me by and everything that I had built up in my mind – all the thoughts of being a useful member of society – have passed me by. Ten years ago, I could never have fathomed that three years after leaving my dream school, and halfway through my twenties, I wouldn't even be within spitting distance of the life I had imagined.

I can see Dr Reckless look at the blank Mental Health questionnaire, but she says nothing.

I guess I really have been out to sea.

GAFFER TAPE

Robert Verhagen

LITTLE FIGHTING HAPPENED during the day. We fought at night, so during the day we played cricket. When working a normal job, the best part of someone's day is getting coffee at 10 a.m. The best part of my day was pulling out the bat and the ball of gaffer tape and drawing a pitch in the sand with my heel.

The bat was a piece of two-by-four that I had shaped back in Kabul. The tape was coming off the handle, but it struck a ball true enough. I carried it everywhere. Believe it or not, it was a great way to win the locals over. Walk in with an F88 and they berate you. Walk in with a cricket bat, and all of a sudden you've got friends. You've got informers.

Not that they ever did any work for us, but the kids loved it when we put on a game, and the kids knew everything. 'He's not from around here,' they might say as you fielded with them – and that was how you got information. That was how you got the bad guys.

Now we were stuck in a very deep valley, on a sparse plain hundreds of kilometres before the hills realised they could be mountains. The snow-dusted peaks of the Hindu Kush were out there somewhere. Places like that reminded me why Afghanistan is called the graveyard of empires. But I also knew there was more to it than barren mountain ranges.

Every emperor from Genghis Khan to George Bush had tried to conquer it – and failed. The Afghans had nowhere to go. They had time on their side. And terrain. Now all those empires were gone – America was leaving – and these days I hear ISIS is moving in there. Let them try, I say. Afghanistan will do more for them than we ever did.

This day, I was bowling, Rich was batting, and the boys who weren't fielding sat around our Afghan translator under a desert pine. The translator had the radio on his shoulder. His smile rose and fell as he listened to it.

'They're commentating the game,' he said.

I looked up at the mountains, the colour of my combat shirt. I looked up at the mountains where the Taliban were hiding, then at the ball in my hand.

'What's Terry saying about us now?' I asked.

It wasn't unusual to trade messages over the radio. We knew each other's positions. When the sun fell, we'd head to the higher ground, exchange rounds with them for a few hours, dig our heels in, and wait for the sun to come up again. It was trench warfare without the trenches. We heard from them a lot, but it was unusual for them to commentate.

'Tell the one bowling,' the translator said, smiling and looking past me, with his ear on the radio, 'he better hope he shoots straighter than he bowls.' I laughed. I turned and bowled for Rich's leg, which covered the crooked sticks we'd stuck in the sand for stumps. Rich beat the ball away, out over the sand. I pinched the bridge of my nose and laughed.

'He says some men are born to field,' the translator called out. I dug my thumb in my chest and mouthed, *Me?*

'Ask him if he wants a hit,' I said in retaliation. 'Go on, ask him. Tell him we can put a wager on it. Loser has to leave the valley.'

The translator shifted. He picked the radio off his shoulder. He was looking at me with a straighter face now. 'Serious?'

I nodded.

He murmured into the radio and waited for the voice on the other end. The voice came through, and he murmured again, nodding as he spoke. Then there was a long pause.

I looked back at Rich, then to the boys in the field, to the closer ones who were listening in, and the outfielders who had no idea what was going on. Then I looked at the fellers under the desert pine, and the steady eyes of the translator who held the silent radio out in front of his body. *Surely not,* I thought. *Surely they're not thinking about it.*

Then a voice came on again. Each word the translator drew out of it was slow. 'If we come down from here, you'll bomb us.' Then he called out to me directly, with the radio off, 'We will . . . bomb them . . . won't we?'

I looked up to the hills. I wondered if I could see the one on the other end of our tin-can line. He had his eye on me, whoever he was, but all I could see were the rich coffee wrinkles of the hills.

I walked out to the sand where Rich had banished the gaffer tape ball. I knew the enemy could see me, standing out there in the dust, a hundred metres from the faint pitch and the crooked stumps, away from the desert pine which covered the translator. I was small and dark and vague to them. And they were invisible to me. *We will bomb them, won't we?* – the question stuck in my head.

'Of course we will,' I said as I got back. I strode about fifteen metres in the other direction with the gaffer tape ball in my hand. 'Of course we will.' I gave the ball a quick toss into the air and when I caught it again, I ran hard towards my batter.

CHILLING

Tanner Brossart

TWO A.M. IN the dead of winter, and there she was, traipsing along the snowy sidewalk. Her breath came out in cloud puffs that drifted upward into the embrace of the nimbuses overhead. She found it calming to clear her head with a nightly walk. The stillness of the world around her sharply contrasted with the tumultuous morning hours. No cars whizzed past, no birds fluttered about the feeders and trees, and the snow showed no sign of any other footprints.

Then she rounded the corner.

She couldn't tell if he had been walking as well, or if he had simply been standing there; she was so absorbed in her thoughts that, for all she knew, he could have just materialised on the spot seconds ago. Regardless, the two collided just the same.

'Oh, sorry!' the woman stammered, instinctively shuffling a couple of steps back. 'I didn't mean to bump into you.'

The man chuckled with a warm smile. 'No need to apologise.'

'There . . . usually aren't many people out this time of night,' she explained sheepishly.

'Really, I completely understand. In fact,' he added as he pointed behind her, 'I was just out on a late-night stroll myself. Care to join me?'

The question came as a surprise, to say the least. She quickly looked him over; his face looked oddly familiar, though she couldn't quite place where she had seen it before. And while she wasn't sure if it was her apologetic nature or the underlying pangs of loneliness talking, the woman eventually nodded and began walking across the street with him.

'What's your name?' he asked.

'Oh, it's Alice.'

'Ah,' he said, smiling again and offering his hand. 'It's nice to meet you, Alice.'

Alice shook it and quipped, 'So, is this the part where you try to murder me?'

This time he gave a heartier laugh. 'I won't try if you won't.'

'Sounds like a deal.'

'Coincidentally,' he said as they rounded another corner onto the next street over, 'did you know that people are less likely to be murdered in the winter?'

'Really?'

'Really! Crime rates go down in winter, and experts think it's because – get this – it's too cold outside for would-be criminals!'

'That's . . . actually kind of funny.'

Alice hadn't expected her walk to turn into a meet and greet, especially since she typically avoided strangers like they were unsolicited phone calls, but she was starting to feel glad that she had run into this man. In spite of the turn in conversation – or perhaps because of it.

After a few seconds of silence, she asked, 'So, what has you walking around so late? You can't sleep either?'

'Pretty much,' admitted the man. 'My work schedule has me up at odd hours, so it's difficult to stay asleep on my days off. You?'

'Me? Oh, you mean, why am I awake?' She let out a sigh, which came out like a plume of smoke from a train engine before evaporating. 'I just moved here a couple months ago, actually. Figured it would be a nice change of pace from my parents' house, you know?'

The man nodded.

'Anyway, I've just been really stressed, I suppose. I mean, I'm almost thirty, I don't even have a job in my field, and it's all so . . .' Alice shook her head. 'Sorry. I shouldn't be venting so much with someone I just met.'

'No, no,' the man countered. 'It's good to let these things out. Plus, it gives me an excuse not to talk.'

'Oh, how sweet,' teased Alice with a grin. Then they both laughed and the resulting puffs of haze mingled under the streetlamps. Her eyes wandered back to his face, drawn in by the nagging sense of familiarity. Had they actually met before? If they had, it may have been in passing. Perhaps she had even admired his handsome features then, too . . .

She caught herself staring a bit too long and quickly ducked her head, hoping he hadn't noticed.

'But really,' the man said, 'I get where you're coming from. Being on your own . . . it's a struggle, to say the least. I was lucky and got a decently paid job right after school, so I was able to live the life of solitude I thought I always wanted.' A sigh. 'After a while, though, you start to wish that something, *anything*, would break the silence.'

Her head perked right back up. 'Oh my god, I know exactly what you mean. Or how, like, "indoors" quiet is different than "outdoors" quiet?'

'Yes, exactly!' He beamed. 'Like tonight. Out here it's so serene, so peaceful. But I guarantee that when we both head back to our homes, the silence will feel . . . heavy. Oppressive.'

Alice nodded along. They made another turn, back toward her street. 'Umm, maybe . . . you could spend the night at my place, then? I'm just up on Berkley here.' She blushed and shook her head with a laugh. 'Oh my God, I can't believe I just said that to a stranger.'

To her surprise, the man also blushed. 'I'm flattered, really, but . . . I do think I should head back home. But I can walk back with you, at the very least.'

'And what, make it even more awkward for me?'

'That wasn't my intention, but if you insist . . .'

It went like that for the remainder of the walk, the two teasing one another in a way that just felt so natural, so right. Alice didn't feel the cold or see the sky clear up; every bit of her focus was on him.

When the steps to her apartment came into sight, it didn't even feel out of place to kiss him goodnight.

As they pulled apart, Alice said, 'You know, I've been trying to figure this out during our walk, but . . . do I know you from somewhere?'

'If you do . . . it's probably from seeing me on TV,' he answered.

'Really? Are you an actor?'

'Not quite.' He paused. 'Would it help if I said I was on the news?'

'*Ohh*, you're that new anchor?' She tilted her head. 'No, that's not right. Oh, wait! You—'

Then the realisation settled in, as did a bone-deep chill. She immediately recoiled a few steps, back toward her apartment. From this angle, the man's face was now half concealed in shadow.

'Y-you're . . . does this mean I'm . . . you're going to . . . ?'

His smile, once so warm and amicable, now looked menacing. 'Like I said earlier,' he replied, 'it's too cold out.'

With that, he continued walking down the sidewalk, placing his steps carefully in the impressions Alice's had made not long before.

TORQUE

Bill Gaythwaite

I'M ON MY weekly Zoom call with my dad. He's trying to tell me the plot of some old movie he saw about thirty years ago, except he can't remember the name of the actress who starred in it.

'Your mother loved that woman, whoever she was. I got dragged to her films whenever they came out.'

'Oh!' I say, with more energy than is required.

'But you know your mother. She said, "Jump." I said, "How high?"'

This is *not* how I remember their relationship at all, or my mother, whose powers of persuasion lean heavily on Southern charm, not boot-camp directives. But I don't disagree. My father's memory has made some adjustments since their divorce ten years ago. My mother has reinvented herself too. For one thing, she left New Hampshire and moved back to Chapel Hill. She finished her Master of Art History and now lectures on the Renaissance. Before the lockdown, she was giving tours at local museums, rattling off anecdotes about Titian and Tintoretto. She lives with a guy who teaches in the Department of Classical Studies at Duke, and a couple of summers ago, she accompanied him to Tuscany for an archaeological dig. This was when my father started referring to them as *Indiana Jones and the Temple of Doom*.

I want to get him away from the past, so I tell him about my Boston neighbourhood where it seems everybody is still not wearing their masks. My dad grunts when I tell him this, which I assume is because he isn't complying either. I imagine my father wears a face covering to get into the grocery store, but then he probably yanks it down so it resembles a wrestler's chin strap. I don't ask whether he's scheduled for a vaccination yet either. It's tough to know what will set him off. I complain about my electricity bill instead, which has risen ever since I've been working from home and need to keep the ceiling fans on all day.

'Ceiling fans shouldn't cost you much,' he says. 'Most run on magnets.'

'What do you mean?'

'What do you mean "what do you mean?"' he says.

'I didn't know this about magnets and ceiling fans.'

'Of course you did.'

'No. I really didn't.'

He leans in close to the camera and peers at me, perhaps wishing that his real son has slipped into a Zoom breakout room and he is speaking to some imposter. Then he sighs and begins to tell me about magnetic fields, opposing polarities and the concept of torque, which sounds like it's straight out of a comic book, but I know better than to mention that.

'Thanks for enlightening me,' I say when he's finished.

'You know,' he says, 'your mother used to say the same thing. Now look where she is.'

I don't know what that's supposed to mean, and my father might not either, because he's gone back to explaining the plot to that old movie he got dragged to. I give up after that, letting him sink into the past. I nod at the camera and motion for him to keep talking. After all, it's the least I can do.

THE GRIEVER

Jacinta Dietrich

IT IS 11 P.M. The buzzing vibration of a phone breaks the silence of the bedroom. They are both exhausted: Sam didn't leave work till late and Eve had been studying all day. Neither wants to answer the phone. They let it ring, hoping the caller will give up. They don't. Reluctantly, Sam searches through the bed sheets until he finds the phone.

'It's Mum,' he grumbles.

Sam's mum is notorious for calling until he picks up. There is no hope of waiting her out, best to just answer. He rolls his eyes as he lifts the phone to his ear.

'Hey Mum.' He mouths 'sorry' to Eve as he gets up, kisses her on the forehead and wanders out of the room, closing the door behind him. She knows he will get his mum off the phone as quickly as possible with promises, which he will not fulfil, of calling her back tomorrow.

Eve rolls onto her side and stretches her legs out where Sam's had been. It is still warm. She picks up her phone and idly swipes through Instagram. She stops scrolling when she reaches the photos already marked with red hearts. She is a serial liker.

Twenty minutes pass. Sam hasn't come back to bed. Eve's eyes start to burn. Aching for sleep, she heaves her body off the bed and goes to find Sam, dragging the blanket with her.

Eve finds him sitting on the verandah. His shoulders are slumped and a thin stream of smoke snakes through the air behind him. She

175

had only seen him smoke once before, when family turmoil last led him to self-medicating his anxieties. Again, the cigarette fits naturally in his left hand. The cigarette butt blazes against the dark night as he inhales deeply, his chest rising as it fills with smoke.

'Pop's gone,' he says, exhaling the smoke through his lips.

She sits beside him on the bench and wraps the blanket around his shoulders. His skin is cool against hers where he rests his head against her shoulder. She can smell whiskey on his breath.

They pack the car in twenty minutes. Eve drives. Seven hours and fifteen minutes later, Google Maps tells them they have arrived at their destination. She pulls into the driveway of Sam's childhood home. He doesn't move, just sits beside her, cradling a now empty bottle of whiskey and the beginnings of a hangover.

The house stands alone and empty. The curtains are drawn, and the front door is closed. Sam inhales deeply. Eve cuts the car engine and there is silence. They sit in the car and watch the sun rise over the roof.

* * *

Eve stands in the hallway and takes three deep breaths.

'You alright?' Sam asks, poking his head out from around the door. She can only see him from the neck up, and his half-knotted tie swings like a pendulum beneath his floating head. She almost laughs, but she doesn't. She nods and his head disappears.

She wanders the hallway while she waits. The walls are lined with family portraits, school photos and sport participation medals. All the things that become especially treasured when kids move out of home. She stops in front of one of the family pictures. Judging from the decorations, it was Christmas, and a hot one at that. The Christmas tree is wilting and Sam's family are all wearing singlets. She stares into each of their flushed faces. *Who are you? Will you like me?*

She moves on, watching Sam's family age across the frames. She stops at a recent photo of Sam. He's got his arm around an unfamiliar girl. Eve pulls out her phone and flicks open Facebook. Her practised fingers quickly find the mystery girl's profile. She scrolls down and sees that the girl dated Sam for a year in high school. Satisfied, she puts her phone away.

Eve continues down the hall, picking out each face. There is a pattern to the faces. If she spots an older man, she only needs to look to the next face to find Sam. She pauses on a photo of Sam at his graduation. Her eyes move across to the older man standing shoulder to shoulder with Sam. His face is lined, but not how she expected. His wrinkles do not show the end of a life, but the shallow crevices of life still to be lived. Sixties, maybe seventies. Young for a grandpa. Not unusual in a small town.

'Is everyone coming back here to get dressed?' she calls out. She rubs her thumb across her sweaty palm, slowly working away little beads of skin.

'Nah,' he calls back. 'They're staying with Gran. They don't want to leave her alone in the house.'

Sam leaves his room and stands beside her. He slips his hands into his pockets and stares at a photograph on the wall.

'Sorry, this has all been so rushed. Pop always said people shouldn't drag this stuff out. He would've wanted it done quickly. No fuss.'

'It's fine. So, I'll meet them when we get there then?'

'Yeah, most likely afterwards. It sounds like Dad isn't coping, which means Mum's not coping. I'll come find you at the end.' His words linger. There's silence between them, and Sam keeps staring at the photograph. He nods slowly to himself then begins to move.

'Alright, I'll be ready in a sec,' he says as he walks back into his room.

Eve's already dressed: black flats discovered in the boot of her car; black stockings found bunched in the bottom of her handbag; a plain black dress from Kmart that cost twenty-five dollars; a black blazer from Target that cost thirty-five dollars. Both purchases were made at the shopping centre that morning. They're last-minute purchases she would have preferred not to have made. She kicks herself. *This is a last-minute event that no-one had wanted. Your sixty dollars don't matter, Eve.*

'Are you ready to go?' Sam asks. He stands in the doorway wearing an old, ill-fitted suit. She can see the tops of his socks and his wrists peeking out from the arms of the jacket. He must have been shorter when he bought it, and he probably hadn't needed a suit since then. She wishes he didn't need a suit now. His eyes are bloodshot, a mix of little sleep and too much whiskey. She knows hers are red too.

'I'm ready when you are,' Eve replies.

* * *

Eve watches the back of Sam's head. She sits a few pews back, behind the family but before work colleagues and other community members. It's further forward than she expected to be. She would've been more comfortable at the back.

The pews start to fill around her. To her left, two couples start exchanging greetings and condolences.

'Have you seen the family?' one lady asks.

'We haven't had a chance. They've been caught up with everything. We've invited them over for a cuppa when they're ready though. Have you?' her friend replies.

'We saw Barry down the street yesterday. He's doing the best he can, but of course it's been tough. Quite a shock for the family. Sixty-four and full of health, they still expected plenty of years.' Only the ladies talk. The men sit in silence, facing forward.

'Yes, quite a shock. How's Rose?'

'Barry said she's doing okay. She must be struggling, though. She was very close with Barry's family, especially after her own father passed away. It must feel like she's lost two fathers in one lifetime.'

Eve remembers that Barry and Rose are Sam's parents. She hasn't met them yet. She wants to write their names on her hand so she doesn't forget. She doesn't have a pen.

'It's nice that Sam has come home to be with them. Family is important during times like these.'

'And they were always so close.' The lady's tone is appropriate for funerals, solemn and quiet. She leans in close to her friend and starts speaking softly.

'I heard he's brought his new girlfriend back home.'

A man behind her coughs. The ladies' chatter stops. They turn in unison to find the noise, but their eyes find Eve instead.

'Is that her?' one of the ladies whispers.

'I think so. She's doesn't look like a city girl – a bit drab.'

'Why couldn't he just find a nice girl here? This one looks just like Nancy's daughter anyway,' she says gesturing toward Eve.

They turn and look at Eve again. Other heads turn to follow. A wave of whispered gossip swells around the room. Eve can feel their small-town eyes on her. *Is this why Sam had never brought me home before?*

She is jolted back to reality by the buzz of her phone. Her handbag half muffles the sound, but she still feels the vibration through the material. The gentleman beside her frowns while the ladies in the next row turn to give her an icy stare. She knows she can't check it, but her fingers still itch to. It's probably nothing more than a photo of someone's brunch. She can see it later.

Sam turns and their eyes meet.

'You okay?' he mouths.

'Yeah. You good?' she mouths back.

He winks at her and turns back to the front. Eve smiles, then stops. *Don't smile at a funeral.*

Eve's eyes move beyond Sam's head and rest on the coffin. She wonders how people buy coffins – do they come with a funeral plan? She imagines a coffin department store, aisle upon aisle of coffins on shelves. *Maybe IKEA does coffins.*

She is grateful for the closed casket. It would be such an intimate thing to see a person in death but not in life, greeting them when they are cold and empty. A photo sits on top of the coffin. It is a black and white shot from decades earlier, the time before children and grandchildren. The face is different to the one she saw in the hall, but only slightly. It is smoother, tighter. The eyes are the same, a distinctive almond shape that Sam inherited. *What did they looked like when he laughed, or watched a sad movie or woke up in the early morning?*

Instinctively, Eve lifts her hands and rubs her own eyes, wondering if they are still red. They feel itchy. She had squirted in some eye drops in the car, but that had only made them wetter.

Glancing around, she sees that the church is decorated with vases of stiff faux flowers. A price sticker dangles from one of their bright green stems. A missed detail in the rush of it all. She wants to remove it, to rip it off and discard the evidence. She wonders how much they cost, and what the family will do with them after? *Would you keep them after the funeral, in your lounge room or kitchen? Maybe they can store them away until they need them again?* She cringes at the thought.

Eve's eyes fall on Sam's parents in the front row. His dad is hunched over, ready to fold in on himself. He looks like he could use a drink. She watches as Sam rests his hand on his dad's shoulder, and the man turns to face his son. His father's face is worn, textured from years of working outdoors. Eve has never worked outside, always cubicles or when she's lucky, an office. *Will Sam's dad respect me less for having not worked outside? Think that I'm lazy or undetermined, not ambitious enough for his son?*

Sam's mum sits on his other side. Her back is straight against the wood. She looks tense, like she's almost at breaking point. Her hair is pulled back and tightly tucked into a ponytail. Judging from the photos, and her appearance now, Sam's mum is the practical one. She was always holding the picnic basket or carrying the birthday cake. She'd been smiling in the photos, though. She isn't smiling now.

The music fades and an elderly priest approaches the lectern, signalling the start of the funeral. Eve watches as Sam shifts in his seat before drawing himself up, bracing himself. His dad shrinks further down into the pew. His mum doesn't move at all.

Eve closes her eyes. She just needs a small rest.

* * *

After the service, Eve stands in line with Sam's family. They are gathered in a green field dotted with engraved blocks of aged grey stones. Gum trees stand like an honour guard along the church-yard driveway.

She is pressed between Sam and his mum. She can feel their heat, the soft black fabric of their clothes. Eve shuffles towards Sam, conscious of his mum's arm pressing against her. His mum hasn't looked at Eve yet. Her blank gaze only stares forward. Sam's hand finds Eve's and he gives it a gentle squeeze. He hasn't cried once today.

The surrounding speakers crackle to life as someone presses play on the iPod. Frank Sinatra's 'My Way' plays over the sounds of nearby birds. A group of men slowly bear the coffin from the hearse. Sam's dad is among them. The man behind him has familiar eyes, probably an uncle or cousin. They all grunt in unison as they lower the casket.

As the coffin reaches the ground and Sinatra hits his peak, Sam's mum lifts her hands to her face and starts to cry. Long heaving sobs shake her shoulders. Sam tightens his grip on Eve's hand, and she feels his body begin to tremble.

Eve tries to focus on her breathing. In. Out. In. Out. In. The last breath falters and catches in her throat. Her face feels wet.

She is a false griever for the deceased. It is not her place to cry today. Her phone buzzes and the vibration shakes through her hand-bag and down to her bones. She doesn't move.

I TRAVELLED THIS FAR BECAUSE I LOVE YOU

Zach Murphy

'THE ANTARCTIC COLD definitely feels a lot different from the cold in Idaho,' Adam said.

'Sure does,' Rodger said as he flicked the mini icicles off his thick moustache. 'Once we cross this next glacier wall, we'll have reached the edge of the earth.'

Adam and Rodger trudged on with their overstuffed backpacks through the wintry terrain, looking like a pair of snails with shells full of climbing equipment and survival supplies.

'I really think we should turn around,' Adam said.

'But we're almost there,' Rodger said. They could see the peak of the glacier approaching.

Rodger pulled out his map. A harsh gust of wind swept it off into the snowy distance.

'See!' Adam said. 'Even the wind is telling us to go back!'

Rodger checked his compass. The needle was frozen stiff, as if the cold had inspired it to give up on its one and only job. Rodger tapped the glass face of the compass, but the needle wouldn't budge.

'It's so cold that the compass broke,' Adam said. 'If that isn't a sign, I don't know what is.'

'It's not broken,' Rodger said. 'It's just confused.'

Adam sighed and rolled his eyes. 'How much further do we have to go?'

Rodger pointed ahead with the focus of an Olympic athlete. 'If we keep moving, we should get to the glacier wall within an hour,' he said.

Adam came to a halt and forcefully planted his boots into the snow. 'I have something to tell you,' he said.

'What?' Rodger asked as he hiked on.

'I don't really think the earth is flat,' Adam answered.

Rodger choked on his own snot from laughing so hard. 'You're kidding,' he said.

'Rodger! It just doesn't make sense!'

Rodger stopped. 'Wait,' he said. 'You're being serious?'

'Yes!' Adam replied.

'Did you not watch the YouTube documentary I sent you?' Rodger asked.

'No-one ever actually watches videos that people send them,' Adam said. 'Especially when they're two hours long.'

'Then why did you decide to come?' Rodger asked.

Adam took a deep breath. 'I thought it would be a good bonding experience.'

Rodger squinted. 'A bonding experience?'

'I just feel like we've been drifting apart from each other the past few years,' Adam said. 'Like, there's this fracture growing between us.'

Rodger took a seat in the snow. 'I've always wanted to accomplish something amazing before I turn thirty,' he said. 'You know, to prove that there's something special about me.'

'Please don't go all Marlon Brando in *On the Waterfront* on me,' Adam said.

'It's true,' Rodger said. 'I feel like my life has been disappointment after disappointment.'

'You've been my best friend for almost my whole life,' Adam said. 'That's a pretty awesome accomplishment.'

Rodger entered into a deep stare. 'I'd shed a tear right now, but it might freeze,' he said.

Adam smiled. 'Let's go,' he said as he held his hand out to Rodger. 'Let's get to that glacier wall.'

Rodger grabbed Adam's hand and popped up from the ground. 'To the glacier wall!'

Adam dusted the snow off his coat. 'After that, I'm not going any further.'

'There is no further,' Rodger answered.

Adam took another deep breath as they travelled on.

* * *

After scaling the glacier wall, Rodger and Adam pulled themselves to the top of the summit and gazed ahead. The miles and miles of frozen expanse gently glistened in the sun's fading rays.

Rodger dropped to his knees. 'It's not the edge of the earth,' he said.

'But it sure is a beautiful view,' Adam said, as he placed his hand on Rodger's shoulder.

OPPORTUNITY

Michelle Kelly

WHAT FOLLOWS IS the true report of a passenger and a gentleman. There was nothing I could do to intervene.

There were four of us in the carriage. The father sat facing me; the son, a boy of eighteen years or thereabouts, sat beside me. The mother sat next to her husband, like a far, fair angel. No other configuration would have been proper. I could feel the boy's thin shoulder press against my upper arm. He was bowed, listless. Awfully, the man's widespread knees pressed into mine.

The family had been in place when I embarked at Lombard Street and since then, our moods had sagged. Early in the journey, in the evening, lethargy had swathed us all, and our transit had been palatable, but now we had been disturbed by some strange vexation and we each sat restlessly in our place. 'Hie, hie—!' – we heard the coachman urge on his horses through the thin wooden panel of the coach. It was several hours before the sun would rise.

We were jolted sharply, and the woman's elbow struck the window frame. The man cursed. The boy moved in his seat and sighed disconsolately. This mode of transportation apportioned us like livestock in a hull. Thus cramped, I felt as fretful as a beast. Who had thought to design this monstrous contraption, a kind of inverted, demeaning compass, so that one was forced to look into the eyes of perfect strangers for hours? It was insupportable.

As I watched, the woman gave a gentle smile to the boy. I thought of the young lady awaiting me at Woodlands. I hoped and trusted that Ann and I would bring each other happiness and prosperity. Our courting was at an end. The arrangements with Ann's father had been acquitted satisfactorily; the final proposal issued and accepted. There was something about this woman traveller that reminded me of my betrothed. The passenger was pale and slight, but she had a soft and kindly air about her. Her hair was tucked smoothly behind her ears and her hands rested easily in her lap. Of our little crew, she was the most jostled, but the locomotion seemed to affect her least of all.

The older man slid forward in his seat, pushing his legs out and my knees further back. 'It's as tight as all blasted in here,' he said, apparently to his wife, but looking straight at me. There was a stain on his lapel. The man's apparel was fine but his bearing slovenly and, as I stole glances at his dark menacing countenance, I resolved instantly and with a kind of horror that this will never be me. I will be respectable, and not some filthy tyrant who incites foreboding in the hearts of those around him. I vowed that my house would be kept decently; my family would be prudent and content. His wife was lovely: contained and trim. But he was insufferable – his thick upper arms and thighs beneath the soiled but well-made garments; the hairy sides of his face, worst of all his temples where sparse thick black strands seemed to draw attention to the coarseness and pockmarks of the surrounding skin. His witless resentment of neat, respectable young men on their way to meet their fiancées was apparent from the eye he gave me. There was a faint air of mutton about his person.

The man continued to regard me baldly. And I came to see that his vigilance was not unmotivated. As well as keeping a watchful eye on the boy, the woman's gaze fluttered toward me on regular occasion over the next hour. It was hard to see in a carriage illuminated only by the moon and the outside lamps, but I saw. She was like a small, bright and curious bird.

Our witching hour agitations seemed to be dissipating. The guard's horn sounded once or twice as we approached a toll. We stopped briefly to change the horses. Muted cries suggested the driver attacked a particularly precipitous slope with something akin to anguish and despair. We sat silently with little movement throughout it all. Our eyes turned outwards, and after a time the older man, blessedly, closed his. Someone cleared their throat. Someone's breath caught as they reckoned with the edge of sleep. The hills around us started to reveal their long low slopes in a sombre light. I discerned the indistinct shapes of scattered cottages and stables. The woman began to rearrange herself and her belongings in a manner that signalled she was preparing to alight.

The coach came to a halt. Grunting as he recovered himself from his ponderous slumber, and with a surly bid to his wife to stay as she was, the older man exited the vehicle. I heard him exchange words with the coachman and the mail guard. It was a small landing party as there had been no outside passengers on this trip; no rambunctious youths bothering the driver for a turn at the reins. Bags were unloaded, and the three men moved off, likely to the inn to settle some business of the journey.

It was at this moment the atmosphere in the carriage shifted decisively, trumping the subtle ebbs and flows of energy I had marked throughout our travel. The boy beside me sat up abruptly, determinately, like a snake rising out of the grass. This movement was shocking, tidal – completely untoward. I felt overpowered by his definitiveness; the purpose he betrayed. He stretched out a thin hand and took hold of the woman's knee and then, rapidly and without pause, reached farther forward, as though her leg were a rail to her lap. I cannot tell you anything other than it was instantaneous. She gasped. I gasped: I had misapprehended the entire situation. He was not her son.

The woman held herself still and a queer look came into her eye. A thought flashed through my mind, unbidden and unaccountable: we three were quite, quite alone. The woman reached down and slid her fingers underneath the young man's seeking hand. Shocked, I looked on. What ghastly licentiousness was I to bear witness to?

I felt frozen to my seat. Should I yell out to alert the husband, the coachman? Could I—? I plucked at my trousers. The woman raised the boy's hand, slowly, toward her face, placing it on her cheek and curling her fingers around his.

I glanced at the boy. Never had I seen wantonness that compared with the wantonness on this young man's face in this moment. And the woman's own expression seemed now to be at ease, pliable. She, so proper, so delicate and solicitous, seemed actually to be quivering slightly. Lord help us, was she accepting his impertinent attentions? I sat up straighter, leaned forward, my own hand twitching. She pushed her chin outwards to nuzzle in her paramour's hand – before twisting her long neck and sinking her small teeth deeply into the tender parts between his thumb and fingers.

The boy let out a yelp and struggled to wrench his hand back from her maw. She was certainly quivering. I understood now – this poor beleaguered lady, forced to defend herself in so unbecoming a manner! This gentlewoman, and this wretch! What scurrilous and beastly behaviour from one so young. Without a doubt, the husband and the sheriff must be informed! And yet perhaps this was not the good woman's desire. It was not for me to tell; she was already gathering herself and her few small parcels to leave.

She was half out of her seat when her unkempt companion reappeared at the carriage door with the words: 'Come, Amelia.' She lightly touched her husband's large arm as she stood, utterly self-possessed. Toward the boy the man tipped his hat, and a brief expression of confusion crossed his face as he gleaned the new demeanour of the scourge, who was now hunched over, one fist balled high into his armpit and the merest suggestion of a grimace on his lowered brow. Without undue pause, however, the husband turned and bid me good day quite gallantly. He moved aside, and the coach rocked slightly as the good lady descended without a glance at either of us remaining. There was silence.

Not for any price could I regard or converse with the figure on my left. I heard the couple move away and the coachman return and take his mount; the mail guard followed at the back soon after. Presently we were away again. Never before had I borne witness to such a happening and I was severely discomfited. In my wildest imaginings I had not conceived that such delicacies, or rather indelicacies, might be exchanged in such transitory and opportune moments. That poor woman! And the boy – had he chanced such a caper before? Whatever had possessed him? Had he met, in the past, with success? From nowhere I saw the image of one man's questing hand joined by another's. In my own mind I hardly knew where to look. With effort, I turned my thoughts to Ann.

INTERMISSION

INFLATED

C G Myth

ONE DAY, I woke up without my left arm.

I am not sure how it happened. I do not believe someone came and sawed it off while I was asleep. I am sure I would have felt that.

Even so, my left arm is gone. I have no feeling on that side of me, no phantom limb or pain in my shoulder, just a missing arm.

I went to see my doctor, and he told me to go to the ER. The blood pooled on the floor as it leaked from the hole on my left side. There was no pain, though. He said I already should have bled out.

The ER nurses lost their minds when I walked through the door. I was put on fluids and connected to two blood bags. The space under my skin started to swell up like a balloon.

Why's he growing?! one nurse said.

I am not sure, the other nurse said. Turn off the fluids. Keep him on blood.

They filled me with donated blood until blood started leaking from my tear ducts. They weren't sure what to do when the blood began dripping down my cheeks.

I sighed. Thanks for all your help, ladies, but I really must be going.

Inflated and red, I walked toward the door of the ER.

I guess some people just lose their arms.

FIX

Lauren Schenkman

THE COUPLE – A man and a woman, Caucasian, ages thirty-four and thirty-two – were locked in a 64-square-foot room at 6:53 Greenwich Mean Time and given a ladder, a pail, two ration bars and a pair of scissors. Via a metal chute in the ceiling, the first stimuli were introduced: stuffed animals of the kind given out at fairgrounds, followed by a collection of plastic dinosaurs, followed by a continuous shower of packing peanuts. The couple took on these first stimuli with great gusto, the woman diligently hacking off the plush toys' heads with the scissors; the man ingeniously using his saliva to wet the packing peanuts so they could be mashed down to a smaller volume. It was obvious right away that the plastic dinosaurs worried them. The man fumbled, trying to stack them together in a way that took up less space, but abandoned this project as more packing peanuts came through the chute and began accumulating on the floor. The woman, not having sufficient saliva to wet them all, tried a different method, spitting into her hands and massaging the packing peanuts between her palms. The man stuffed them into his mouth and then spat them into the pail as soggy pulp, pressing them to the bottom, then pulling them out to form packing-peanut paving stones, which he placed carefully on the floor. Increasing the flow of stimuli even slightly sent them into a panic; diminishing the flow put them at ease and encouraged them to fuss with the plastic dinosaurs again, although that was clearly a lost cause.

All of this they abandoned, of course, once the dead fish were introduced. At first, the man and the woman simply stared as the carcasses of mackerel and sardines spewed out of the ceiling chute and thwacked wetly onto the floor. Then the man put on a determined sort of face and moved the ladder closer to the chute and climbed a few steps, as if he were planning to tackle the problem at its source. But at that point a dead pancake batfish flew out of the chute, hit him in the face and knocked him right off the ladder. Shaken, he dragged the ladder back to the wall while the woman – whose expression said, 'While you've been fooling around with the ladder heroics, I've been doing something actually useful,' – began, while holding her nose, kicking the dead fish into piles in the corners of the room and covering them as best she could with the packing-peanut residue and the insides of the carnival animals. The man followed the woman's lead, ignoring the ladder as if the failure had never occurred.

They were allowed to make headway on this for a little while. Then came the sludge. The sludge began pouring through the chute as just a mere trickle at first, along with the dead fish that still came plopping out semi regularly. Then the flow increased to a thin curtain deceptively resembling a chocolate fondue waterfall, except that the sludge was a mixture of farm runoff and pulped slaughterhouse leftovers. The man, perhaps looking to save face after the ladder fiasco, went immediately for the bucket in order to catch the sludge as it fell, but the smell apparently became too strong for him – a notable occurrence, given that his senses should have already been dulled from the fish – because he put the bucket down and sat against the wall of the room and put his head between his legs. The woman jumped up to grab the pail and began to make trips back and forth between the wall and the centre of the room where the chute was placed. It seemed that her strategy was to transport the sludge away from the man in order to minimise his contact with it for as long as possible. Now the woman began talking loudly and energetically, and though she could not be heard through the soundproof walls of the chamber, it seemed like she was saying something along the lines of, 'Great idea smashing down those packing peanuts, genius. We could have really used them right now.' In response, the man's mouth began to move rapidly, probably saying, 'You seemed to like my idea just fine five minutes ago.' In response, the woman's mouth moved even more quickly, probably saying, 'You never take responsibility for anything,' after which the man probably retorted, 'Why bother when you always end up blaming everything on me anyways?'

It looked like game over. The woman was still running back and forth from the chute to the side of the room, but she was getting sloppy with the pail, while the man, his head between his legs, continued to yell at her.

And so, the test substance was turned on. Everyone reacts differently when they see it. This time, the woman leaned against the wall warily. The man remained immobile, too exhausted to move. They watched the white stuff, which resembled cotton candy, come out of the chute. Then their expressions changed, indicating that the stenches were being absorbed, which is what the test substance is engineered to do. The woman sat down next to the man, and soon they were smiling and hugging each other and laughing, settling down more comfortably into the fish carcasses and sludge.

We were thirty-two minutes in. Within fifteen minutes, we knew from previous trials the toxins in the air would put them both into vegetative comas. But at this point in the experiment, the subjects usually find themselves to be unaccountably hungry, which is what the ration bars are for – the ethics committee's idea. But because people always stash them away at the beginning – looking nervous, because there are only two, and they're wondering how many days the experiment runs – they never find them. Nobody guesses they will only have, tops, fifty-five minutes to live.

The man gestured to the woman – he was hungry; couldn't she find him something to eat? The woman looked around obediently, and then scooped up a handful of the test substance and offered it to him.

Because all the scents had been neutralised, they really couldn't be blamed for getting confused. The man took a morsel of the fish- and shit-soaked foam and took a bite. He shrugged – not delicious, but good enough. The woman smiled modestly, pleased to be useful, and soon joined in.

It happened this way in every trial. This was trial number 999, which might be called overkill, but with something this serious, this final, we couldn't afford uncertainty.

We looked at the chief scientist, who nodded. The results were indisputable. We would advise leadership to move forward with production.

This is a relief – even for us, who know more than most – what's in store for us. Before, there was grief, and anguish, and bargaining. There was existential despair, there were questions, there were last-minute Hail Mary solutions, there were prayers offered up to various gods.

But we're past all of that now. We're in another phase. We'll content ourselves with this fix.

At least now, none of us will have to smell it anymore. What's piling up around us every day, every minute: up to our knees, up to our waists, up to our throats.

ENDINGS

PLATINUM BLOND

Toby Remi Pickett

WHEN TONE STARTED fading away, we moved into his father's beach house in Fairhaven. His father lived in Singapore and managed a division of Rio Tinto. It was just us there – me and Tone. It was the end of summer and I had finished two years of college, which struck me as a waste, and I wanted to go away for the final week. Neither of us had anything better to do then: no dates, parties, friends or places to be. We had been spending our days sitting in the sterile, totally white lounge room of his South Yarra house. The sun was peeking through the venetian blinds and illuminating the veins beneath Tone's skin. All he had consumed those weeks were Coca-Cola and gin – he wasn't in a good state. Tone's hair was bleached platinum blond, and his arms and legs looked skeletal, as if they were barely there. He kept whispering about the beach. He would lay back on one of the leather recliners, slip his Ray Bans on and mutter as the day disappeared slowly into night. I wondered what it must look like to a stranger watching us from beyond the large glass windows in that lounge room, seeing our tragic silhouettes, as if we were a study of isolation. So it wasn't much of a discussion that we'd leave together. It wasn't even to fix things; we were well beyond that.

* * *

We talked the entire drive to the beach house, mainly me. Tone replied softly about who was screwing whom, who was using drugs, the Polo Lounge, B-list celebrities, artworks he was planning – they always involved a lot of red – and his plans for the following semester. He was going to visit me at college and then we would go on holiday down to Lorne with some old, forgettable friends. We could drink all day and end up drunk, sprawled along the bland foreshore near an old empty fisherman's cottage that we were convinced housed ghosts. Occasionally, Tone would turn up the radio so we could listen to the new Lana Del Rey or Troye Sivan song. I didn't want to tell him, but none of the plans we entertained would happen. I figured he already knew. There was little worth in making plans for anything because he was dying, but we were young and we didn't know any better. That day I forgot Tone's name; he became only the dying boy to me.

* * *

As we arrived at our windswept destination, we turned down a long, pebbled driveway enclosed by high fences, frosted glass and carved hedges. The house overlooked Bass Strait and was a monumental white building that exuded affluence. I had spent my youth at a Caulfield private school, which gave me a sense of what is ugly about the people who lived in these types of places. I could smell it as we unpacked our bags from the car. The inside of the house had the same odour. It was clean and sparse, except for a massive fake Modigliani painting in the dining room. From the hallway, I could see large French doors that led out to a shimmering stone-tile pool. Behind the pool stretched an enormous leafy garden. As I walked around the house, the dying boy checked the security camera footage. I thought he had bigger things to worry about. I asked what he was looking for, but he wouldn't say. He just asked me to get out the tanning lotion.

* * *

Each day felt like a tragic, slow-motion replay of the last. The dying boy would sit in the rocking chair by the pool, gazing toward the beach while smoking long, reaching drags of his cigarette. Meanwhile, I played pool and darts, watched Stanley Kubrick movies on the Apple TV, drank pilsners, listened to The 1975 and slowly became overwhelmed by a sense of hopelessness. I was happiest when we were ignoring each other. He would roam around in a Ralph Lauren dressing-gown that used to be mine. It was far too big for him now and draped across his wasted body. I made him plain toast, the only thing he requested, but he still wouldn't eat it. He instead drank tea – one Country Road mug each morning. The steam would rise to his face, except he waited until it went cold before taking his first sip. Then he would smoke. We occasionally walked down to the beach together. He said he couldn't feel the sand on his feet and only I went swimming; it was freezing. When we returned to the house in the evening, he went down on me, bathed in the half-light of the lounge room. Nothing felt right. Once, he murmured that he probably loved me and that he was sorry, but I pretended to be asleep. When I knew he'd drifted off, I got up and went for a long walk along the beach. The sky changed colours from blue to purple to black. The surrounding trees trembled in the wind.

* * *

In the final days of our vacation, the dying boy would call out in his dreams, screaming incoherent words. One was about him as a young boy being attacked by a swarming circle of crows. He was shaking and I just lay there. I sometimes tried to comfort him by caressing the curled strands of his hair. The bleach was starting to whiten up. Mostly, though, I spent my nights sprawled on the lounge, limbs spread out like I had been crucified. The aircon made the room biting cold but I never turned it off. I got stoned and watched the bubbles in my glass of San Pellegrino dissolve into nothing. In the mornings, I turned on the large LED TV to watch *Rage*. Changing the channel meant seeing violent images of a bombed-out town somewhere in the Middle East or advertisements for *Hawaii Five-O*. I tried to meditate about how I should care more and how bright things blinked and vanished away. I wondered how to escape. I resolved that the following morning I would leave the dying boy for good.

* * *

The sun was an apocalyptic red the morning that I left. I told him that I had to go, and made up something about a party and paying off some debts. A feeling of mourning sat heavy in the bedroom. His eyelids were shut and I stood still, studying the creases in the bedsheets. He was pale white now and remained in bed, puffing his cigarette with short, desperate breaths. I stood in that room for what felt like hours. I felt chained to his side but there was nothing else to do. When I arrived home two hours later, it was dark and there was no moon in the sky. I stood in the driveway. I was alone. I thought of the dying boy and how I now knew what death looked like. I had left him back in the bedroom by the beach, the bay windows letting in gusts of sea salt and the shadows moving across his still body until it was dark, and he was invisible once more.

* * *

I do still think about the dying boy. Standing in the smoker's lounge at Flamingo Club; dancing with our eyes shut tightly, strobe lights flashing around us; passing out at Brighton with him on top of his father's Mercedes GLA; kissing him, feeling the clenched bones in his jaw; nights in Brunswick drinking Veuve Clicquot and singing along to The Wombats and The XX; the endless stream of cigarettes; the carved lines of his muscles and the electric blue of our friend's jacuzzi; the scent of weed and semillon; how yellow he had become by summer from using too much tanning lotion; shooting zombies on the Xbox; fingering a SparkNotes book of *As I Lay Dying*; trying to mellow out over cappuccinos on Johnston Street, and a spray-painted sign across the empty road reading THE FUTURE. But they're only memories.

DARLA

Joseph Edwin Haeger

GRACE GOT ME Darla as a wedding present. We married young and neither one of us had a lot of money, but she was able to do odd jobs around town to secretly build up enough of a nest egg to sneak down to the general store the Tuesday before our wedding to buy the gun. We were living together – much to the chagrin of both sets of parents, but what could we do? We were in love – and so on the morning of our wedding she left before I got out of bed. She wanted to keep certain traditions alive, and me not seeing her before the ceremony was one of them. The shotgun was left on the kitchen table with a note: A little something for my one and only. I expected her to make a joke in the card, but instead it was a sincere declaration of love. She knew how much I'd sacrificed, and how much I was prepared to sacrifice, so she wanted to do something just for me before our life began in earnest. I knew it was my big day but couldn't stop myself from going into the basement to get gun wax for the stock. I put Darla – a name that came to me right away, Darla from my darling – on my lap and moved the wax carefully across the wood. The gun was brand new, so cleaning her wasn't necessary, but it felt like a declaration of love to Grace. This gun would be this shiny for the rest of my life. A Model 48 Topper. The dark finish on the wood nearly matched the black barrel. Sure, it was constructed from multiple parts, but here, all put together, it looked like it was chiselled from one big slab of power. I imagined the expert who assembled it – a pipe, probably a Chesterfield, hanging out the side of his mouth as he sucked in the smoke without bothering to reach a hand up to it. He probably tapped and measured this specific gun with as much care as the first perfect gun he'd ever built, and now this made-up man was pumping out perfect gun after perfect gun. It was a single-shot, break-open. I dropped the barrel and looked through it right at our floor. We'd need to sand and re-stain the hardwood, but that was a project months, even years, away. First, I needed to clean Darla, and then I needed to go marry Grace. It had turned out to be a perfect day.

I kept Darla in my home office for years. On the weekends, I'd sneak away to hunt grouse or, on the rare occasion, ducks. I'd opt for small game, knowing I didn't need a dog or a child's help to get the job done while Grace stayed home, perfecting the piecrust recipe her grandmother had tucked away in one of her passed-down cookbooks. The love we had for one another was enough to sustain the power of our marriage, and we didn't think we needed to overload it with a child or a dog. In the end, we were happy with just the two of us, so we never bothered with other responsibilities, and hunting ducks is best done with one or the other. All that would have happened is we'd've been crushed under the love in our life. And so, it was like that, that our happy life moved forward.

Then my arthritis caught up with me. The cold mornings bore their way into my joints and bones, and I had to hang the gun up, letting all those little grouse families walk free. We sunk two hooks into the brick above our fireplace – the same one we ate grouse pies in front of – for Darla while Grace told me all about the neighbourhood kids. They loved using our driveway as their start line for their little bike races. It never bothered me, and hell, I'd've encouraged it if I was ever home when the kids were playing. I knew how much Grace thrived on seeing those children happy, and it made me happy to see her happy. Her joints also caught up with her, but whereas mine were stiff and painful, hers birthed something a little worse, and before we knew it, she was too far past anything for the doctors to do. Sure, we were getting up there in age, but Christ, if we'd known thirty-two was going to be our middle age, then maybe we would've done things differently. How? Hell, I don't know. I loved her completely, and the best way I could think to honour her throughout our life was to be home every night. It was to sit across the table from her as we ate our meals. It was holding her hand in front of the fire while she chipped away at a crossword puzzle. And so, I had to say goodbye to Grace and then go home and look up at Darla. I loved her with all my heart, and Darla was proof that she loved me with all hers.

My rational brain told me we were nothing more than the grouse I shot during all those weekends in the woods. One moment they're breathing and alive; the next, they're not. Hearts pump and then they don't. I always kept Darla oiled and waxed. She never looked her age. I could taste the oil now – from today to yesterday to the Saturday morning on the day I was to be married. Years stacked upon years, embedded in the metal of this gun. The position was awkward, but wasn't life? One day you're seventeen and in love. The next she's moved on without you. But it wouldn't be too long. I wanted to pray to the god Grace believed in, but I didn't know how. I sat there a moment longer, sucking in the bitter smell of gunpowder. I thought about what brought me here. Then I didn't.

THE RIDGE

Gail Holmes

Dedicated to Millie.

IT'S ME WHO keeps Claudia company on the long nights when she walks away from him.

We hurry along the ridge with its hive-buzzing sodium lamps, oblivious to the views over the Clyde Valley and Glasgow's city lights. Claudia keeps glancing back over her shoulder until we've left the housing estate behind.

Sometimes, like tonight, we have a milky coffee in Luigi's Café. Luigi lets us stay after closing time while he cleans up. He shows us to a booth with curved wooden seats. Claudia unwraps her scarf and teases her cinnamon hair with her fingers. She always holds the glass coffee cup with her pinkie curled.

God, she's pretty. I love her, but I never tell her.

* * *

When I met Claudia and Sean, they had been married for a while.

I distrusted his charming smile from the start. I always try to stay on the other side of Claudia whenever Sean's in the room. Sometimes he makes an effort to get me to like him by singing to me – he has a good voice. Still, I've never warmed to him. You just know, don't you?

'It's not wise to argue with him, Lorrie,' Claudia cautioned one day.

'I'm just standing up for myself.'

She looked at me for a moment, her brows knitted as if I was getting at her.

'There's more than one way to do that,' she said softly.

Those words coil around me still, then tighten up so suddenly I can't breathe.

* * *

Claudia's watching the steam rise now, swirling over her cup. She's left Sean before. He tracked her down and brought her back in a borrowed Ford. She's always trying to figure out how to get away from him. Her eyes mist up as another plan dissolves into the curling steam.

I want to reach across the table to her. Instead, I steady my frozen fingers around the latte glass. Luigi brings two biscuits in orange wrappers. He lets his hand rest on the table a moment.

'What about your brother?' he asks Claudia quietly.

'Peter?' She looks stung. 'He emigrated to Australia.'

'Au-stra-li-a,' Luigi says, in long curly syllables. He brushes some crumbs from the table and nods unhappily. 'That's a long way.'

A stirring of hope warms me. When Luigi leaves, I lean towards her. 'Could we go there? He'd never find us.'

For a moment her eyes glint, and a smile kisses her lips. Then she bites the inside of her lip. 'I don't even know where he is now. Perth, I think. He hated Sean.'

* * *

The sky is heavy and starless as we walk slowly back up towards the ridge.

Claudia stops in the shadows between the streetlamps. She stares over the murky, swishing grasses that heave and shift, fluid as the sea. The city smoulders in the valley. In the distance, the red aviation light on the television tower flashes slowly on and off. She watches the light flicker for some time.

She's not afraid, but I am.

The grasses hiss and crawl towards me. The buzz from the street-lamps fills my head so I can barely think. We're stuck on this ridge forever, locked in a moment that keeps repeating. I put my hands over my ears, waiting for her. She tugs her scarf higher and thrusts her hands into her pockets. I imagine tendrils of grass slithering up and pulling her in.

I stagger back nearer to the light. The drone intensifies. My body trembles – there's nowhere that's safe.

'How can you stand this?' I cry out.

Claudia sweeps out her arm as she turns to me. 'There's no-one here,' she says steadily. 'There's nothing to be afraid of.'

I look around, breathing hard, trying to see the lights as she does. Trying to ignore the swarm.

'I can't keep coming with you.'

She nods at me as if she's always known this.

'It's alright, Lorrie,' she murmurs, then stares back out towards the light.

* * *

Sean sings 'Danny Boy', tears rolling from his eyes as if someone has died.

I think he must be crying for his father, but then I think of Danny. He and Sean used to laugh and drink till the bottles lay tipped on their sides on the rug like abandoned spin-the-bottles. I remember Danny taking a cigarette from his silver case, lighting it and handing it to Sean. A smile chiselled into Danny's face as Sean's eyes met his. Claudia twisted the tea towel tight as she watched this from the kitchen doorway.

Tonight, it's just Sean and the Johnnie Walker Red Label. He sits back in the armchair, tapping his fingers on the arms. The changes happen faster these days. First, it's the fists slowly clenching and unclenching. Then the knuckles flinch back from the armchair. Burning fluid seems to race through him, drying up the smoothing wax and making his hair stand up. He turns Danny's silver cigarette case over in his hands. My throat constricts as the colour in his face deepens.

I twitch back the curtain. Sleet splodges against the window. I glance at Claudia. She stands, vigilant as usual, in the kitchen doorway. Earlier, she lifted my coat and boots and placed them near hers by the front door.

Sean is on the edge of his chair now. His long arms are bent, hands clawing at the chair arms, eyes protruding – a mantis ready to pounce.

He's up. He kicks an empty bottle over as he swaggers towards me. I thrust my hand over my paper.

'What is that?'

'Nothing.'

'Let me see it.'

Claudia takes a step towards me.

'What the bloody hell is that ugly thing?' Sean says.

Before I can stop myself, I thrust out my chin and look right at him. 'It's an insect that preys on others.'

His skin creases near his mouth as if he's about to speak. His arm twitches.

I glance at Claudia in alarm.

'The water's hot for you now, Sean,' she says.

Sean is fastidious. Nails, hair, skin – he usually scrubs all the work dirt off as soon as he can. But tonight, the water was cold.

He scowls at me then turns to Claudia.

'I'll have a bath,' he says. 'Bring me in another drink.'

Claudia and I listen as the water pummels into the bath.

His boots are tossed against the wall. There's the sound of ringing metal as something hits the towel rail. Water sloshes violently as he gets in.

'Let's go, Lorrie,' Claudia whispers.

We pull on our boots and scarves behind the front door. Claudia's breath is fast against my ear. She is about to open the front door, when she stops.

'Come on,' I urge.

She holds a finger to her lips. Along the hallway, the bathroom door seems to pulse in its frame. The only sound is the erratic tick of the wall clock that needs winding.

A dull pain grows in my head.

'It's too quiet,' Claudia whispers.

'He might be listening for you. For us.'

She looks as if she's considering this, then she shakes her head and tries to pass me. I grab her arm.

'Let go, Lorrie. Something's not right.'

'So?' I tighten my grip and hold her gaze.

'What?' She narrows her eyes.

'This might be your chance, Claudia.' The words slither out and sneak along the walls. I lean in to her ear. 'No-one would ever know.'

Her eyes close.

My mind races with plans. We'll walk across the ridge. We'll get on the bus, so the driver sees us. Then we'll go to Luigi's. We'll act the same as normal.

Claudia opens her eyes. She stares ahead, fixed on something I can't see. A shiver creeps up my spine. The walls sink into the heaving darkness till all that's left is Claudia and me and a distant high-pitched drone that's swarming towards us.

She turns her gaze towards me. She doesn't know who I am. She stares down at the shackle of my hand, cauterising, until slowly I unfurl my fingers.

I fall backwards, my heavy coat pulling me down. My hands clutch my head to stop the insane buzzing. It's all around. Why did I come back here? I turn towards Claudia. She's running. Her boots thud along the hallway. Too loud, Claudia, I want to call. He'll hear you.

She leans her head against the bathroom door. 'Sean?'

She opens the door.

A stark shroud of light falls onto Claudia. She glances towards me, her face ashen. Her lips form a silent word, telling me to go. She doesn't want me to see. She steps into the bathroom.

My heart thunders in my ears and my blood crushes everything as it charges through me. I can do nothing. I am caught between tick and tock.

There's no decision. Yet there must have been, for my body is moving. I pull open the front door.

The wind screams at me. An icy blast wrenches the door from my hand and slams it against Sean's metal toolbox. That's when I hear Claudia call, 'Lorrie, help.'

I stand tottering in the wind, tears stinging my face, wondering what to do. I throw open Sean's toolbox and grab his Stanley knife. It's cold and hard in my hand as I run along the hallway.

The bathroom floor is a pond. Sean's boots lie on their sides where he tossed them, towels in a sodden heap near them. Water seeps over the rim of the bath. One end of Claudia's scarf hangs down from the bathtub. Claudia leans over the tub, gasping for breath. Her beautiful hair covers her face like tangled weeds.

The Stanley knife falls from my grip and clatters to the floor.

Claudia's under again. Her hands are wedged against the bath. Claudia's levering at his shoulders, trying to heave him out. Sean's staring up – his eyes wide, bloodshot.

I pull her back. She gulps in air, her nose streaming with bathwater.

'I can't get to the plug.'

'Leave him,' I scream.

'He's drowning.'

She takes a breath and goes under. She hauls at his wide shoulders. Her hair splays out across the surface.

I look at Sean, still unsure of him.

Claudia shakes the water off her face. She looks around for something to help. Finding nothing, she grabs his head and pulls.

She's muttering at him angrily, 'Not like this.'

Their faces are inches apart. She gazes at him, until she realises that he's already gone. Sean's eyes are still open as Claudia lets go of him.

Claudia's scarf and hair are twisted around her as she keels over on the floor. She clutches at the sodden scarf, cradling it against her chest.

'Not like this,' she sobs.

I've never heard Claudia cry before.

I look at Sean lying lifeless in the water and notice plaster debris floating around his head. Above him, holes gape in the wall. The metal towel rail lies on the floor.

'I'm sorry, Claudia. I thought he was trying to hurt . . .' My voice cracks and echoes in the frigid room.

Her eyes are puffy and defeated when she looks up at me. 'It's alright, Lorrie,' she says.

THE AFTER

Elisabeth Gail

YOUR ARMS BUCKLE and give out under his weight and you both fall, thumping against the cold, wet ground. Everything aches, your body throbbing to a staggered beat, but at the same time you feel strangely numb.

You can't help but stare at him as you catch your breath. His skin has turned mauve, and his limbs are covered in dark scabs turning colours you'd rather not think about. He has never looked less human. Well, maybe once. But you push that memory away.

You lean him against a tree so that he's half sitting, then you tilt his head towards the stars. They feel endless, hovering just above you. You went on a date like this once. He wrapped his arms around you and told you how beautiful you were. But you're the one who has to do this now with his limp arm resting over your shoulder. It's strange to be so close to someone, yet feel so distant. The smell of his cologne has gone and so has his warmth, but you pretend for a little while like it's still there. It's nice. The stars are nice too, and you try to forget. You know it's dangerous, but right now you don't care.

You whisper things like, 'I love you' and 'I'm sorry'. And as you look into his eyes, you feel for a moment like he's really there – like he's still living. Not breathing, but living nonetheless. There was always life in those soft brown eyes.

But he's dead now, and you need to live with that. You can't pretend forever. You pull yourself back into the present. You have a job to finish; life cannot be simple anymore, and you know that.

You get up and you dig a hole.

GHOST TOWN

Tanner Brossart

THE FIRST THING the town saw was a pair of men cruising onto the main road from a dusty side trail around noon. An older man in a blue plaid button-up drove the truck, his brow furrowed as if straining to remember something. In the passenger seat sat a younger, indifferent man, his thirty-year-old grandson; his dark suit was reminiscent of a funeral-goer or – in an amusingly similar sense – a businessman.

The two men passed a weathered wooden sign to their left that read: WELCOME TO LAMONT, AMERICA'S LITTLE SLICE OF HEAVEN! Beyond the sign stood a plethora of equally dilapidated buildings: one- and two-storey structures that had once been homes and shops. The grandfather eased off the gas, giving himself time to take in their surroundings as the truck ambled forward. At the same time, he rolled the windows down, which proved to be a better relief from the summer's heat than the air conditioning. After fifteen seconds of cruising, he let out a plaintive sigh.

'Can't believe how much it's gone to shit already, Franklin.'

Franklin, who had just put his phone away, sighed with him, though for different reasons. 'Yeah, Gramps. Sure is something.'

'Hendersons used to live there, but those trees weren't in the front yard before. And that was the old candy shop, you remember that? 'Course, you were pretty little then . . .'

The buildings in question had been stripped of their original paint long ago; in their place grew the dank greens of mould and moss. Yet despite the obvious signs of time and nature's methodical deconstruction, the area was motionless. No other creature, aside from the occasional sparrow or robin, entered Lamont. Not even the wind dared to survey the ruins alongside the two men. Franklin found it calming, lonely and eerie all at once.

He cleared his throat a little too loudly. 'So, guess the news was true. Completely abandoned. You wanted to go see the old house, right? Then we're out of here?'

'Where's the hurry?' replied Gramps. He continued to stare out the windshield, not noticing Franklin pulling out his phone once more. 'Flight doesn't leave 'til tomorrow, right?'

'Yeah, but . . .' Franklin grumbled. 'I dunno, just figured we should get back before it gets too late. Took us a while to drive out here and all . . .'

Gramps nodded, but still took his time turning the wheel and going down the small grid of roads that crisscrossed Lamont. Even though the radio had dissolved into static long before they had reached town, the lack of music felt especially prominent now. The farther along they went, the more cracks appeared in the road. Weeds sprouted through, as if eager to taste fresh air after so many years of being suffocated by the asphalt.

Finally, Gramps parked the car in front of a small derelict farmhouse in the south-west corner of town. He left the engine running as the two stepped out, looking the house over. The spots with paint still on them were sun bleached to a pallid baby blue. Roughly a third of the roof's shingles were cracked or missing, and one of the gutters hung limply off the left-hand side. Surprisingly, the porch swing still appeared intact, though Franklin didn't dare consider testing it out. Beyond the windows was a dark absence – the kind that fit better in a haunted house than in a bucolic barnyard. In a way, it felt like the two had stumbled across a dead body.

Franklin turned his head to gauge his grandfather's reaction. He thought he had seen a tear trickling down the old man's face, but when he tried to get a better look, he saw nothing.

Gramps coughed. 'Guess we should head over, then. See how the folks are doing.'

On the edge of town stood a small cemetery. Gramps parked the car on the grass across the street, at the edge of the forest. A row of paper birches, spindly and white like finger bones, formed a natural fence separating them from the rest of the woods. Somewhere within, cicadas screeched at one another. The men didn't even bother to look for oncoming traffic as they made for the tombstones.

'Guess this don't look too different,' Gramps said. Then he let out a breathy chuckle. ''Course, just goes to show how bad that Miller kid was at doin' his job, don't it?'

'Kid?' pondered Franklin. 'I'm pretty sure he's the same age as me.'

Gramps's laughter sputtered out into a cough. 'Yeah, well . . . figured he could've mowed round here at least one more time. Show 'em some damn respect, for Christ's sake.'

He headed for the right side of the lot. There, every headstone displayed the same last name: Meyer. Franklin stayed behind at the last row of non-Meyer graves, while his grandfather shuffled along and bowed his head for a minute at each one. He stopped for an especially long time at one grave toward the back. Franklin didn't need to ask to know who it was. When Gramps showed no signs of budging, the young man approached, stopping at a headstone one row behind.

'She was the one who picked out your new place, you know. Knew she was getting on in years and thought you'd be lonely without her.'

'You don't need to tell me,' the old man growled. 'Only heard it a hundred times.'

'Are you upset that you, you know . . . couldn't be put alongside her?'

No response. The silence between them thickened like a bubbling soup in the summer heat. A steady breeze seemed to pick up across the road; overhead, the forest's leaves flickered like candles. Franklin had never been part of a seance, but he imagined that he would feel the same unnerving static in the air were he to attend one.

'This was our *home*,' snarled Gramps. 'It was meant to be home for all of us. Always. Born here, die here. If I wanted to be in some cushy big city, I'd've pushed our damn house there myself with my bare hands!'

'Gramps—'

'But then your father had to go and marry that bitch what got it in everyone's head that livin' in a city was some sort of *paradise* . . .'

'Don't talk about my mother like that!' Franklin spat. 'She had nothing to do with it!'

Franklin's grandfather wheeled around. Flecks of sweat dotted his face and forearms. His squint did little to hide the film of tears covering his eyes, held back as if his dignity depended on it.

'This place wasn't going to last, Gramps. Maybe you don't want to admit it, but it's true. Even before we moved out, Lamont was going downhill. Remember that year when Mo's bar burned down, and it took the whole county to find the money to rebuild it? Or when the Hendersons had to take the whole Delaney family in because they couldn't find enough work to afford their own house? That could have been us! You—' Franklin held his tongue for a moment, seeing the hurt behind his grandfather's stoic facade. 'I mean, honestly, it was probably good that we got out when we did.'

'So?' the old man countered. 'You think it's okay to give up on somethin', just 'cause it gets a little tough? This here was a *community*, Franklin. The sort of thing you ain't gonna find in a city.'

'Then why didn't anyone stay, huh? You saw for yourself, just like you said you wanted to. The whole town is cleared out. And it's probably because they were all thinking the same thing. This place was fine growing up, sure, but there was never anything here for us. It's just farmland that a factory could probably manage.'

Gramps stared at the ground and mumbled, 'You never could appreciate the little things, could you?' He shook his head, continuing to mutter to himself. 'All the little things . . . never could . . . never . . .'

Franklin dismissively fished his phone from his pocket. 'We'll be getting back to town late if we stay for much longer.' An exasperated sigh. 'Look, how about I buy dinner tonight before I head back to the hotel? And I'll promise to visit you more – I'll even bring the kids with me next time. Just . . . get your keys and let's go, okay?'

The old man's grumbling diminished to little more than a breath as he reached for his back pocket. Thinking he was grabbing the car keys, Franklin started walking away.

The last thing Franklin heard was a gunshot.

WHAT HAPPENS WHEN WE
DON'T KNOW OUR NEIGHBOURS

K L Lyons

THE FIRST TIME Simone saw the thing with yellow eyes, she almost pissed herself.

She was in the backyard with her dog and the thing was in her neighbour's window. It was shaped like a person but had yellow orbs where the eyes should be.

But she brushed it off, telling herself it was an old Halloween decoration or a trick of the light. When her dog had finished doing his business, they went inside.

Simone did not know her neighbours. She was not especially outgoing and it seemed like as soon as she learned someone's name, they moved away. She was perfectly content to live in her own little bubble while they lived in theirs.

Because she did not know her neighbours, Simone didn't notice they were gone until the mail started to pile up. But she brushed this off too. After all, they could be on vacation.

Simone's neighbours were Jules and Harriet. Years ago, they'd gotten married after only six months of dating and had been together ever since. They fought occasionally, mostly over little things, like whether to store the big spoons and little spoons in the same spot in the drawer. They were, all in all, pleasant people who did not deserve what happened to them. But such is the truth about life: none of us get what we deserve.

Simone had heard that there was no sign of them by the time the police arrived to perform a wellness check. But their wallets, keys and phones were still there. An investigation was opened, but with so little to go on, it went nowhere. Eventually the house was cleared out and a FOR RENT sign was posted out front, so she knew it was empty when she saw the thing with yellow eyes again.

The next time, she was doing the dishes when she looked out the window and saw it staring back at her. She immediately pressed herself up against the opposite wall, out of its line of sight. She stayed there until she convinced herself she was being ridiculous. She returned to the kitchen sink, eyes down, and stuck her hands in the warm water. When she found the courage to look up again, it was gone.

That night she dreamed she was drowning. There was a boat near by, but the sky was as dark as the water, and they could not see her. She tried to scream and slipped under.

She woke up with her skin clammy and her heart racing. She focused on the warmth of her dog sleeping next to her, grounding herself with the weight of his body and the smell of his fur. Eventually, she was calm enough to go back to sleep.

In the morning, her dog was gone. Usually when he got up first, it meant he needed to go outside, so Simone jumped up to see if she could catch him in time. She called his name, going from room to room, but she couldn't find him. She even looked outside, as if he might have let himself out somehow. But he was gone, just like Jules and Harriet.

Now this was harder to brush off. She was crying when she called in sick. She didn't tell them how her dog died, but by the time she hung up the phone, she knew what she would do.

She sat in the living room to wait for the thing with yellow eyes. She knew it was coming for her. She knew it would keep going until someone stopped it, but she was not going to be that person.

Because Simone did not know her neighbours, no-one noticed she was gone until the mail started to pile up. But they brushed this off, at first. After all, she might be on vacation.

ALONE, ALONE

Dominic Burke

NOTHING WAS WRONG. Cloaked in the shade of the olive tree, how could anything be wrong? The leaves overhead cast their dancing circles of light that breathed and waved with the breeze. Grandad was inside, getting his spades, his buckets, two boonies for work under the sun. That day we were planting tomatoes. But, inevitably, so too did we check up on his herbs, checked if any of his caterpillars had become butterflies, and checked if the flowers still looked towards the sun.

'It is selfish and cruel,' he once said, 'to imagine that the garden is for us alone. What of the other living creatures? Don't they deserve their due?'

Grandad already had several tomato plants whose vines wound around their wooden guiding poles, whose fruits were plump and red. But he needed more for all the grandkids he was expecting. He kept a white-and-brown goat with a star on its head, whose name I never learnt because Grandad never called him over. The goat would trot and bleat and follow him around the garden with neither prompt nor cue. I can't imagine a goat needing a name. The grass, as a consequence, was always short and green, and once in a blue moon Grandad would make goat cheese – soft and white. Next to me at the base of the olive tree was a Grecian amphora. It was the colour of the earth in those lands that looked out over the Aegean Sea: a pale reddish brown that flaked and chipped with age. I wondered what would happen one day when all the paint chipped off.

I'm sure Grandad would just repaint it. Grandad told me that the vase and the olive tree reminded him of his homeland, and I believed him. That's why he planted the tree and placed the vase, if only for a faint impression of home. I asked often if one day he would take me.

'Sure, why not?' he always replied with the same smile he wore when he saw me first thing in the morning.

The strangest day of my life was when I realised that I didn't speak my grandad's native tongue. He never used to speak it around me, as if he was trying to keep a shameful secret. He had said something to my mother in a language that sounded curly and soft with sounds I had never heard before. The longer he talked, the more confused I became – as if another soul had spoken with his body. It made me cry. His English was always broken and considered, like the words only came to him in waves. He was a different man when his mouth curled around those strange sounds. He spoke rapidly with supreme confidence and laughs that came from his belly, and with smiles that weren't meek and shy but great beaming things that wrinkled his eyes. I wondered for a long time, after seeing who my grandad refused to be around me, if I could really be considered his grandchild. He loved me – I could tell by the way he hugged me, and the fire behind his eyes – but was it really the same? After all these years, I know these to be stupid thoughts – I know he loved me all the same – because if they were to be true, life would be unbearable.

The wind rustled the branches again, bringing with it the scents of blossoms and blooms and scattering the loose leaves from the olive tree. I looked to my left to the grape arbour he had built many years ago. It was small, and every year my grandad would declare that no grapes were to be eaten, and that they were to be saved for the wine, for he dreamed of one day bottling wine. He had made his own *pigeage* tub with the wood left over from the arbour. But every year the grapes were eaten; the *pigeage* tub had begun to rot around the edges. This year would be the same. I reminded myself to ask Grandad about the chickens he used to keep in the back corner of his yard because I wanted to know where they had gone. I pulled at the grass and crushed and rolled it around in my hands.

Finally, I heard the flyscreen door open and close and I knew it was Grandad with his buckets and spades. In my eyes, he was still as strong as an ox, and the years had left his strength untouched. I never knew a man who worked harder than my grandad. He was someone who never really retired, someone who only promised to stop working in the grave. But it wasn't his fault. One day, he took me aside and told me there's no point being alive if you can't work. I've never known him to exaggerate, nor was he a man swept up in the stories of others, so when he told me that he'd sooner be dead than lead a life where his garden wilted and he could no longer support his grandkids, I believed him.

He wore his loose-fitting linen shirt with the sleeves rolled up, and slacks with a chestnut-brown belt. I'd never seen him wear anything else. He had the figure of a farm worker or a galley slave, with muscles built up over time from toil. Each time he saw me, he told me how tall I was getting, how I'd soon be taller than him. I was already up to his chest. We both knew I didn't have far to go.

When I looked up, I could see nothing of his face but an infinite blackness – a void that rippled and swam with the sounds of his voice. He beckoned me to get up, and told me that it was time to work. He took my hand. I was dragged along by the faceless man who was wearing my grandad's clothes. We walked to the plot he had reserved for the tomatoes, and together we drove the stakes into the black earth. The work passed quickly, as if it hadn't even happened.

'Good job, my boy! You're a big strong man now, aren't you? My big strong man!'

And through the blackness I saw the outline of his smiling eyes. Only slightly protruding, then they receded just as fast. I tried to cry out but all I could do was stare at where his eyes ought to have been, and where they appeared to have left their impression. From his smile broke a laugh. I can say that, despite not having seen his smile in that moment, because he only ever laughed after smiling, I heard his laugh. It rattled in my ears and I could see the blackness swimming around where his mouth should've been. The sound echoed off the cloudless sky. I remembered suddenly that there should've been a goat there, too. Grandad hadn't yet butchered the goat with the star on its head, and he'd never get another goat again. I broke my stare to see the goat bleating and trotting just like she used to do, in a spot where she wasn't bleating and trotting just a moment ago. The seeds were already scattered before I knew what was happening – maybe while I was still looking at the goat – and I felt my grandad's hand on my back. The sun had set. We were going back inside for dinner.

THE LAST SOUL OF IRAQ

Abdullah Aljumah

Dedicated to the lost souls of Iraq.

Baghdad, Iraq, 1991

THE NIGHT SKY was ablaze with bombs and whistling missiles flying and roaring overhead. The old man pushed his cart with its unsold vegetables into a tumbledown shed toward his home. He walked in and removed his chequered *ghutrah* from his head, hoping to rest a little. He looked around and rolled his eyes, calling several times for God's protection. He sat down and his hand passed over the face of the youngest child sleeping near by. He kissed him. He sighed and his hand rolled over the other grandchildren. They were all asleep, but every now and then one of the children would shiver from the noise outside. They'd open their eyes, terrified, but when they'd see their grandfather, they'd be reassured and fall back asleep. As he prepared his bed, he looked at each of them, one by one: there were two girls and two boys.

In the corner of the room, his daughter-in-law, cloaked in her prayer shawl, sat on a dog-eared prayer mat, counting rosary beads in her right hand and muttering faint prayers. He looked at her with pain.

'Why haven't you slept yet, my dear?' he asked.

Halima didn't answer. She was sunk deep in her thoughts.

'Sleep. It's getting late, my dear!'

As she looked at her father-in-law, her voice cracked and tears rolled down her cheeks.

'Will I ever see him again?' she asked wearily.

'May God Almighty protect him.'

The conversation between them didn't last any longer. His final words left a lump in his throat.

* * *

'Ahmed, I want you to make me a slingshot.'

'What do you need it for, brother?'

'I want it.'

'Wanna hunt birds with it?' Ahmed laughed as he teased Ali.

'Yes, 'cause we haven't had chicken or meat for a long time.'

'That's a brilliant idea. I'll make you one. Go, get me a knife. Let's do it.'

* * *

I'm sure he'll make it back. He always does. Like he did back in the war of 1986. I still have my pink dress I wore when I first met him by the old palm tree. I am sure he still remembers it. I'm gonna embroider a white shawl that I'll adorn with pink flowers to go with it.

Halima stood up, delighted by her wandering thoughts. She took a few steps towards a dilapidated wooden cabinet to fetch her sewing kit. Suddenly, a loud rumbling sound came from overhead. She froze.

* * *

'Ahmed, I want you to carve my name on the slingshot.'

'What do you wanna do that for?'

'So no one claims it as his own when I lose it.'

'But you won't lose it.'

'I might. Someone could find it when we're gone.'

'Who told you that?'

'I overheard our mother during her prayer say we might all be gone soon.'

'Ali, it's *haram* to eavesdrop. Besides, God could hear you, you know that, right?!'

'I am sorry, but . . .'

'It's okay. Let another boy find it when we're gone.'

'No! No!' Ali protested.

'Let someone have fun and play with it. It's okay to share.'

'No! I want you to carve my name on it, and I wanna tie it around my waist – it's mine.'

* * *

'Where's my father, Mum?' Halima's youngest daughter asked, her eyes wide.

'He's working far away, sweetie.'

'When will he come back?'

'At the nearest opportunity, my dear.'

'And when is that?'

'Once circumstances allow him to do so.'

Halima tried to assure her with warm but weary eyes. She checked on her other children. All four were inside the house.

She looked at them together as if she was saying goodbye to them for the last time. She knelt and kissed each of them, one by one.

And it was the last time. The walls and the ceiling kissed the ground. Their youth vanished before its time.

The rescue team found the family among the rubble: a chequered headscarf; an unsewn shawl with a stitching yarn; Ali's slingshot buried underneath his small body. It was all a mixture of blood and tears. Their lives were silenced.

* * *

The soldier returned but didn't find a soul waiting for him.

EVERARD

Bruce Meyer

EVERARD IS MY hometown, designed in the shape of a wheel, all its avenues leading to a treed square with a crumbling gazebo, where those who have taken a wrong turn find themselves driving around the green in circles because they have somewhere else to go but do not know how to get there. The house fronts line up to face the world and the porches jut into the streets like stages on which the small dramas of promises and last kisses and cricket silences on summer nights once played.

On those summer nights, when the sun sank and lit up the golden leaves of sycamores, it was possible to believe that Everard was the promised land. Now, just before the sun sinks behind the abandoned First National Savings and Loan bank, the rays strike the gates of the town's cemetery, where I work, and which fill me with a vision of hopeless redemption.

When the graveyard was established by the town's stewards, the choice places were at the back. But as time passed, and the sad homecomings of the bodies of men whose flesh and bones returned without their souls, their progeny moved on to better places on the coasts or the big cities where memory only lasts as long as polaroids left in sunlight.

The few who remained in Everard now fill the front rows of the cemetery, and so many buried close to the gates are the bodies of friends I have known and lost: the white tablets of soldiers. Then there are the discreet low bronze plaques of girls and boys who met with misfortune as they attempted to seize adulthood by the hems of graduation gowns and rented tuxedos. And there are the stones laid flat on the ground for people who spent their lives working and saving so they would have a final resting place where the grass tries to grow over their names until their stones are almost swallowed by the ground. I keep those markers trimmed. I feel I owe it to them.

For years, Everard was a single-employer factory town. Most of the men on the assembly line and the women in the stenographer's pool spent their lives caught up in what the factory made, which is of no consequence now because there is no longer a use for the product of their labours. They took the secrets of gears and oil, order forms and remittance slips, and (finally) closure notices to their graves with them. I have loved this place too much to love it less now that the town is beyond salvaging.

My best friend Bobby's mother teared up when I mentioned the factory to her before she passed on. She shook her head in denial without offering a word. Instead of being known for its production, Everard now meets the world with a decaying billboard on the side road off the highway. The sign is overgrown with sumac and scrub pine. Its centre is missing and it says, 'Welcome to Everard. Home of the_____'

Bobby was a brat. He'd been named Bobby at birth, then he was called Rob in the lower grades until the other kids taunted him about being a bad guy straight out of the cowboy serials we watched on the local TV station on Saturday mornings before the ball games began and our fathers chased us outside. Then he became Bob, the guy who was everyone's friend in high school, but who considered me his shadow and told me I was dumb for wanting a simple life. And finally, as he too was laid to rest, Robert was the name written on the granite marker as an upright afterthought to all his names. His parents never thought he would exhaust all the variations of Robert, and they never thought they would outlive him.

We both got summer jobs courtesy of the town. Sometimes we picked up garbage from the square or slapped a coat of paint on the gazebo to quell the rot, but most of the time we serviced the cemetery. Bobby would lie down on someone's grave and watch me pushing a gas mower among the headstones.

'You know,' I told him, 'I could really get into this.'

'You're a fool. Is that all you want to do with your life?'

'Yes,' I said. He didn't realise then the importance of keeping the town's past sacred. I read once in the *Farmer's Almanac* about Homer, who was blinded as a ten-year-old and taken to an island where he became the memory of populace. I could see history all around me. I could see it dying. History ought to be a living thing, but all living things run their course and have to end sometime.

Everything that happened to Bobby coincided with the death of Everard. We were born in the era of grand hopes, when we were going to the moon, not because it was easy but because it was hard.

Bob earned high grades. He could have become anything he set his mind to. He won a scholarship to a university 400 miles away where he studied sciences. Sciences were supposed to be the future, but then someone dropped a canister of science on a village on the other side of the world and burned the clothes off a young girl who ran screaming past a photographer. Bob protested the war and got tossed out of university. His parents said it was a disgrace he'd never live down.

He moved closer to home, and managed to learn a technician's trade that he took directly to the factory where he met the best-looking young woman on the assembly line.

It was a bitter day when the factory had to close.

The Legion bugler showed up and the flag beside the front steps of the executive building was hauled down for the last time as the Legion man played the Last Post. The sky darkened and heavy rain no one expected burst out of nowhere and drenched the men from the corporate headquarters who were there to offer meaningless plaques of merit to workers who realised they had forsaken their futures for a fruitless cause.

No one cared that we were all dying when the plague hit. When I left school without much of a future in town to look forward to, I was lucky to find the only job Everard had to offer. I worked in the town graveyard and I buried each of them: my best friend Bobby, his parents, their neighbors, my parents, and even the bugler.

I tamp down the mounds of the cemetery and level the graves that are so old they have sunk. I stand well back during services for the plague victims. I am not ready to enter history yet. My job is to remember. I wear a mask. I wear a facial shield and a white suit with a hood and booties. I wear rubber gloves when I handle the caskets. I burn the rubber gloves after each committal. And I walk backwards out of the burial ground.

Maybe I think I am undoing time by watching everyone I have lost recede before me, but I am adamant I will not become part of the past. I will not become a front porch or a crumbling band shell. The future is what I cannot see behind me.

It may be dangerous to walk backwards but I know every inch of ground in the graveyard and I know wherever I go within its bounds I will not fall into an open grave. But just in case I do, I carry a shovel with me so I can dig my way out. It is a yellow shovel. I wear an orange workman's vest, a green hard hat, and a red plaid shirt hanging over the top of my blue jeans. Caution comes in many colours and I always stop and marvel when a rainbow forms over the town and frames the graveyard.

Rainbows are a sign from God or a postcard from Bobby promising terrible things won't happen again to Everard. And I will keep backing away from everything I have known until I have backed away far enough to say, 'That was the past. Now show me the future.'

The future insists I'm a blind boy, a walking, talking encyclopedia of the town's story. I tell the future I am not blind but just a hostage here. I saw what the future was doing to us all. The future says it will make amends.

When I am ready to see what lies ahead, I am certain it will be so enormous, so complex and astounding I will wish I had another life to take it all in, not as what has been but as what will be. And I will follow the rainbow over Everard to see where it ends.

A BOY IN THE SNOW

Tom Roth

AS SNOW FELL, Liam thought of seeing his son, but Connor was dead. He sat on his kid's bed, watching a thick layer of snow pile up on the ranch houses and trees, his mind buried in his only boy.

'It's ready,' Molly called from the kitchen.

'Be down in a sec,' Liam said.

Liam itched his bald spot and turned away from the window to face the dim room. It was a ritual of his, entering the room before supper, as though he'd find Connor in front of the Kurt Cobain poster on the wall, playing his guitar beside the small desk piled with song sheets. He'd listen to his son jam out before saying it was time to eat.

'Time to eat,' he said out loud anyway, touching the dusty strings of the guitar. Liam had promised himself he'd learn to play in honour of his son, but the few times he'd tried his fingers shook on the neck.

'I'm having a beer,' Molly said. 'You want one?'

Liam didn't answer. He walked over to the window one more time. Twilight fell, casting blue shades on the snow and, far down the hill, Liam could see distant houses aglow behind white thickets. No tyre tracks marked the road, just a desolate slope of layers upon layers of snow. He sat down on the bed again, folded his hands and tried to pray to Connor.

'It's on the table,' Molly said, cracking beer cans.

He was about to answer when crunching snow – the sound of footsteps – stopped him. Down the road, out of the falling snow and

234

twilight and woods, appeared a little boy in a red hat and red coat and dragging a toboggan.

'Liam?'

The boy struggled through the flurries as he passed the house, then tripped and tumbled into the deep white spread above his knees. Liam could hear soft sobs as the child got up and pulled the toboggan down the other side of the hill, leaving a track of footprints behind him as he descended out of sight.

Finally, Liam got up from the bed and hustled down the hallway of floral wallpaper. Molly was at the table breaking crackers into her tomato soup, a worried look on her face.

'There's a boy in the snow,' Liam said.

He pulled his beige field jacket off the coat rack on the wall and glanced out the window.

'What?' Molly said, her short brown hair curtained around her face. She got up and looked out the window behind her. Snow had already covered the tracks of the toboggan. The boy's footprints were gone. 'You saw a boy out there? When?'

'Just now,' Liam replied. 'Pulling a sled. He was crying, Moll. He looked cold.'

'Liam,' Molly said, 'sit down.' She placed her hand on his chest. They stood at the window, watching as night brought more and more flakes, torn shreds against a purple curtain. 'Would you sit down and eat? I'm sure he's just going home now.'

They sat at the table. Molly dipped her sandwich in her soup and bit a corner off. Sipping his beer, Liam stared out the window behind Molly and thought about the boy in the snow. He imagined the kid wrapped in a blanket on their couch, a cup of hot chocolate in his hands, while Liam asked the boy where he lived. He wondered if the boy liked tiny marshmallows in his hot chocolate the way Connor had.

'What?' Molly asked, seeing his eyes.

'Who do you know has kids out here?' he said.

Molly put her sandwich down.

'No one else on this road ever had kids except . . .' Liam stopped for a second, fingers pinching his eyes behind his glasses. Living out here they had worried Connor would get lonely without other kids around. 'Except us.' He shook his head and stood, and pulled his jacket on again. 'That boy's lost, Moll.'

Molly got up and took her coat off the rack.

'I'll be fine by myself,' Liam said. 'Finish your meal.'

'You think I'm going to let you go out there alone? After what happened?'

They held each other in the kitchen. Connor didn't play sports. He got a job at a guitar shop in town and spent most of his free time after school there, giving lessons and selling guitars. Their son wanted to own a shop when he got older, to play in a band at dive bars on weekends. Connor was down-to-earth; he never talked of rock-star dreams, he just wanted to be around music. Molly kissed Liam's cheek.

'Let's go find that boy,' Liam said when they parted.

After brushing off the black Chevy Tahoe, Liam and Molly pulled onto the darkening road, the big SUV powering through the snow, slipping a little on the way down. Liam tightened his hands on the wheel and focused on the roadside, watching for a red hat or sled marks or footprints. No sign of the boy appeared. They reached the bottom of the hill and went farther down the long road between the woods. A wall of flakes ripped across the headlights.

'He couldn't have gone far,' Molly said. She surveyed both sides of the road. 'He went this way?'

'Yeah,' Liam said, 'dragging a toboggan.'

'You sure you saw him?'

'Yes, Molly.'

He caught Molly looking at him. On nights like this, with a great snowfall upon the woods, she'd study his face. He'd know she was waiting for him to open up about Connor, but he had buried his grief and his guilt, and sometimes he could hardly meet her eyes. She turned away.

On the right, a very narrow side-road branched off the main one, snaking into the forest. Liam saw a mark on the ground and veered onto the road that bent above a steep wooded hill. He drove slowly, flakes blinding his vision as the Tahoe struggled around the curves, through snow and trees.

'What are you— Liam, we can't go this way.'

'He took this road. I saw his footprints.'

'What footprints? You can't see a damn thing out here!'

'I don't need you yelling at me,' Liam said. 'He's here, Moll. We're close.' Liam honked his horn a few times, hoping the kid would hear.

'We shouldn't be on this road.'

'He's here,' Liam said again, his voice soft and low, almost a whisper. 'We're close.'

The road curled up a hillside. Liam pressed the gas and the Tahoe swerved, slipping near the edge of the road and a deep drop of woods. The day Connor died, it had snowed like this. Liam had just come home. Molly was asleep on the couch, *Seinfeld* on the television. Hearing his son's guitar, Liam had gone to Connor's room and watched him play a solo.

'I'm about to head over to the shop,' Connor said. 'Are the roads bad?'

'They're a little slick,' Liam said. 'Just get home before dark.'

Climbing the hill, foot on the gas, Liam scanned the forest for any sight of the boy in the red hat and red coat. He recalled his last words to Connor, how he had allowed his son to get on the road that day, how he had waited on the couch watching Molly sleep.

The Tahoe slipped again, a back tyre off the edge of the road.

'Oh God!' Molly said. 'Liam, pull over!'

He continued up the steep curve, seeing no boy on the road, and then parked. Getting out, he started up the wooded hill on foot, entering trees thick with snow.

'Liam!' Molly shouted. 'Where are you going?'

'We're close,' Liam said, his voice very low, speaking only to himself. 'We're close.'

'Liam, wait!'

Liam marched through the steep, snowy forest. Molly's voice faded behind the flakes, but he could tell the snow was letting up. Soon the night would settle, buried in a white silence, and soon, very soon now, he'd find his way back to his wife, and show the boy that one only needed to follow their footprints to get out of the woods.

THE SACRED HEART

Elle Lane

IT FELT LIKE a cruel joke. *He* was the one with the high blood pressure and the purple face, but she had the heart attack. His wife and now his daughter, lost. Maybe his temper was radioactive.

He snatched her body and remade her in his image, giving her the same suit and short-cropped haircut. Gone was that messy bob that she never conditioned and the eyeliner that was never quite even.

Seeing her was devastating. From Justin to Justine and back around again. We had never all been in the same room together, but her family and friends welcomed me with solemn smiles and nods. I wanted them to accost me and chase me from the church. It was nice, though, that we could all get along.

I set down the green carnations I bought for her. The flowers looked artificial in the light shining through the stained-glass windows, too green to be real.

He was watching me from the front pew, smirking. He was waiting for my reaction. A more empathetic woman would feel rage. A better woman might have said something. I was neither, so I let the hopelessness envelope me. With a sour smile on my lips, I sat in the back pews.

Five minutes into the ceremony, a woman in a black blazer and pencil skirt floated in, taking a seat in the pew opposite me. She didn't sing along or pray when we were told to, yet she would stand before being called, with robotic precision. I wondered if she was one of Justine's work friends.

They started talking about Justin: where he was born, where he went to school, when we got married, how he loved *The Big Bang Theory* and Robin Williams. It was strange to hear someone's life broken down into a list of facts. I expected someone to interrupt the service, but nobody said anything. We let her go into the next world as Justin. We failed her, and I felt guilty.

It was stuffy and claustrophobic inside the church, but outside it wasn't much better, at least in the presence of the procession.

'I only smoke at funerals,' the woman in the pencil skirt explained, lighting up and taking a desperate drag. 'Nasty habit, I know. Same chemicals in this are in her body right now.' She paused. 'Sorry, that was inappropriate,' she added. 'I go to a lot of these things. I'm Anne, by the way.'

'Are you the funeral director?' I asked, waving away the smoke.

'No,' she laughed. 'I'm here to protect people like Justine. Well, we're supposed to. Sometimes there's not much we can do.'

'Like today?'

'Exactly like today. There's no will, so her next of kin gets to make all the decisions.'

Anne shook her head and took another drag, her fingers shaking.

We stood there in silence for a long time, watching the hearse drive off.

'You going to join them?' she asked.

'No.'

'Why not? *He* was your husband wasn't *he?*'

'He was . . . but that's not him,' I said, tracing the cracks in the cement with my shoe.

'She told me about you, Meghan. About some of the things you said.'

'Oh.'

'You really hurt her. People like Justine, they don't have a choice. You can't expect her to hide who she is forever. Even if it would be easier for you.'

'But that doesn't mean I have to follow her,' I argued, tears in my eyes.

'You don't, even though she would have wanted you to. She loved you very much. She was afraid that she'd never find another woman like you.'

'I-I know,' I said, holding back sobs.

'But I don't want you to blame yourself. I just want you to know that she loved you.'

We didn't speak for a while after that.

I watched her cigarette burn down to its base.

'Did you know there's formaldehyde in cigarettes? Same with coffins,' she said.

'How can you smoke, then?'

'I need something to do with my hands. Looks like you could use something yourself,' she said, pointing to my twitching fingers.

'I'll solve it when I get back.'

'Alcohol will pickle your brain, same as tobacco,' she said, taking a final drag before putting it out on the metal banister. She tossed the cigarette butt at the church doors.

'Places like this do a lot more harm than good,' she said.

'That's not true.'

'You know who else lived two lives? Who'll rise from the dead in their true form?'

'Who?'

'Your husband,' she said. 'She might have been buried a man, but in her heart she was always a woman. What's that symbol you Catholics have? The heart with the thorns?'

'The Sacred Heart.'

'That's it, the Sacred Heart. That's what she had. They can cover her in thorns and prick her with arrows, but she will live on.' She paused for a moment. 'Anyway, I'm headed back to Columbus now. It's been good meeting you, Meghan. I hope you have a good rest of the day,' she said, shaking my hand before walking away.

He called me later to ask why I didn't show at the cemetery. I made up some excuse about feeling overwhelmed. He didn't believe me, but it didn't matter. He had no-one left to control now.

RUAN LINGYU

Chris Neilan

A Spray of Plum Blossoms. The Goddess. She answers an ad, fifteen-year-old daughter of a house servant, fifteen-year-old daughter of the Republican-era, daughter of the Three Principles of the People. The Qing dynasty had crumbled when she was barely a year, as if she'd heralded the collapse herself. She answers an ad, fifteen-year-old girl, skinny servant's daughter, from the Mingxing Film Company. A year later and she's on the screen: *Married in Name Only.* She is effervescent, they say, impressively elegant, they say – sixteen-year-old daughter of a house servant widow and a decade-dead father, unskilled worker, from Asiatic Petroleum, in the after-life now, throwing Mahjong with her other ancestors. Fatherless from six. We lose the ones we love. We lose the ones who love us. Sometimes, all we have is our elegance.

She is a daughter of Sun Yat-sen's new era, a starling of the Republican dawn. Her eyes are elongated opals, overspilling hurts. Sometimes, to the dark rooms of workers in Shanghai, Guang-zhou, Beijing, Chengdu, it will seem as if she is emerging through the screen, her image twenty feet tall and glittering grey, and if you know her story, you will see her dead father and her servant mother just under her two-storey surface, as the camera presses in. Women will find their breath has caught, men will stir at the shift of her dress, sixteen-, seventeen-, eighteen-year-old daughter of the servant widow. The fourth son of the family her mother serves will take Ruan to court, claiming that she is his wife and a thief.

Her new partner, Tang, the tycoon, will already be engaged in an affair with another actress. The fourth son, a gambler, will launch a second lawsuit, accusing Ruan of adultery. It is the third decade of Sun Yat-sen's new era. The newspapers know a good story when they see one. They fill their pages with the fallen Goddess. Margin to margin, on factory floors in Tianjin, tea shops in Wuhan, libraries in Beijing, street stalls and markets in Yunnan and Hunnan, thief, adulterer, whore, harlot, fraud, servant, pleb, slut, cheat, fraud, thief, liar, witch, gold-digger, harpy, dog. Her films continue to play, re-screened in the cities, the provinces. In *New Women*, she plays an actress destroyed by circumstance. In *A Spray of Plum Blossoms*, true love somehow evades her.

Her suicide note reads:

gossip is a fearful thing

The procession for the funeral, Ruan's funeral, twenty-five-year-old Ruan, skinny effervescing Ruan, sixteen-year-old *Married In Name Only* Ruan, six-year-old daughter of ghosts Ruan, is three miles long. As the cart bearing her small body is pulled by six horses through the crowds, numbering in the tens of thousands, three other women take their lives. Three daughters, wives, who cannot bear the young Goddess's absence. Three daughters who understand shame, caprice, and roomfuls of men. They take their lives. Take? They end their lives. They die right there, in the crowd, with Ruan, as if to say: me too.

She will be played by Maggie Cheung sixty years later, and Maggie Cheung will win Best Actress at Berlin. Her name will not appear in Western histories of the silent era, daughter of the Three Principles, who effervesced, a teenager. To look at her, you feel, would be to look back at ourselves, and see ourselves killing the thing we love.

ABOUT THE AUTHORS

Abdullah Aljumah

Abdullah Aljumah is a bilingual and bicultural writer with a Masters Degree in Linguistics from Eastern Michigan University. His short stories have been published in anthologies and literary reviews such as the *Running Wild Anthology of Stories* Volumes 3 and 4 (2019/2020), *Rubbertop Review* Volume 11 (2020), and *Writers of Tomorrow* (2021). He writes short stories and poems revolving around childhood experience, hypocrisy, religious conflicts, and forced or arranged marriages.

Chloe Allen

Chloe is a writer and educator from Florence, Alabama. She has an MA in Creative Writing from University College Dublin, Ireland. Chloe is currently studying and teaching at the University of North Alabama as an Adjunct Professor and PhD hopeful. When she is not teaching, studying, reading or writing, she enjoys drinking coffee and taking her pet tortoise for long, slow walks on the beach.

Charlotte Armstrong

Charlotte Armstrong is a recent graduate student of the University of Melbourne. She has been published in *Farrago* and was the winner of the *Farrago* 2020 Jack Musgraves Memorial Award for her work creating horoscopes. She has a strong interest in mythologies, having undertaken an Honours thesis on the subject. Charlotte's quiet evocative stories take mundane events and inject an element of magical realism in the hope that she will encourage others to see the magic of the world.

Scott Beard

Scott has both a BA in Creative Writing and an MA in Curriculum and Instruction from Wichita State University. His writing has appeared in *The Report, LEVITATE Literary Magazine, Dime Show Review, Please See Me*, Military Experience and the Arts, The Showbear Family Circus, and *Abstract*, to name a few. His literary criticism has been published in the October 2019 edition of *Coffin Bell*. He enjoys fishing, hiking, reading, writing, travelling, and ice hockey. Learn more about Scott by visiting his website: www.carethbeard.wixsite.com/scottbeard.

Samuel Bollen

Samuel Bollen is a writer living in Playa del Rey, California. He is an alumnus of Princeton University and the author of *The Ghostwriter* (forthcoming from Running Wild Press). His screenplay *Roswell '97* placed as a finalist in the Reno-Tahoe Screenplay Contest and the Sunvale Screenplay Contest.

Paul Bowman

Paul Bowman has worked as a bartender, lumber salesman and nursing home maintenance man. He writes plays and fictions. His stories have appeared in *Burnt Pine Magazine, Chiron Review, Downstate, Green Hills Literary Lantern, Trajectory*, Southern Fried Karma, *Fleas On The Dog* (his favourite title for a journal), and elsewhere. Because he shuns fame and fortune, he refuses to write a bestselling novel.

Redfern Boyd

Redfern Boyd often writes about travel, pop culture and things famous people have said when they thought no one was listening. She holds an MA in English Literature from Central Connecticut State University. Her poem 'Igor Stravinsky Awaits the Arrival of Dylan Thomas' won *Blue Muse Magazine*'s Leslie Leeds Poetry Prize in 2018. Her work has appeared in publications including *Atticus Review, Plainsongs, Boudin, Outrageous Fortune, Route 7 Review, Riza, Uncomfortable Revolution, A Feast of Narrative* (volumes 2 and 3) and *DoveTales*. A New England native, she now lives in Berlin, Germany.

Tanner Brossart

Tanner Brossart is a writer currently based in Seattle, Washington. He graduated with a BA in English and Creative Writing from Coe College in 2016. He has also had poetry published in the college's internationally renowned anthology the *Coe Review*. Currently he writes articles for *Game Rant*, an online video game publication.

Dominic Burke
Dominic Burke is a student at the University of Sydney, majoring in English and Philosophy. His first publication was in *The Foundationalist*.

Mark Crimmins
Mark Crimmins is the author of experimental travel memoir *Sydneyside Reflections* published by Australia's Everytime Press in June 2020. His short stories and flash fictions have been published in thirteen countries in over fifty journals, including *Columbia Journal*, *Kyoto Journal*, *Quarterly Literary Review Singapore*, *Queen's Quarterly*, *The Apalachee Review*, *Confrontation Magazine*, *Chicago Quarterly Review*, *Pure Slush*, *Flash Frontier: An Adventure in Short Fiction*, and *Flash: The International Short-Short Story Magazine*.

Kaitlyn Dara
Kaitlyn Dara is a writer, musician, athlete, comic artist, filmmaker and animator currently double-majoring in multimedia and film at Corban University in Salem, Oregon. She is an Asian-American with Vietnamese and Laotian heritage on her dad's side. When she has time outside of school, she often works on webcomics as Kaiden Kae.

Jacinta Dietrich
Jacinta is a writer and editor with a passion for sharing authentic stories. Her debut novel *This is Us Now* was published by Grattan Street Press in 2021. When not working as an editorial assistant or freelancing, she's developing ideas for her next project. She is currently working on a middle grade novel about a circus, and a young adult novel about alchemy and family. She lives in Melbourne with her boyfriend and their house rabbit Wallenby.

Chris Dixon
Chris Dixon graduated with a Bachelors degree in Creative Writing from the University of North Carolina, Wilmington in December 2020. He works part-time as a taxidermist and has been writing short stories, novellas and screenplays in his spare time.

Sam Elkin

Sam Elkin is a writer, event producer and radio maker living in the western suburbs of Naarm (Melbourne). Sam has been a Wheeler Centre Next Chapter fellow and his essays have been published in the *Griffith Review*, *Overland Literary Journal* and *Kill Your Darlings*. He is currently co-editing *Nothing to Hide: Voices of Trans and Gender Diverse Australia* and working on a memoir.

S J Elliott

In addition to his 'day' job S J Elliott has written for a myriad of journals and his writing has appeared in *FilmInk*, *Southerly Magazine* and *The Big Issue*, among other publications. He also hosts his own podcast, 'The Write Way', which you can find on Spotify.

Joel Fishbane

Joel's novel *The Thunder of Giants* is available from St. Martin's Press. His short fiction has been published in a variety of magazines, including *Witness*, *New England Review*, and the *The Saturday Evening Post*. For more information, you are welcome to visit www.joelfishbane.net.

Kate Fleming

Kate Fleming is a writer, graduate student at the University of Melbourne and founder of *The Mindful Materialist*. Kate's work has been featured in several magazines including *Judy's Punch*, *Farrago* and *Ablaze*. She is currently a content writer for the University of Melbourne's *Antithesis* blog.

Steven G Fromm

Steven is from New Jersey and his work has appeared in several publications including *Salamander*, *The Columbia Journal*, *Midwest Review*, *Juxtaprose* and *The Ocotillo Review*. Steven received two Pushcart nominations in 2020.

Elisabeth Gail

Elisabeth is a writer and poet from Melbourne, currently completing her Honours in Creative Writing and Literature. She loves to find interesting ways to incorporate gothic and horror aspects into her writing. She has been published in *WORDLY Magazine*, *Gems*, and *The Creative Issue*.

Bill Gaythwaite

Bill Gaythwaite's short stories have appeared (or are forthcoming) in *Subtropics, Chicago Quarterly Review, december, Grist, Mudville Diaries: A Book of Baseball Memories, Oyster River Pages*, as well as other magazines and anthologies. He was a winner of Glimmer Train's Best Start Contest and his work has been nominated twice for the Pushcart Prize. Bill is the Assistant Director of Academic Affairs at Columbia Law School.

Angela Glindemann

Angela Glindemann is a queer writer living in Melbourne, Australia. She works in educational publishing and has written for *Archer Magazine, un Projects* and *Asymptote*. She won the Short Story category of the 2020 City of Melbourne Lord Mayor's Creative Writing Awards.

Stephanie Gobor

Stephanie is a writer, artist, keen gardener and radical homemaker. She is an active member of the Ballarat community in Victoria, Australia, where she resides with her husband and menagerie of pets. She enjoys the stereotypical romance of writing on her laptop in cafes without wi-fi.

Grace Gibbons

Grace Gibbons is an author and playwright. She has had humour essays published in *Women in Comedy* and *Funny Pearls*, is the co-author of *From Access to Equity* and has contributed many articles and humour essays to a newspaper published in the Boston area. She holds a Master of Fine Arts and teaches at the Culinary Institute of America.

Travis Grant

Travis Grant lives in Northern Alberta, Canada.

Joseph Edwin Haeger

Joseph Edwin Haeger is the author of *Learn to Swim* (published by University of Hell Press, 2015). He has had work published in *The Inlander, Drunk Monkeys, Hippocampus Magazine* and others. He lives in the Pacific Northwest.

Clay Hardy

Clay Hardy is a fiction writer based in Portland, Oregon. When not drinking coffee or cheering for the Portland Trail Blazers and Timbers, Clay is usually hanging out with Porter, his golden retriever. You can find him on Twitter @_ClayHardy and on Instagram @clay_is_writing.

Gail Holmes

Gail Holmes is an emerging writer and graduate of the Master of Creative Writing, Publishing and Editing program at the University of Melbourne. Originally from Scotland, Gail worked all over the world in engineering and business before calling Australia home.

Maggie Nerz Iribarne

Maggie Nerz Iribarne practises writing in a yellow house in Syracuse, New York. Her story 'Somewhere Else' won a finalist prize in the 2021 Zizzle Literary Flash Fiction contest. She keeps a portfolio of her published work at www.maggienerziribarne.com.

Breanne Jade

Breanne Jade is a student at Aquinas College in Grand Rapids, Michigan. She is studying theatre for social change, business administration and writing. Her work has been published in *Teen Ink*, where she has also received two Editor's Choice awards.

David James

David's fourth and fifth books, *A Gem of Truth* and *Nail Yourself Into Bliss*, were published in 2019. *My Torn Dance Card* was a finalist in the 2017 Book Excellence Awards; his second full-length book *She Dances Like Mussolini* won the 2010 Next Generation Indie Book Award for poetry. He has published six chapbooks and has had more than thirty of his one-act plays produced in the US and Ireland. He teaches writing at Oakland Community College.

Christine Johnson

Christine Johnson is an undergraduate student at the University of Maryland, and an emerging short story and flash fiction writer. She is a musician, beekeeper, runner, and lover of ballroom dance. When she's not writing or reading, she's usually studying environmental science, because that's what her degree is actually in. Her work deals frequently with how societies mould families and how families mould individuals.

Amy Kayman

Amy Kayman is a flash fiction writer and graduate student at the University of Melbourne. Amy's work has been featured in publications including Melbourne-based *AGORA* magazine. Her writing is informed by her own experiences and the way short-form writing is at the intersection between prose and poetry.

Michelle Kelly

Michelle Kelly is a scholar and emerging creative and critical writer living on unceded Wangal land (Sydney). She has been featured in *TEXT*, the *Sydney Review of Books*, *Writer's Bloc* and *The Incompleteness Book* (published by Recent Work Press).

Jonathan Koven

Jonathan Koven is a technical writer and head fiction editor at *Toho Journal*. He is the author of *Palm Lines* and his fiction and poetry have been featured in *Goat's Milk Magazine*, *Night Picnic*, *Iris Literary Journal*, and more. His debut novel *Below Torrential Hill*, a winner of the Electric Eclectic Prize, releases in December 2021. He lives in Philadelphia with his best friend and future wife Delana, and cats Peanut Butter and Keebler.

Elle Lane

Elle Lane is an internationally published LGBTQ writer and poet. She received her BFA from the University of Cincinnati, which she represented at the 2021 Reiss Colloquium. Her work has appeared or is forthcoming in *SOS Cincinnati*, *LUPERCALIA Press*, Issuu Magazine, and The Dead Mule School of Southern Literature.

K L Lyons

K L Lyons is a writer from Tulsa, Oklahoma and a citizen of the Muscogee Creek Nation. Her poetry has appeared in *Anomaly* and *wards*. You can usually find her hiding in the kitchen or on Twitter as @dystopialloon.

Maria McDonald

Maria McDonald is an avid reader who loves to write. Mother of adult children and grandmother to two, she spends her time writing. Maria's short stories and articles have been published in *Woman's Way* and *Ireland's Own*, but she dreams of the day she will see her novels in bookshops. Find her on Twitter @mariamacwriter.

Linda McMullen

Linda McMullen is a wife, mother, diplomat, and homesick Wisconsinite. Her short stories and the occasional poem have appeared in over one hundred literary magazines. Linda received Pushcart and Best of the Net nominations in 2020. She may be found on Twitter @LindaCMcMullen.

Helene Macaulay

Helene Macaulay is an actor, writer, filmmaker and award-winning documentary and fine art photographer living in the American Rust Belt. Her writing has appeared in *86 Logic*, *LEON Literary Review*, *Gyroscope Review* and *The Commonline Journal*. Her films have been broadcast on PBS affiliates throughout the Northeastern United States and her photography has been exhibited internationally including in The National Portrait Gallery, London. Her acting credits include numerous films on the festival circuit as well as appearances on network and cable television and nationally syndicated radio.

Samuel Marshall

Samuel Marshall is an author and poet from the UK. He is the author of *Scribbles on the Bedroom Wall*, a film and book review blog with a focus on horror. His biggest literary inspirations are Bret Easton Ellis, Douglas Coupland and Charles Bukowski. You can follow Samuel on www.scribblesonthebedroomwall.wordpress.com/blog.

Bruce Meyer

Bruce Meyer is an author of books of poetry, short fiction, flash fiction, and non-fiction. His stories have won or been shortlisted for numerous international prizes. His most recent collection of stories is *Down in the Ground* (Guernica Editions, 2020). He lives in Barrie, Ontario.

Rebecca Moore

Rebecca Moore is a writer based in Washington, DC. Her work has appeared in *Fluent Magazine* and *Five Stop Story: Short Stories to Read in 5 Stops on Your Commute*. She was a finalist for Glimmer Train's Short Story Award for New Writers. She works as a senior brand content producer at the news and media outlet POLITICO.

Marija Mrvosevic

Marija Mrvosevic is an aspiring author and graduate student at the University of Melbourne. She has been writing for more than ten years and has had short stories published in her native country Serbia, most notably in the *White City Wordsmiths Vol. IV* anthology published by The Balkan Writers Project. In Australia, Marija's strange, funny and sad flash fiction was published in *Farrago*, and her short atmospheric non-fiction piece was published in *Inkspot*.

Zach Murphy

Zach Murphy is a Hawaii-born writer with a background in cinema. His stories have appeared in *Reed Magazine, Ginosko Literary Journal, The Coachella Review, Mystery Tribune, Ruminate, Ellipsis Zine, Wilderness House Literary Review*, and *Flash: The International Short-Short Story Magazine*. His debut chapbook *Tiny Universes* is available via Selcouth Station Press. He lives with his wonderful wife Kelly in St Paul, Minnesota.

C G Myth

C G Myth is a poet, fantasy writer and jewellery maker from south Florida. They cherish making stories for queer and disabled people to enjoy. They hold a BA from the University of North Florida and are now pursuing an MFA from Stetson University. When they aren't writing, they're usually listening to music and petting their service dog. They can be found on Instagram @clay.teeth.

Chris Neilan

Chris Neilan is an award-winning author, screenwriter and filmmaker. He was shortlisted for the 2016 Sundance Screenwriters Lab and the 2021 Sundance Development Track. He was awarded second place for Short Fiction in the 2017 Bridport Prize, shortlisted for the 2020 Aurora Prize and has been nominated for the 2021 Pushcart Prize, the 2021 Shirley Jackson Awards and the 2021 Best Small Fictions anthology.

Kellene O'Hara

Kellene O'Hara is currently pursuing her MFA in Fiction at The New School in New York City. Her writing has been published in *The Fourth River, Marathon Literary Review, South Florida Poetry Journal*, and elsewhere. Find her on Twitter @KelleneOHara and online at www.kelleneohara.com.

Helena Pantsis

Helena Pantsis (she/they) is a writer from Naarm, Australia. A full-time student of psychology and creative writing, they have a fond appreciation for the gritty, the dark, and the experimental. Her works are published or forthcoming in *Voiceworks, Island Online, Going Down Swinging*, and *Meanjin*. More can be found at www.hlnpnts.com.

Martha Patterson

Martha Patterson is a writer living in Boston, Massachusetts. Her work has been published by Smith & Kraus, Applause Books, *Sheepshead Review*, Silver Birch Press, Pioneer Drama Service, *The Syndrome Mag* and others. Her new collection of twenty-seven stories titled *Small Acts of Magic* was published in 2021 by Finishing Line Press. She has degrees from Mt Holyoke College and Emerson College. She loves being surrounded by her books, radio and laptop. Her website is www.mpatterson125933.wixsite.com/martha-patterson-.

Toby Remi Pickett

Toby Remi Pickett is a writer and undergraduate student at the University of Melbourne. Toby is the winner of several awards for creative writing including the Prose Award for Newman College's Peter Steele Prize and St Patrick College's Thomas Keneally Prize.

Boshra Rasti-Ghalati

Boshra Rasti-Ghalati is the author of several poems and short stories that have been published online and in paperback including *Together, Apart, South Florida Journal of Poetry, Literally Stories* and *Surry Seen – Surrey Art*

Gallery Anthology. When she is not writing, you might find her reading about political discourse and human rights. Her debut novel, *Surrogate Colony*, is forthcoming. You can find more about Boshra on her website: www.boshrawrites.wordpress.com.

Seth Robinson

Seth Robinson is a writer, podcaster, and creative producer living in Melbourne. His creative work has appeared in *Aurealis*, the University of Sydney Anthology, *TCK Town*, *Farrago*, and *Woroni*. His debut novel, *Welcome to Bellevue*, was published by Grattan Street Press in 2019. He is a graduate of the Australian National University and the University of Melbourne, and is currently completing a Doctor of Arts in Creative Writing at the University of Sydney. You can find out more about Seth and his work at www.sethrobinson.ink.

Tom Roth

Tom Roth received an MFA from Chatham University in Pittsburgh, Pennsylvania, where he was also awarded for Best Thesis in Fiction in 2021. His short stories are published in *Fictive Dream*, *Foliate Oak Literary Magazine* and *Riggwelter*. He has a publication forthcoming in *Great Lakes Review*.

Lauren Schenkman

Lauren Schenkman is a writer, journalist and translator. She has been published in *The New York Times Magazine*, *Atlas Obscura*, *Tin House*, *TED Ideas*, *Granta*, *The Hudson Review*, *Writer's Digest*, *Electric Literature* and *The Kenyon Review*, among other places. She has co-produced radio stories for Afropop Worldwide and Public Radio International's 'The World', and her fiction has been performed on NPR's 'Selected Shorts'. She was a reporter and editor at *Science* magazine and a Fulbright grant recipient in Nicaragua, her mother's homeland.

Paulette Smythe

Paulette Smythe is a writer and visual artist who divides her time between Melbourne and the Strzelecki Ranges. She graduated from the University of Melbourne with a PhD in Applied Linguistics and has taught English to migrants and refugees in a variety of settings. In her writing, she seeks to capture the mystery and paradox that lie beneath the surface of ordinary life. Her work has appeared in *Verandah, Bewildering Stories, Eureka Street, Coffin Bell, Shuffle: An Anthology of Microlit, Prometheus Dreaming* and *The Nasiona.*

Arundhati Subhedar
Arundhati doesn't consider herself an author, but she enjoys reading and writing imagined worlds and heartwarming characters. She holds a BA in English and a Masters in Publishing and Communications. She also works as an editor for children's and YA fiction, and for fantasy and sci-fi novels. Above all, she loves a good story.

Jen Susca
Jen Susca is a graduate of the University of New Hampshire where she studied English and psychology. She currently lives and works in Boston. You can read more of her work at www.jensusca.blogspot.com and follow her on Instagram @sopranosundays.

Joanna Theiss
Joanna Theiss is a freelance author living in Washington, D.C. Before becoming a freelance author, Joanna Theiss worked as a public defender, a government attorney and a healthcare researcher. She has had articles published in academic journals and magazines, and short fiction in literary journals such as *Inkwell Journal* and *Barren Magazine.*

Robert Verhagen
Robert Verhagen is an emerging author, English tutor and bookseller at Eltham Bookshop, north-east of Melbourne. He is a current graduate student of the Master of Creative Writing, Publishing and Editing program at the University of Melbourne. Robert has published two works, *Murder at the Mountain Rush* (2016) and *In the Company of Madness* (2020). He also chairs the not-for-profit community news magazine *Mountain Monthly* in the Kinglake Ranges.

Jasmine Dreame Wagner
Jasmine Dreame Wagner is an American writer and multidisciplinary artist. She is the author of *On a Clear Day*, a collection of poems and lyric essays, and is the recipient of fellowships and residencies from the Connecticut

Office of the Arts; Foundation for Contemporary Arts Emergency Grants; Kimmel Harding Nelson Center for the Arts; The Lighthouse Works; Marble House Project; The Millay Colony for the Arts; and Virginia Center for the Creative Arts (VCCA). Wagner's writing has recently appeared in *BOMB Magazine*, *Colorado Review*, *Denver Quarterly*, *Fence*, *Guernica*, and *Hyperallergic*.

Tejan Green Waszak

Tejan Green Waszak was born in Mandeville, Jamaica. She is a cross-genre writer, editor, and educator. Her work has been published or is forthcoming in *Narrative Northeast*, *The Grief Diaries*, and *The Caribbean Writer*, among other publications.

Pei Wen

Pei Wen is based in Singapore, an island in Southeast Asia where eternal summer is interspersed with intense and satisfying thunderstorms. When she's not writing or reading, you can find her relaxing in a jacuzzi or drinking bubble tea. Drop her an email at peiwenwrites@gmail.com.

GRATTAN STREET PRESS PERSONNEL

Semester 2, 2021

Editing and Proofreading
Jack Ahdore – Copyeditor & Sales Associate
Jake Dell'Arciprete – Copyeditor & Content Writer
Liza Hughes – Lead Copyeditor & Sales Associate
Izzy Smith – Copyeditor & Content Writer
Arundhati Subhedar – Chief Proofreader & Production Associate

Design and Production
Joanna Bloore – Production Manager
Collin Vogt – Production Associate & Content Writer

Sales and Marketing
Cordelia Egerton-Warburton – Sales Manager
Kate Fleming – Sales Associate & Book Reviews Editor
Rachel Grey – Marketing and Events Officer & Proofreader
Richard Hanson – Marketing and Publicity Officer & Content Writer
Freya Long – Marketing Manager

Social Media
Neha Joseph – Social Media Associate, Submissions Assistant & Proofreader
Xuan Wei Yap – Social Media Manager & Proofreader

Submissions Officers
Aleks Burgess – Commissioning Editor & Proofreader
Robin Harper – Commissioning Editor & Proofreader

Website and Blogs

Lily Miniken – Blogs Co-editor & Proofreader

Claryss Kuan – MZ Editor

Katherine Tweedie – Publishing Blog Editor

Academic Staff

Sybil Nolan

Katherine Day

Alexandra Dane

Susannah Bowen

Mark Davis

GRATTAN STREET PRESS ACKNOWLEDGEMENTS

This semester, Grattan Street Press connected with writers across the globe to produce a collection of original stories for our first short-story anthology. While we had intended to produce this book back on campus, face-to-face as you do in a regular publishing setting, we were thrown into another lockdown. The restrictive conditions forced us to yet again renegotiate our working model and adapt to the demands of a completely online publishing process. This semester's students rose to the challenge and we couldn't be prouder of the outcome.

We began preparations for *Intermissions* at the beginning of the year, when the Semester 1 Flash Fiction submissions team – Ian Dudley, Frieda Hermann and Sophie Raphael – curated a list of works from emerging and established writers from Australia, the US, the UK, Jamaica, Qatar, Ireland, Canada, Hong Kong, Singapore and Saudi Arabia. We'd especially like to thank our talented authors for their contribution, enthusiasm and collaboration. Collecting, editing and printing over 60 short stories is no mean feat; the timely cooperation of our stable of contributors made the process smooth and enjoyable. Editing the texts has also required a high degree of organisation and skill, from copyediting to proofing pages. The copyediting team, led by Liza Hughes, comprised Jack Adhore, Jake Dell'Arciprete and Izzy Smith. Arundhati Subhedar led the proofing team comprising Aleks Burgess, Robin Harper, Neha Joseph and Xuan Wei Yap.

The production team, led by Joanna Bloore with Collin Vogt and Arundhati as co-typesetters and designers, created a beautiful cover and sample setting reflective of their newfound design talents. Cordelia Egerton-Warburton and associate, Kate Fleming, did a great job providing anthology research and generating sales of our other titles throughout the pandemic – with book buying becoming a solely online event without the ability to visit local bookshops. Kate has also kept us informed and entertained with a number of book reviews from contributing blog writers.

The book-review section, while relatively new, can be found within our existing blogs: MZ and the Publishing blog. Both blogs are updated each week and allow us to connect with our readers and industry networks. Finding and editing content is a constant task, but the blog editors this semester – Lily Miniken, Katherine Tweedie and Claryss Kuan – embraced the opportunity to be part of the wider discussions around what concerns our Millennial and Gen Z readers, and what's happening in publishing.

Our submissions editors, Aleks Burgess and Robin Harper, worked hard to publicise GSP as a publisher supportive of emerging writers, exploring various writing groups and gaining good traction with our biannual Pitch Our Tent event. We look forward to potentially sharing the fruits of their labour in the coming semesters.

The Pitch Our Tent event this year was also coordinated by the ever-efficient Rachel Grey, our events manager, who formed part of the marketing team, led by Freya Long with Richard Hanson as publicity officer. Together, they have done a terrific job of getting the word out about our books. Not only did we host Pitch Our Tent, but we managed to successfully host an online event – a Q&A between the talented Lee Kofman and Jacinta Dietrich. The event would also not have been possible without the skills of our social media manager, Xuan Wei Yap, and social media associate, Neha Joseph, who offered our followers engaging and comprehensive social media updates.

A heartfelt thanks to colleagues in the Master of Publishing and Communications program who continue to support GSP: our program coordinator Alex Dane (who is also GSP's digital publisher),

Mark Davis and Beth Driscoll. A special thanks to Susannah Bowen, our industry associate, who taught in the subject this semester.

Thanks to our Head of School, Assoc. Professor Paul Rae, his EA, Jacqueline Doyle, and to our School Manager, Charlotte Morgans, who were gracious in the face of processing over 60 author contracts. Thanks also to Kerin Forstmanis, who was integral to drafting the contract. Finally, thanks to IngramSpark who have been our printers and distributors from the beginning and continue to help us realise our creative vision.

Katherine Day
Managing Editor at Grattan Street Press

ABOUT GRATTAN STREET PRESS

Grattan Street Press is a trade publisher based in Melbourne. As a start-up press, we aim to publish a range of work, including contemporary literature and trade non-fiction, and re-publish culturally valuable works that are out of print. The press is an initiative of the Publishing and Communications program in the School of Culture and Communication at the University of Melbourne, and is staffed by graduate students, who receive hands-on experience in every aspect of the publication process.

The press is a not-for-profit organisation that seeks to build long-term relationships with the Australian literary and publishing community. We also partner with community organisations in Melbourne and beyond to co-publish books that contribute to public knowledge and discussion.

Organisations interested in partnering with us can contact us at coordinator@grattanstreetpress.com. Writers who are interested in submitting a manuscript to Grattan Street Press can contact us at editorial@grattanstreetpress.com.

CPSIA information can be obtained
at www.ICGtesting.com
Printed in the USA
BVHW032320071221
623424BV00008B/725